"Do you want to dance?"

Alice stopped tapping her foot, and turned to Hugh, who'd caught her unawares.

And he did catch her unawares, his appearance startling to her every sense. It still seemed impossible that he had returned to Swaffham. And after all this time, it should have been impossible to be so affected by him. And yet, she was.

Tonight his clothes were as fine as any nobleman's. None of which softened the hard slant of his jaw or his piercing storm-filled gaze.

"Which dance?" Her eyes strayed to the lock of hair that fell loose and soft over his forehead.

A quirk to his lips. "The one that's beginning right now."

Aware of eyes on their exchange, Alice carefully chose her words. "Yes, I would like a dance."

"Then let's begin this," Hugh said, taking her hand in a sure grip. His palm pressed to hers and their fingers entwined, his calloused tips brushing her wrist. He drew her closer as they joined the other dancers, holding her longer than the dance provided. A dance she knew well, but, for the first time, somehow didn't know at all.

Author Note

Finally, Hugh's story is being told! How could he possibly be book six, when he first appeared in *The Knight's Broken Promise*, which is book one in the Lovers and Legends series? Well, I'm not writing these stories chronologically. In fact, as stand-alones, the books can be read in any order.

But that doesn't explain why it took me this long, so I'll tell you. Hugh's past is so tormented that his story was difficult to write. Add in the fact that at the end of book one he's committing treason, and I wondered what heroine could possibly understand him?

That's when I found Alice, who has been valiantly trying to save Hugh since she was six years old. The only problem? Alice has the king of England threatening her life...

NICOLE LOCKE

—

Her Christmas Knight

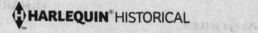

HARLEQUIN® HISTORICAL

Recycling programs
for this product may
not exist in your area.

ISBN-13: 978-0-373-62977-0

Her Christmas Knight

www.Harlequin.com

Printed in U.S.A.

Nicole Locke discovered her first romance novels in her grandmother's closet, where they were secretly hidden. Convinced that books that were hidden must be better than those that weren't, Nicole greedily read them. It was only natural for her to start writing them—but now not so secretly.

Books by Nicole Locke

Harlequin Historical

Lovers and Legends

The Knight's Broken Promise
Her Enemy Highlander
The Highland Laird's Bride
In Debt to the Enemy Lord
The Knight's Scarred Maiden
Her Christmas Knight

Visit the Author Profile page at Harlequin.com.

To my Brother—

Thank you for teaching me the value of kindness,
the virtue of perseverance and the worthy ability
to tie my shoes. You're the absolute best.

Chapter One

October 1296, London

She wasn't going to make it.

Heat prickled down her back. Her hands, clutching a seal to her chest, grew damp. Alice stopped running, pressed her back against the stone wall and let out a steadying breath.

She was going to make it. She had to. She had come too far. It was the labyrinth of passageways that was making her anxious. She didn't know where she was going.

It was the dark…which was more heavy and cold than the stone she rested against.

How long had she been running? She should never have agreed to the game—never agreed to visiting Court in the first place.

As if she'd had a choice. King Edward needed gold and her family—wealthy wool merchants—were being heavily taxed for it. To soften the blow, the King often invited her family to Court. Beyond delighted, her father had always taken the trips alone. This time round, however, the King had formally invited *her*. And one could not avoid a direct royal command.

But she could have avoided the seal-seeking game. Noting that the King wasn't in residence, she had tried to avoid the game. But someone had put her name in the bowl and it had been pulled. Then she and the others had been shoved into various darkened hallways to find a seal and solve the riddle.

Which should have been easy. Even if she didn't know and couldn't see where she was going, she'd thought she could depend on her ears to hear the lapping of the Thames or the running of the other seal seekers. But her ears had failed her. All was dead silent.

She rolled the seal in her hands, hoping the unusual shape would distract her from her thoughts. The seal was neither round nor square, and it was much too large for her hands, but it had to be the correct seal. She was sure that she'd understood the riddle: *Find the door that holds the light.*

A door couldn't hold a light unless there was a light behind that illuminated it, and yet she had opened so many doors and there had been only more darkness.

Her breathing hitched. She mustn't think about her fear of darkness. She must consider only the light and where she hadn't been. If she concentrated on the riddle maybe she could forget the dark. *Maybe.*

Laughter. High-pitched and suddenly snuffed out.

Where had it come from? It had burst out and disappeared too quickly for her to tell. Was it the other seal seekers or someone hiding in the shadows?

She pushed away from the wall and walked to the left. She might be going in circles, but she had to move.

The riddle had hinted at additional seals. The others might be ahead of her.

Not daring to run any more, she quickened her steps. If the other seekers were close and she slipped and the seal fell she would never find it again. But she couldn't be too cautious. If she was quick enough she'd have the prize—she'd be out of the dark.

Another step and another—until the floor dropped.

Stairs?

She swiped at the dark with her hands and feet until the corridor curved into a staircase. Keeping a hand on the stone wall, she shuffled her way down until she found her way to a heavily latched illuminated door.

There were more sounds, too—murmurs and whispers of a crowd trying to be quiet. This was the door! She brushed her free hand against the smooth wood until she found the latch.

Other noises were reaching her ears—more laughter, and footsteps behind her. No time to waste. She placed the seal beside her feet, and used both hands to lift the latch. It held, as if someone on the other side was preventing it from opening. Did she dare call out?

No, the footsteps behind her were too close.

She jumped and used her body to press down on the handle. The latch broke free, but the clank echoed in the quiet corridor. The footsteps behind her changed direction.

No time to lose.

Grabbing the seal, she rushed into the too-bright room. Images of people and flames flickering in elaborate wall sconces distracted her. She collided with a wall wearing chainmail and started to fall backwards.

Thick arms wrapped around her waist and lifted her.

Clutching the seal against her chest, she felt her feet leave the ground as she was pressed against the unmistakable curves of a trained warrior. Winded, and blinded by the sudden light, she felt his flat abdomen against her own, her breasts rubbing abrasively against interlocked steel, and still the warrior pulled her up... and up.

She was being held much too closely. She breathed in to catch her breath, to protest, and smelled leather and metal, and a scent that was this man's alone. A scent that hovered on her memory...elusive, familiar. It filled her with such a sudden wanting that she clamped her mouth shut.

Images blazed in her mind. It couldn't be him. It *shouldn't* be him.

Another feeling assaulted her, more powerful than the embarrassment of being held too closely. It was even more deeply pitted in her stomach than her sudden inexplicable wanting.

She felt fear.

She blinked her eyes to focus and was caught by the bluest eyes she'd ever seen. No, not the bluest eyes she'd *ever* seen, because she'd seen these eyes before. Years ago. The fear went down her back all the way to her heels before it raced hot and fast to the top of her head.

She blinked again. No, these eyes were not the same—even though they were the crystal blue of a summer sky, so bright and too piercing to be real. These eyes had had that light taken from them. They were as clear and stunning a colour as to be almost impossible, but these eyes held something else—some darkness—as if an unseen storm was about to break.

Other features of this warrior were different, too.

His blond hair did not wave around his shoulders, but was cut short, its curls tamed to just behind his ears. His skin was not pale from the clouds and mists of a small town, but was sun-baked. Underneath the torch-light his face was all hard, lean planes and too fierce for softness. There were lines, too, around his eyes—not from laughter, but from determination. His lips, which curved sensuously and were made for smiling, were instead turned down deeply.

None of this seeming harshness hid the sheer beauty of his features. No, this man's perfection was marred by a nose that crooked a little to the left.

The seal slipped in her suddenly damp hands. She knew that nose. She had broken that nose. Reluctantly, against her will, she raised her eyes to his again. He was still studying her.

She felt permanently latched to him. She could not move even to let air into her lungs. Oh, she didn't want to, but she knew those eyes. And they knew her. There was no confusion in their blue depths, there was only… waiting.

But he couldn't be the man she knew. She hadn't heard from him or seen him for more than six years. She'd thought him dead. She *wanted* him dead.

'Hugh?' The name escaped before she knew she still had a voice, and the corner of his lips lifted.

She knew that crooked smile. She knew that smile all too well.

The bright room blurred. Her body felt like a whirling spindle. She felt the instant tightening of his hands against her back and his body bracing itself against her sudden lack of strength.

She was fainting.

A sharp pain in her back, a sudden shove forward, and Hugh shifted to keep their balance. It was all she needed to break eye contact. The dizziness left; the room turned bright again.

They were surrounded by heavily perfumed people. The courtiers' dress of—multiple colours along with the copious amounts of gold and silver—glinted and glared in the torchlight. They were all staring at her. Their mouths moved, but she couldn't hear their words above the roaring in her ears.

She pushed away, but Hugh did not immediately release her. Instead he slowly lowered her to the ground. If possible, the chainmail was more abrasive and his body was harder than a stone wall. Her breasts tingled inside her chemise; swathed in her heavy skirts, her dangling legs entwined with his.

It was all too intimate, too heady. When her feet touched the floor it felt as if he'd dropped her from that imagined cliff.

Unsteady, she pressed her hand against his chest. Her body shook with the rise of his breath, the strong beat of his heart. Hugh's hands returned to her sides, and they were all too familiar, too proprietorial. He didn't have a right to such touch. He had refused her offer to have a right to such touch.

'Release me,' she said, not looking in his eyes.

He stepped away. The crowd moved into the space before her. Their voices finally reached her ears. The circular room was clanging and echoing with cries of protest, outrage, laughter, loud talk.

The courtiers stared and pointed at her chest. Embarrassment warmed her skin. Had the ribbons around her dress loosened as Hugh held her so tightly? Had she become undressed—here, in public, at *Court*?

She looked down, but nothing was indecent. The light green ribbon that wound round her chest and sleeves still held her blue linen dress together. She was intact; there was nothing to cause her shame.

And she still had the seal clutched to her body.

The seal. She had the seal.

How could she have forgotten the game? How long had she been held by Hugh, staring at him as if she... as if she *wanted* to see him again? Embarrassment did more than warm her skin. This time she knew she turned red. Something she couldn't control. But what she could control was what she did about it.

Putting as much coldness into her features as possible, she looked up. He wasn't there. The crowd had surrounded her and was pushing her forward. Digging her heels into the flooring, she struggled against the crowd until they suddenly opened before her. With a last shove she was released into a small opening.

She righted herself, running one hand down her crumpled dress, and turned to glare at the courtiers— but a glint of red and gold at the corner of her eye shocked her into stillness.

Disbelieving, she turned towards the red and gold of the King's throne. It wasn't empty. Instead there was a very tall, very thin, bearded man reposing on the ornately carved chair.

Fighting the instinct to hide, she dropped in a deep curtsey. King Edward had returned to the Tower of London and he was staring right at her.

'Rise, my lady. It appears you have something of mine.'

She rose, her knees unsteady, her hands trembling. In fear of dropping it, she pressed the seal to her belly. King Edward barely glanced at it.

She was suddenly acutely aware of falling very short of Court decorum. Hair tangled from running, purple dress crumpled by the crowd, cheeks flushed with bewilderment. Even her mind was in disarray.

But none of this was fair. She'd neither seen nor heard any formal announcement of his arrival. Literally, she'd been in the dark.

As if conjured by its name, darkness swirled around her chaotic thoughts. Was she about to faint?

No!

She raised her chin. Damn the dark and—if she could—damn the King, too, for making her feel inadequate. After all, it was his stupid game she'd been playing. What did he expect? And whoever had heard of a king taking so long to gaze upon someone's appearance?

But he wasn't looking at her appearance. He hadn't noticed the crumpled silk or the tendrils of hair that strayed out behind the silver circlet around her head. The King hadn't noticed her physical appearance. The King seemed to be assessing her.

She *was* going to faint.

'Who are you?' King Edward's deep voice echoed in the unnaturally quiet room.

She desperately wished her mouth wasn't so dry. 'Alice of Fenton, sire.'

'From Swaffham?'

'Yes, Your Majesty.'

He chuckled. 'Well, it seems you have won a prize.'

Alice didn't know how to answer. Despite the King's

laughter his brow remained furrowed, and it gave him a troubled look.

She chastised herself. Perhaps he could not rid himself of worry when there were such heavy matters to deal with in the north. But with such concerns, why was he bothering with a courtly game?

His chamberlain was suddenly on her right. In his hands was an elaborate ivory hunting horn. Even in the great glitter of Court the horn glimmered bright, its three bands of carved silver sparkling like stars. If this was her prize for such sport, every extravagance her sister had told her about Court was true.

She bowed her head. 'Thank you, Your Majesty.'

He inclined his head, but looked beyond her shoulder. She would have looked, too, but the chamberlain was handing her the horn. His manner was overtly stiff, his arms barely extended. It forced her to bend low and forward to retrieve it, or look as if she was refusing the prize.

She was practically wrapped around him when she heard his message, whispered so softly only she could hear.

'You will go to the antechamber when the third song starts.'

Startled at the words, she didn't react as the chamberlain grabbed the seal, shoved the horn into her hand and disappeared.

When she looked up from the horn the King was gone. She had not acknowledged a *king* leaving the throne. What was wrong with her?

Courtiers swarmed around her, but her ears and eyes were numb to their excited chatter.

She heard music faintly in the background. Had she missed a song?

No, the chamberlain had just left, and the people around her were moving into a dance. It was the first song.

At the third song the King commanded a private meeting with her. Although the chamberlain had not said so, she knew this was not something to be repeated. Not that she would tell any of the people crowding around her to admire the horn. They were strangers all, and she had never felt that fact more than at this moment.

She tried to accept their congratulations, but mostly she waited for their interest to wane. It did so in very little time.

Soon she was left alone, while people danced, gossiped and flirted. She had never understood until now what it meant when it was said that people twittered. She watched people laugh too gaily and talk too loudly. If they would simply be quiet she could concentrate.

Two, she counted. She knew this song.

There wasn't much time before she must reach the antechamber. Certainly not enough to collect her thoughts, which were now more crumpled than her dress. She didn't know why she was being summoned, or why she had felt the King was measuring her.

Maybe by her winning she had caught his eye. The Queen had been dead for years and he had yet to remarry. Was that why he had been assessing her? Did he wonder if she'd make a suitable mistress? Her heart lurched. It was an honour, but one that she had never hoped for; she certainly hadn't wanted to win the game that much.

She searched the crowd for bright golden hair. But she didn't need her eyes to know that Hugh was not in the room. Her awareness of that man was something she had carried most of her life.

There was no one for her to confide in. She had thought herself lucky that she had an entire week without her family prodding her to dance with men they thought suitable. But right now she would have appreciated a familiar face. What good was it to have a large family if none of them were around when she needed them?

The second song was ending. It was time for her to go. She was too frightened to look around—too worried that people would see where she was going and know what would happen to her.

The guards at the door seemed reluctant. They only stepped slightly out of her way, and opened the door the merest slit. She was forced to turn sideways to fit through. She certainly wasn't an honoured guest.

Once inside, she heard the door shut with a heavy metal clank. Immediately, the crowd and music were muffled. It was too late for her to realise that she had taken comfort in the noise and people.

The room was lit by tall, narrow stained-glass windows. The natural light was calmer than the glitter and torches of the throne room. The sun had not set, which surprised her. It seemed that more time had passed since she had started the game.

The walls were finely decorated with red fleur-de-lis. Dark green velvet draperies hung from an elaborately carved four-poster bed. The huge fireplace was not lit, but shone brilliant white from many cleanings. On the

far wall was a small round nook that was overpowered
by a large golden cross.

King Edward sat in the middle of the room, next
to a rectangular table that was laden with fine pewter
and food.

There were no guards, no nobles nor courtiers vying
for his attention. They were alone, and this was not an
antechamber but his bedroom.

It was not these facts that gave her pause. It was the
feeling of the room. Fine refreshments on the table, the
King sitting and enjoying a repast, drinking wine… It
was all so private, so…personal.

He turned his head to her. Bedroom or not, she was
still before a monarch. She gave another curtsey.

'Come, there will be no formality here.' He waved
for her to sit across from him at the table.

She did, her eyes never leaving his. His face remained unreadable, his eyes shadowed.

'Would you like some refreshment?' he asked, his
eyes resting on the horn she had laid in her lap.

'No, thank you,' she replied, as deferentially as she
could. She wouldn't be able to get anything down her
throat even if she tried. She was surprised she was able
to speak.

'You are nervous,' he said.

She hesitated. 'I am.'

King Edward sighed. 'It cannot be helped. I wondered how you would fair, being of the softer sex.'

She was being judged. Had she disappointed him by
being nervous? She had every reason to be uneasy—
even to fear him. He was one of the greatest rulers in the
world. But she realised that her nervousness stemmed
from something more than simply knowing his power.

She was in a situation she couldn't comprehend. Why would a king come back from war to play a game, and why she was in his private counsel, alone with him in his bedroom?

'My fear is for what is expected of me, Your Majesty, not necessarily at your august company,' she said.

He set down his goblet and raised surprised eyes to hers.

Her answer had gone too far. She had practically challenged a monarch.

'I did not mean—' she began.

King Edward gave a low chuckle and shook his head. 'No, do not recant your answer. I am pleased with your honesty and I am relieved that you have no fear of me but of what is expected of you.'

'I did not say that I did not fear your company—simply that I fear what I am doing here more.'

He leaned back in his chair, his creased brow softening. 'Ah, it is good to know that you are wise. It would be remiss of me to say you should not have fear.'

She boldly strode on. 'What is expected of me, sire?'

He reached for the flagon of wine between them and gave it a swirl. The wine's floral scent filled the air as he poured. His actions allowed her to watch him without his too knowing eyes staring back at her. Although he would not remember, she had been presented to him at Court when she was very young. He had changed much since she had last seen him. The shadows under his eyes and the cynical way he held his body told his age more than the grey of his beard.

'How did you escape my guards?' He set down the flagon.

It took her a moment to realise he was talking about

the game. 'I waited in the dark until they were occupied by the other players, Your Majesty.'

'Although I am not pleased that my guards should be so easily distracted, it is good that you show both intelligence and patience,' he said. 'You will need both.'

She didn't reply. Being the last of three daughters, she had learned patience. The King was weighing his words and she was still waiting for an answer to her question.

'Did you enjoy finding the seal?' He grabbed a loaf of bread and tore it. The crumbs scattered across the table.

'I did, thank you.'

He chewed slowly. 'You hold your prize as if I will take it back,' he said. 'I promise that it is yours, but I do desire you to place it on the table so that I may enjoy it in these last moments.'

Her eyes fell to the horn still clasped in her hand. She placed it on the table.

He set down the bread and pointed at the horn. 'You have not looked at it closely, have you?'

There had been little opportunity for her to inspect her prize. She shook her head, fearing she would offend him.

'Did you not find it odd that the prize is a hunting horn?'

'No, Your Majesty, it is a fine prize.' She glanced at it, and noticed that numerous pictures had been carved into the thick silver bands.

He picked up the horn and turned it in his hands. 'There are many tales told here.' He touched the smallest band by the mouth of the horn. 'This is the resolution of the story, although how it is resolved makes little sense in comparison to the tales told by the first two bands.'

'And those tales, sire?' she asked.

The King seemed in little hurry for their meeting to be over. And if he thought he was putting her at ease by talking about a decorative horn he could not be more wrong. She felt tighter than the silver bands.

He gave a slight shrug. 'It tells of kings warring and lovers being torn apart. It is a typical story for troubadours.'

'And what is shown in the resolution that does not make sense?' she asked.

'We only see the lovers joined again, their arms cradling a child between them.'

'And this does not make sense?'

He set the horn down and reached for his wine. The liquid sloshed against the sides of the blue glass. In the light streaming from the stained-glass windows the dark red colour looked like blood.

'We do not see what happens to the kings. I have to admit I am biased, but there should be some balance between the two tales.'

She glanced at the perfect workmanship of the horn. 'Perhaps a band is missing.'

'Or the craftsman didn't think what had happened to the kings of different countries was important enough to depict.' He drained his goblet. 'I want you to know that I do not hold to such a belief. I could not care less what happens to the lovers, or to individual people. There are greater risks than the lives of two people. How old are you?'

'I have known twenty-two summers, Your Majesty.'

'You are old enough for what I need of you. You

showed cunning and care in pursuit of the seal and you live in the very town that plagues me the most. So, although you have no training for such a task, I am ordering you to take on a mission of the utmost importance.'

'I do not understand.'

She shifted in the seat that was no longer comfortable. Her first instinct was to leave the room, but she could not rise without his permission. Maybe she should not have been so clever in the game-playing. But she was coming to realise that perhaps it hadn't been a game.

'I want you to know that what I speak of now is between us. If this information becomes public before your duty to me is accomplished, you and your family will be placed in this very tower—and not as guests.'

She wished now that she had taken his offer of wine. The liquid would have quenched her suddenly parched throat. She nodded her head to let him know she understood, although she didn't, not fully.

'No need to lose your courage now. I am not asking you to break any commandments with God.'

Her heart did not ease. Maybe she wouldn't have to commit murder, but it was something grave. Something that was important enough to bring the King back to London. Something that he felt necessitated his making a threat to her family.

'In any war, information is as important a part of winning as the ability with a sword,' he continued. 'Right now there are letters that are passing secrets from this very chamber to the usurpers in Scotland. For distinction, or for pride, all these letters are sealed with the impression of a half-thistle.'

She could not be following this conversation correctly. It was too private, too important. The King of England was telling her that he had a traitor in his court. And the traitor closed his treacherous letters with a seal. A *true* seal.

'The seeking of the seal...the riddle,' she said, 'it wasn't a game.'

'No, it was a test. I thought that whoever was cunning enough to find and escape with a fake seal would be cunning enough to find a real one.' He tapped the table and smiled. 'And, in case you were wondering, none of those seekers were randomly chosen to play the game.'

She had to concentrate on his words and not on the image of her sisters locked in the Tower. 'What is it that you want me to do?' She forced the words from her lips.

'I think it should be clear to one who has beaten my best guards and won a testing game. It is the reason the winner's prize must be a hunting horn. I wish for the winner to be a hunter.'

She must be shaking her head, for the King raised his hand and nodded.

'Yes, Alice of Fenton from Swaffham. I wish you to find the Half-Thistle Seal,' he continued. 'Whoever has this seal will be the traitor. We believe that this traitor is in *your* very town—might indeed be among the people you know.'

She stopped breathing. This couldn't be happening to her. He couldn't possibly mean what she thought he meant.

'I wish you to become a spy,' he finished.

Oh, spindles—he did.

Chapter Two

The next morning was too clear and pretty for Alice's dark mood, so she took comfort in the night's damp that was still making the morning unpleasantly cold. Rubbing her arms, she walked briskly out through the iron doors and into the enormous courtyard.

The light had not yet crested the horizon and the courtyard was bathed in a glow somewhere between night and day. The dim light did not matter. She knew where she wanted to go. The kitchen gardens would be empty of courtiers and servants at this time. She needed the privacy. Better yet, she desired the ugliness of lacerated chopped vegetables and herbs. A mutilated barren garden might lighten her mood.

She had spent most of the night trying to resolve what the King wanted of her. When she hadn't been able to, she had tried to sleep. Nothing had worked. The night had not been long enough for her to resolve anything, and the dark had made her already nightmarish thoughts more frightening.

She rushed up the inclined hill, and turned to walk through the lavender-hedged entrance.

The kitchen gardens were empty. She pulled her skirts tight against her to walk the narrow paths between each planting. She didn't know why she bothered. Tearing her dress might be a welcome distraction.

In fact, she'd welcome company, too. She longed for Esther, her most loyal of servants, but she was too old for this trip. Esther's cantankerous company would have kept her occupied with menial chatter. She'd would even have taken her father's flighty personality for a diversion.

Then she wouldn't have to worry about the task she had been ordered to do: to spy on her friends, to expose one of them for the enemy they were.

It would be impossible. The King was not asking her to delve into the personal belongings of strangers, but of *friends*. She would have to search their homes, their carriages, their wardrobes to look for a hidden seal. How could she betray her friends' trust?

A crunch on the pebbled path announced that she was no longer alone.

'Couldn't sleep?'

She did not need to turn around to know who was behind her. His voice, as familiar to her as her own, confirmed her other nightmarish thoughts. She had indeed seen Hugh again. In the night, she'd hoped she imagined him because of the unfamiliarity of Court.

Releasing her grip on her skirts, she turned to face him.

He stood closer than she'd thought was possible on the pebbled footpath, and the morning light was strong enough to illuminate what she could no longer deny.

His lean, rugged body was solid; the blond hair that had once curled around her fingers was bright. Everything about him was all too real. Including her sharp anxiety at seeing him again.

It was as if six years had been stripped away and she was sixteen again. Sixteen and spilling out her naïve adoration with no reserve, with no thought that her affections would not be reciprocated.

She remembered every inflection of his sneering reply.

Shame flooded her limbs. She wanted to flee, to turn away, at least to lower her eyes—but she could not.

He approached her slowly, stealthily. The blue concentration of his eyes burned away her confidence. Even her skirts hung limply, as if the very clothing she wore was as insignificant as she felt.

'So it *was* you,' she whispered.

He took a step closer. The glint of the morning sun softened his features, or maybe it just hid the harshness she had glimpsed last night.

'Did you doubt it?' he answered. 'When it was I who had you in my arms again?'

Hot embarrassment swept through her. It had not only been the King's mission occupying her thoughts throughout the night. Hugh's arms, his slightly crooked nose and all her embarrassing confessions to him had haunted her dreams and had her wishing for the light of day so that she could pretend he did not exist.

She had almost convinced herself, too. When the King demanded so much of her, she didn't need her thoughts occupied by her childish vow to marry him. Certainly she never wanted to re-live her begging him for a kiss when she was sixteen.

And now he stood right in front of her, like a mocking reminder of her foolish youth.

A reminder of how he had rejected her.

But that did not mean she had to listen to him or repeat the mistake of conversing with him. He had purposely made it sound as if her running into him had been a clandestine affair. As if she would ever consider such thoughts again!

She looked pointedly around him and lifted her skirts—but he blocked the only exit from the garden. For one flaring moment, she fought the terror of feeling trapped. No doubt he had done that purposely, too.

'Let me pass,' she said, proud that her voice didn't betray her true feelings.

'After this long time, that is all you have to say to me?'

'I'd say less if you would let me by,' she replied.

'You have changed much, Alice. You used to be more talkative.'

'Maybe I thought you were someone worth talking to.'

She took a step in his direction. She'd force him to move if she had to.

He didn't move. 'I merely guessed that you couldn't sleep. It was either that or you never made it to your bed. But you have changed your gown. I was always partial to that colour grey on you. It almost matches the colour of your eyes.'

'You have been too long at Court,' she said. 'Save your pretty words for the more feeble-minded.'

'Just as well you didn't wear grey yesterday, for it seems the King prefers purple,' he replied, as if they were carrying on a normal conversation. 'Did you return to your room last night, or did one of your many servants bring you a change of clothing?'

Why was he talking of her clothing? He was close enough that she should have been able to know what he was thinking, but his eyes were like opaque glass—reflective, revealing nothing.

She didn't need this confusion.

'Why are you here?' she demanded. 'I know it wasn't to talk of my dress.'

'After we had run into each other in the hall, I thought we could meet once again—but then you spent time with the King.'

'Are you following me?' she asked.

'Only enough to see you.'

His eyes held hers and his lips curved almost sensuously, almost as if he wanted her.

She couldn't take his looking at her like that—not now, not when she was too tired to keep her defences up. Why was he acting as if he cared? She knew that he didn't, and never had.

Treacherous tears were building. She would embarrass herself if she stayed.

But he wasn't going to let her pass. He was going to stand there with his beautiful smile and his confusing words. A thought occurred. Something... No. *Someone* had brought him here.

'It is the King, isn't it?' she asked, although she knew she was right.

'The King?'

'You want to know what the King wanted of me. You don't want *me*.'

Some emotion flitted across his eyes like a jagged cloud. His intensity towards her vanished and he shrugged. 'You cannot blame me for trying.'

Oh, yes, she could. If she hadn't already wished him

to hell, she was doing so now. Callous, cruel, arrogant...
She was glad his words had cut so quickly into her softening feelings. Her tears had dried and she could leave
without another embarrassing scene.

'I owe you no words, no explanation,' she retorted.
'I owe you less than that—I owe you nothing.'

'Oh, do you?' he replied. 'In front of all those courtiers you would have fainted from exertion if I had not
been holding you up.'

Let him think it had been exertion and not his presence that had caused her to feel faint.

'You cannot keep me here for ever.'

His stance changed, became more relaxed. He had
that air of boredom she had seen in the other courtiers.
But Hugh didn't fool her.

Oh, he was dressed as ornately as any courtier. The
green of his tunic, woven very fine, lay perfectly over
his chest and tapered slightly at his waist. His tan leggings fitted seamlessly over his legs and his boots
gleamed new. Yet none of his frippery hid what he had
become. He was too unyielding, too rugged to look like
anything but what he was: a warrior.

She had never thought of him that way, although
he had trained for knighthood all his life. She had
watched him broaden into a man, but he had always
been Hugh...a girl's infatuation.

Now he was something more. Something she didn't
understand.

'I do not need for ever,' he said. 'I need enough time
for you to tell me what you did with the King.'

'Did?' she repeated. 'What I *did* with the King?
Don't you mean "spoke of"?'

'Do I?'

He would not let her avoid this conversation. She had wanted—no, *needed* to confide in someone. And here was Hugh, asking her to do so. As if she would ever confide in him again.

'He congratulated me on my winning,' she said.

'Something more happened; the King doesn't just share pleasantries in his private chamber.'

'Nothing of importance.'

'Your blushing gives you away. You were never good at lying.'

She'd have to get good at it. Her sisters' lives were at stake.

'It is of little consequence for you.'

His eyes narrowed and he abandoned his appearance of nonchalance. 'Maybe you haven't changed. I see you have kept your stubbornness.'

She'd have preferred to keep her pride, but it hadn't take long in Hugh's presence for her to know that it was still in tatters.

'I do not see how it concerns you.'

'The King and his friendships *always* matter to me.'

'I am hardly his friend.'

He eyes hardened with a heat that slid along her face, taking in her eyes, the slant of her jaw, and resting on her lips. She felt his eyes there, felt his words as he answered.

'No, I suppose *friend* doesn't quite capture your role in the King's life, does it?' His eyes were back on hers and the heat was gone. 'But I refuse to think you've changed that much. Whatever the King wants of you, you won't be able to do it.'

Shock caused her to ask, 'How do you know what the King wants of me?'

'It isn't hard to guess. You were in his private chamber for over an hour.'

He *had* been watching her—maybe even listening behind a door or a tapestry. The King had made her think it was a private conversation. There could only be one reason why Hugh would be privy to this secret: the King did not trust her.

Well, she'd show them both.

'What do you know what I can or cannot do? It's been six years. Long enough for both of us to change.'

'Not long enough. Not to betray your family like this.'

'It's *not* a betrayal. It's an honour!'

Colour left his face. 'To hell with this pretence. What has he done to you?'

He moved to grab her.

She jerked her arm away. 'Do not delude yourself into thinking I would welcome your touch again.'

Anger blazed in his eyes before he could hide the emotion from her. She fought the instinct to step back. Hugh wasn't pretending he was angry; he was acting as if he hated her.

'No?' He dropped his arm. 'Or maybe it is the King's touch you prefer.'

The insult seized at her thoughts. This wasn't a conversation about her spying. Hugh didn't know what the King had asked of her. He thought she was *whoring*.

Rage whipped and tightened her throat. 'I'd prefer anyone to you!'

'Then you have changed from the girl I once knew,' he said. 'What happened after you threw yourself at me and I refused? Did you throw yourself at another?

Did he refuse too? Or were you simply waiting for the King to notice your...*charms*?'

She clenched her skirts so she didn't strike him. 'If I was, that would be my affair.'

His mouth curved cruelly. 'An interesting choice of words.'

Her fingers bit into the cloth. It didn't matter what he thought. He didn't deserve the truth.

'I don't have to listen to this.'

She stepped over the plants, not caring when her skirts snagged on some rosemary.

He shifted away and let her pass. 'There is no need to ruin your gown in order to escape from me. I will go, but I will stop whatever has been started here.'

'Only if the King wishes it.'

She smiled and knew it didn't reach her eyes. Let him make what he would out of her words. She was beyond caring.

His hands flexed at his sides and he loomed over her before he settled back on his heels.

'He *will* wish it,' he bit out as he pivoted away. 'I'll make sure he wishes it.'

He was out of her sight before she could take two breaths.

She felt rooted where she stood. Rooted. And she was standing amongst the herbs.

A tight rumble rose involuntarily from deep inside her. She bit her lips to seal it in but the sound burst out of her. Then there were more—too fast, too quick to control—until she was laughing and crying in the garden. Hysterics amongst the herbs.

She clamped her hands over her mouth and wiped

furiously at her tears. Frustrated at herself, she brushed at her skirts until she could take large gasps of air.

By the time the sun had risen and the opening of shutters echoed in the courtyard, she could breathe again and felt lighter. Better.

Better than she'd thought she would after seeing Hugh again. Maybe all she had needed was those hysterics to settle her thoughts.

She strolled further into the garden and picked an apple from the arbour.

When she had first come to the garden she had thought being alone would sort out her thoughts, but it was her outpouring that had made two things painfully clear.

The first was that she knew herself better than Hugh did—and in more ways than she had ever guessed.

She *could* do what the King commanded. Spying was no more than discovering information and lies. It was no more than seeking the truth. Her worries over betraying her friends were misplaced.

She would find a way into their homes. If someone she knew was a traitor then searching through their belongings would not be a betrayal of friendship. If treason against her King had been committed, she had already been betrayed.

She couldn't believe she had ever wondered if she could spy. A wrong had been committed. What did she always do when there was an injustice? She made a plan and corrected it. If there was a wrong, she'd set it right. She couldn't believe she had ever questioned herself.

It had to be the surprise of seeing Hugh again that had muddled her thinking about spying.

Her thinking always became ensnared when it came

to him. Their conversation today was proof of that. Over
the years she had imagined many conversations with
Hugh, but in her imaginings the conversations had made
sense.

This conversation certainly didn't. He had never
given her an honest answer as to why he'd sought her
in the garden. The flattery about her dress and wanting
to see her alone had been a lie. He might remember differently, but she would never forget his rejection of her.

She bit hard into the apple. It was mealy from the
cold, but she didn't care. He believed she was the King's
mistress. He thought she whored with other men. He
had come to the garden to find the answer for himself.
Maybe he'd thought she would lie with him as well!

Hurrying her pace, she revelled in the crunch of the
pebbles beneath her feet, but it didn't ease her heart.
And that was the second pain-filled fact she had learned
from her crying.

She was still in love with Hugh.

For six years she had fooled herself into thinking
she no longer cared for him. How wrong she had been.
She might as well be sixteen again, with all her wild
longings.

But she didn't *feel* sixteen around him. There was
something more now. She felt…

She took another bite of the apple. What good would
it be to delve into what she felt around him? Hugh had
ridiculed her youthful declaration of love. And now he
thought she whored with the King.

What manner of man was he?

She knew the answer to that: the wrong manner of
man.

Anger rushed through her limbs and sent heat to her

face. She had been wronged for many years by Hugh. And, no matter how much of a wrong it had been, she could never set her heart to rights.

Pivoting, she strode towards the exit. She had lost in the battle of love, but there was more to her than her heart. There was her loyalty, her honour, her determination.

Throwing the apple core onto some shrivelled clippings, she made her decision.

To hell with Hugh and her heart. No more distractions, deliberations or confusions.

She had a traitor to catch.

Chapter Three

November, 1296

Of course, making the decision to be a spy and knowing how to do it were two different matters entirely.

Alice walked purposefully through the town square to the widest house in Swaffham. Icy rain pelted against her. She clutched her green cloak tighter. It was a futile gesture. The rain had already found gaps around her neck and cuffs, and her dress lay coldly sodden against her trembling skin.

She sped up her walking, aware of other unfortunate drenched souls jumping out of her way.

Two weeks of wasted time at Court and travelling to Swaffham and she only had vague ideas of what she could do to find the Seal. It wasn't as if she could *ask* anyone how to spy. She was sworn to secrecy.

At least she knew what she had to do first. She needed information about the people in town—which meant she needed to be around them and invited into their homes. And there was only one place to go for those types of invitations.

Pushing open the door, she walked quietly into the building that held many town meetings. The hall was a simple large room, filled with chairs and tables. The walls were covered with plain unembroidered panels of green linen cloth. A fire blazed in the hearth under the hood of a huge chimney, and showed light that the narrow windows fitted with oiled parchment could not.

Fresh rushes crunched under her feet and alerted the men whispering in different corners to her presence. Some of them looked up, but most kept to their heated conversations and ignored her.

She pulled her hood tighter around her face and walked briskly to the stairs leading to her sister's living quarters.

When she reached the landing, she knocked on the large wooden door. The moment the servant had ushered her into the private solar her sister Elizabeth flew down the narrow stairs at the back of the room.

'Oh, Alice! I am glad you returned. You would not *believe* what I have been through in the last few days.'

Alice tried to untangle her wet cloak, but her fingers were swollen and red from the cold. The maid who had let her in concentrated on the knot and Alice gratefully lowered her trembling hands.

'What has happened now?' she asked.

Elizabeth took the remaining steps. 'The town council will not listen to John.'

This was a familiar argument to Alice. Her brother-in-law might not have the respect of the town, but her sister had the respect of her husband. 'Do they ever?'

'They *should*!'

'Because he's your husband or because he's the mayor?'

Elizabeth shook her head and gave a tiny exasperated grin. 'Both.' She strode across the hall, her slippered feet slapping against the bare wooden boards. 'He is trying to initiate a law so that householders and shopkeepers are required to clean the streets in front of their houses and shops.'

The maid removed the cloak and herself from the hall.

Alice rubbed the cold from her arms. 'That seems like a reasonable request, given previous laws that have cleaned the inside of the businesses and moved others farther away from residences.'

'I thought so—since it is their own waste they wade through in the streets! With all this rain it makes everything slippery and dangerous. It is a wonder more children do not drown when they fall.'

'You and John have done so much to clean this town, you would think they would listen to this.'

Elizabeth shook her head. 'That is the penalty of working with the bureaucracy of officials and magistrates. Great for regulating guards to watch the ramparts and patrol the streets by night, but if they have to actually *do* something, like clean their own homes, they argue and fight.'

'What will you do?'

Elizabeth winked. 'I have some ideas—but John says they could land me locked in irons.'

'Doesn't that make them *good* ideas?'

'Oh, I have missed you!' Elizabeth grabbed Alice's hands and a frown marred the smoothness of her brow. 'You are freezing!'

She pulled Alice's hands away from her body and looked in earnest at her gown.

'And you are soaking wet. Where have you been?'

Alice looked around at the house. The servants were trying to be discreet, but they were everywhere.

'Is there anywhere we could go that's private?'

'Of course—my bedroom has already been cleaned and—'

She didn't wait until her sister had finished answering, but immediately set out for the second and more narrow flight of stairs towards the family's private rooms.

These rooms were warmer, filled with thick rugs, bright embroidered linens and cushions. It was her sister's touch, but Alice didn't take any comfort in the softness of the room, and she didn't wait for the click of the door before she started talking.

'I walked from the town's gates—' Alice started.

'Why would you do such a thing? It is winter. Is there something wrong with the coach or the footmen? Is it the horses? Father did not order the leaking roof repaired and they are terribly sick! What do you need me to do?'

Used to her sister's rapid-fire questioning, Alice walked to the hearth and poked at the fire to increase its heat. 'No, no, it's none of those things. I merely needed to talk to you in private and didn't want my presence to be noted.'

'Something happened to you in London?' Elizabeth pulled a red and green woven blanket from a chair and draped it over Alice's shoulders. 'You should not have gone there alone.'

She had always been glad that Elizabeth had stayed in Swaffham. She couldn't imagine confessing about going to dances to their oldest sister, Mary, who married into a family with even more land, and who only liked to talk about sheep. Not that she liked confessing anything. She'd rather depend on herself and not communicate any of her worries.

Which was probably why, now that she was here, she didn't know what to say. She couldn't lie and she couldn't tell the truth. Her sister was cunning and knew her too well. She would have to talk in half-truths in order not to raise her sister's suspicion. And she would have to find a reason to get invitations into everyone's homes.

As a wealthy merchant's daughter, she used to receive such invitations, but she had been refusing them for so long she was no longer offered any.

Now, not only did she need to be invited, she needed a reason that she wanted to be invited. Unfortunately, the only thing she could think of would force her to swallow her pride. But what was pride compared to a king's order?

'I think it's time…' she began.

'Time for what? Do not be coy with me. You know I cannot stand it.'

She had expected Elizabeth to interrupt. In fact she needed her sister to interrupt so she would have time to prepare each sentence.

'You know how you are always saying that one day I'll be over Hugh?'

Elizabeth's hands flew to her chest. 'You are not making some cruel joke?'

'I'm not.'

Or at least a part of her was telling the truth. And her anger at him made the lie easier.

'I think that day has come.'

Elizabeth sat down hard on the edge of her bed. 'I am speechless. I never thought I would hear you say those words. Even if you felt that way, I never thought you would actually *say* it. How did it happen? You have met someone? Were you introduced?'

Oh, she'd met someone. She met the man she had foolishly fallen in love with, and he'd thought her a whore. Simply the memory of him tightened her guts and coiled her innards with irritation.

'Nothing like that!'

Her sister's brows rose and she gave her a know-ing look.

Needing to be calm, Alice forced her mind to erase Hugh. She wouldn't tell her sister of seeing Hugh again. There would be no point. It wasn't as if he would ever return to Swaffham. He hadn't returned to the town in years. Here, she was safe from his presence.

If only her thoughts were safe from thinking of him.

'I have met many men,' she amended. 'It was dif-ficult not to at Court. There was eating, dancing and games. I could hardly go to London and not meet some-one.'

'Well, then, who was it that took your eye? Please tell me. Do I know him? You know I always thought Mitchell would be a fine match for you—especially now he's returned from his travels.'

Mitchell was close to her age, and as sensible as her sister's husband. He was indeed a perfect match for her. If only she could force her heart to agree to such a bargain.

She'd have to tell a truth.

'No one in particular took my eye.'

Elizabeth frowned. 'None ever do. You have always

been this way. Ever since that ridiculous incident when you were six.'

'It wasn't ridiculous!'

'You defend him again?'

'I can hardly not defend him. I broke his nose!'

Elizabeth shook her head. 'You did *not* break Hugh's nose; Allen broke his nose.'

'I'm the one who swung my fist.'

'But Allen and his friends lowered you into that empty well.'

'I hate the dark to this day. And if not for Hugh, where would I be?'

'Happily married to a suitable man instead of pining away for years in vain hope. I thought you were over him?'

Alice slipped out of her shoes and placed them closer to the fire. 'I am.'

'Then why are you defending him?'

She raised one foot to the fire and revelled in the warmth seeping into her toes. 'Because, despite what he has done, and despite the fact I'm no longer in love with him, he does deserve some bit of kindness.'

'Truly?'

It was all lies—lies, lies. She was in love with him and he didn't deserve kindness, but she had to continue her story.

'I was scared witless after being left in that well. When Hugh came and fought them off—'

'Getting his nose broken in the process,' Elizabeth interrupted.

'I was so relieved.'

'And that relief manifested itself into some strange infatuation until you thought yourself in love with him.'

Elizabeth stood and paced the room. 'It was childish, making that vow to marry him.'

'I was six!'

'But you made a vow. It didn't matter what age you were. You were always stubborn, always headstrong. You have never broken a vow, never backed down from a challenge. I always feared the moment you vowed to marry him you would stick to it even if you did not love him. Or that maybe you would fool yourself into loving him simply to fulfil your vow.'

Alice looked down. Steam rose from the bottom of her dress. This was not the conversation she'd wanted. Defending Hugh was a mistake, and had only alerted Elizabeth to her true feelings. She needed to change the subject or else she'd never fool her sister.

'Aren't you curious what happened to me at Court?'

Elizabeth's eyes narrowed, but she nodded her head in agreement.

'I noticed men and women talking...laughing. Together. It reminded me of you and John. It was...painful.'

Elizabeth bit hard on her lip, her hands tightly clenched in her lap. 'I did not know you felt that way.'

She didn't. She had always been happy for her and John. If there had ever been an occasional wish that she could be as happy, it had been quickly pushed away so she could concentrate on her projects.

She turned her back to her sister and thrust her feet and hands towards the fire. 'I didn't know I felt that way until I was at Court.'

'Curious that you should feel that way in London. It's not as if loyalty and love are in fashion there.'

'Maybe they seemed happy. Maybe I simply saw what I wanted to see. Maybe I want to be married.'

The squeak of the bed ropes and the flutter of her sister's dress notified her that Elizabeth was moving closer. Alice rubbed her hands and hunched her shoulders forward to hide her features. She felt Elizabeth's eyes trying to prise the truth from her profile, but she didn't dare look at her.

'You could borrow a gown of mine if you are so cold.'

Did Elizabeth suspect? She couldn't, *shouldn't* look at her sister. 'No, I'll warm up in a while.'

'You've turned down so many proposals...'

'I know.'

Elizabeth turned her attention to the fire and rubbed her hands briskly. 'But I believe there are a few of those men still available.'

Alice nodded her head. Even if Hugh hadn't been behind her reason for refusing those marriage proposals, she wouldn't have married any of the men who had applied for her hand. But they were the ones she needed to gain information from.

Elizabeth sighed. 'Alice, are you serious about this? Is this how you truly feel? Look at me.'

Concern creased Elizabeth's brow and troubled her grey eyes. Alice would have to make her performance more convincing if she was to get those invitations.

She smiled. 'It *is* how I feel.'

'Because I do not want you trying to placate your family into thinking you are happy. You know Father would be overjoyed if—

'Do not talk to me of Father and relationships. He's hardly one to talk about the raptures of love.'

Their father was overtly kind and generous with everyone. He loved their mother very much. Unfortunately, he loved many other women as well. It had only been a slight relief that he'd always tried to be discreet on his trips to London, but since their mother had died all discretion had vanished.

'Fair enough.' Elizabeth frowned. 'This is not one of your projects, is it? You are not doing this out of some warped sense of setting a wrong to rights?'

She kept her eyes on her sister's. This, at least, wasn't a lie. 'It isn't.'

'It's not some silly vow you made while you were away?'

'No.'

It wasn't a vow—or a project. It was an enormous promise to the King. She felt the weight of it heavily on her shoulders. Or maybe it was all the lying she was doing.

Elizabeth's hands went to her face and wiped the tears under her eyes. 'I cannot tell you what this means to me.'

Alice grabbed her sister's hands. 'Don't cry.'

'All this time…' Elizabeth's voice broke. 'All this worry. I did not think you would even attempt to find someone you deserve.'

'Please don't cry. Please. I can't take your tears.'

Waving her hands in front of her face, Elizabeth beamed. 'I am *happy* for you!'

Alice clasped her sister's hands firmly together and willed Elizabeth to stop her happiness. Such sisterly joy pressed upon her more heavily than the lies she'd told. She still had more lies to tell, and it wouldn't do if she failed this early in her mission.

'I know you're happy for me, but it means nothing if I don't actually have a husband.'

Elizabeth shook her hands free. 'That is easy to remedy. St Martin's Day is mere days away, and Christmas will soon be upon us. In fact, I can think of many upcoming affairs that John and I have been invited to. I'll simply secure an invitation for you as well.'

Such invitations were exactly what Alice both dreaded and needed. Lies and deceit pricked sharply in her heart, but she'd do anything to save her family.

'I knew I could count on you for help.'

Chapter Four

Hugh stormed through his old house—such as it was. The three-room residence was smaller than he remembered, the furniture rougher and the linens course. Abrasive, just like Swaffham. A small town with sparsely cobbled, cramped streets and not enough amenities where a man could get lost. Or, better yet, not be seen when he didn't want to be.

He had never intended to return to this town of his childhood. A town he had been forced to travel to when his dying mother had written to his errant father and begged him to care for his son.

And so, at the age of five, Hugh had been carted off by travelling strangers. He had left Shoebury knowing he was leaving his mother, knowing he would never see her again. Knowing he was travelling to the care of a man who had never wanted him in the first place.

His father, Clifford of Swaffham, a knight impoverished, had been an abusive drunk. Many a night Hugh had dreamed he still lived in Shoebury with his mother—only to awake to cold and hunger. Many a time he'd thought it would have been better to be left alone in the streets without a parent.

Why his father had agreed to take him, he had never known. To this day Hugh didn't know if he hated his father or Swaffham more. The tiniest comfort he hoped for upon his arrival was Bertrice's food, and that held no flavour.

He rubbed the grit from his eyes. Even with her ankle healing from a recent break, Bertrice's food was better than fine. It was his mood that wasn't. He wanted to crack the clay cup in his hand, but he tipped it to his mouth and downed the ale instead.

Had *nothing* changed? Even his need to drink remained the same. He knew from experience that there wasn't enough ale in all the land to hide his thoughts from himself, and if he drank much more he'd wouldn't be able to keep his thoughts to himself.

Maybe if he poured out all his secrets he'd be rid of their poison.

The thought of finally being free of their crushing weight sent a mad euphoria through him—before hard reason dropped like an axe.

Laughing bitterly, he poured more ale into his cup. Pouring out his secrets would never happen. If it did, he'd be free—but only of his own head.

He renewed his pacing, stifling walls and bitter memories assaulting him from every cobwebbed dusty corner. At Edward's court he shared his room with four other knights, but his suite was generous, its linens and wall coverings fine and warm in colour and purpose.

He kicked one of the thinly plastered wooden walls and a shifting of dust hit his shoe and hose. There wasn't a scrap of colour or warmth in this hovel.

He shook the dust off in disgust. He regretted telling Bertrice not to clean the rooms. She had been insistent, but his bitterness at returning had tainted everything. Now he could see that if he was to spend time here, he'd have to make this hovel hospitable. Pampered soft bastard that he was.

Not that courtly pampering had made him any kinder, or any more of a gentleman. He was an unscrupulous man in a merciless predicament.

He'd been ordered by King Edward to find the keeper of the Half-Thistle Seal. Because private information had been leaked from the King's chamber, Edward had lost a military surprise he'd been strategizing for months.

The Scots had not come as quickly to heel as the King had demanded since he'd won at Dunbar, and Balliol was now at the Tower of London. Since July, the King had relentlessly ordered nobles and clansmen to swear him fealty. Adamantly established sheriffs and governors to enforce his rule.

But that wasn't all Edward had done. He'd also launched spies to infiltrate and report that his orders were being completed.

Hugh was such a spy. His skill with sword and strategy had been noted, but not exemplified.

Hugh had had the honour of gaining the King's attention earlier this year, in April, after the death of the King's favoured knight, Black Robert.

Secrets. Hugh was good at keeping and discovering them. He was good at reporting to the King. He had all the information Edward could ever need, but not everything he wanted to know.

For one, Black Robert was not dead, and was in

fact Hugh's closest friend and currently living on Clan Colquhoun's Scottish soil while married to a Scot.

As for the second secret—Hugh didn't need to travel anywhere to find the keeper of the Half-Thistle Seal. Hugh merely needed to look in a mirror or in the purse strapped tightly to his waist. The small seal had been pressing heavily since it had been hidden on the inside of his tunic. A metal thistle cut in half. One for him. One for Robert. Made so that Hugh could inform Robert of the King's whereabouts and of any royal decrees that might affect Clan Colquhoun.

How had Edward discovered the Seal so soon? Only a few messages had been sent. Necessary to warn his friend of the King's movements. Secretive, but innocent, and certainly not enough to start a war. Merely enough to save lives.

So many lives. The English...the Scots. How long could he protect both? Did it matter?

Ah, yes, it did—and that brought him to his third and definitely most perilous secret: Alice.

A joke on him since he was ordered to pay close attention to the Fenton family. Of all the families in all the land that the King had ordered him to spy on it had to be—

Three sharp blows to the weakened door had pieces of chipped plaster falling to the floor. Turning sharply, Hugh sloshed the ale in his cup as he watched the inconsequential door withstand the pounding. His sole concern was who might be visiting this time of night.

Only Bertrice knew he was in the town. He wanted it that way—wanted to give himself at least a day before he had to face everyone. Face what he had to do.

Another bang on the door...another swirl of dust.

'Hugh, open the damn door—it's freezing outside.'

Hugh recognised the voice, unlatched the door and stepped away as a tall, thick giant of a man stormed into the tiny house and stamped his feet to dislodge the snow that had settled on him.

Blowing on his hands, the man turned. 'It's not much warmer in here.'

'I can open the door for you to leave and find warmer accommodations,' Hugh replied, latching the door and turning to Eldric, a man he had known since they'd fostered at Edward's court.

'I think I'll take my chances in here,' Eldric replied.

'Are you sure about that?' Hugh replied, assessing one of his oldest friends—one he had not seen for many years.

Many young squires had been shoved into the same room back then. There had been nothing to differentiate Hugh from the rest of the boys Edward fostered, but even then Eldric had been huge. Everyone had wanted to be his friend and his partner.

Having known too many tormentors in the past, Hugh had steered clear—which had only got him noticed by Eldric.

It hadn't taken long for Hugh to realise that Eldric wasn't like the children in his past. For one, his friend had whistled—a habit that would have been mercilessly mocked if Eldric had been a hand span shorter. The other thing was that he was always at ease with his place and with everyone around him. From a lowly servant to the King, Eldric took every meeting with a happy outlook.

Such an outlook on life had intrigued Hugh. Growing up in Shoebury and then in Swaffham he had thought his life sheltered though he'd always known his family's past darkened him. He knew it for certain when he heard Eldric laugh with an ease he could never manage.

However, there was nothing at ease about his friend now—and he guessed it wasn't only the cold that caused the certain tenseness to his friend's shoulders and expression.

'What are you doing here, Eldric?'

Eldric pointed to the flagon still on the table. 'Is there any left?'

Hugh knew better than to turn his back to fetch another cup. 'Not much.'

Eldric's gaze took in Hugh's dust-covered boots, his travel-worn breeches and wrinkled tunic. 'I can tell that.'

Hugh knew he was hardly in courtly dress and had drunk deep. But that was his own business, not this town's nor his childhood friend's. Years had passed since he'd seen him, and yet even though Eldric had scarcely been in his presence, he knew exactly how to challenge him.

In these small confines, there was only one way to accept such a challenge.

Turning his back, Hugh fetched another cup and flipped it over in front of Eldric, so that dust, plaster and insect remains fell to the ground.

Without so much as a telling tic, Eldric accepted the cup and poured the rest of the flagon's ale into it.

Hugh's humour lifted. Regardless of the unanswered question of why Eldric was in Swaffham, there was some of the same man he had known. Eldric was indeed still at ease with his world.

'As to why I am here…' Eldric shrugged. 'You have to know news of your presence in this town has spread.'

Gossip. He might have underestimated the power of the small town. 'I arrived today. I thought myself alone for tonight, but that's not what I meant.'

'Ah, you mean why am I in Swaffham?'

Hugh gave a curt nod. 'Not exactly your home town.'

'I've got cousins here now. And, though it is yours, I never thought you'd return.' Eldric took a sip and eyed the empty flagon. 'How can you be still standing?'

'I am my father's son.'

Eldric scanned the room's sparse furnishings. 'You weren't exaggerating about your past.'

'And were you about yours?'

Eldric sighed, his expression resigned. 'Come, this is a gloomy conversation.'

'Without any answers being revealed. It's late, and I'm tired.'

'Well, then, I'll get to the point. I am like you…as you most likely would have guessed by now…if not for the strength of that ale.'

To cover his surprise, Hugh turned to sit. There was only one other chair in the room—his father's chair, but Hugh had broken that long ago though the remains stayed in the corner.

Hugh didn't know if he was more surprised that jovial Eldric was a spy or that he had disclosed it. He had heard that Eldric was commissioned, but had thought it only a rumour.

'Edward sent you here?'

'No, I'm on a…detour.'

'Personal?' Hugh asked.

Eldric gave a small smile.

Hugh didn't expect an answer, but sometimes the most obvious questions slipped into answers.

'Are we friends?' Eldric said.

'Yes,' Hugh replied, surprised that the answer came easily despite himself knowing better. Maybe there was still some of that sheltered and naive boy in him yet.

Eldric nodded, as if Hugh had answered some other question not asked. 'Good to know.'

Hugh sensed that there was more to say, and he intended to wait. After all, he knew about keeping secrets. If he pried too deeply Eldric would do the same. With his silence, it appeared Eldric knew a score of secrets—as did Hugh. Could it be possible that Eldric was a friend in truth? There was only one way to find out.

Shifting in his seat, he said, 'I would think Edward would know better than to employ *you* to carry and catch secrets. It's not as if you can hide.'

Eldric let out a startled laugh. 'You'd be surprised how easy it is to hide in plain sight. People don't equate my handsome stature with intelligence.'

'Your intelligence must be all you're relying on!'

Eldric did laugh then. 'I may not have bested you, but my sword arm is still longer than yours.'

Hugh drained his cup. 'Longer, but not sharper.'

'Sharp enough. And in these quarters you couldn't escape even with that footwork you learned from...' Eldric's voice faded and he shook his head. 'Sorry, I heard the news.'

The unsaid name hung between them. 'Black Robert' of Dent—Edward's favoured knight and Hugh's mentor.

Hugh had been just as surprised as Eldric when Robert, who had been older and already making a name for himself, had taken him under his wing to train him.

Hugh had readily accepted, even knowing that Robert trained hard, and he had been pushed to do the same. Through that time Hugh had tormented himself, wondering if Robert knew of his shame because of his father's drunkenness and lost honour.

But Robert surely had to have done, because nothing was truly a secret at Court—which had made Robert's sullying himself with Hugh's family reputation all the more startling.

Of course Hugh had heard of Robert's own rumoured history. How he might not be legitimately-born, which shouldn't be possible given his knighthood. Still, the vague rumour had persisted and surrounded Robert, despite Edward's affection for him and his alliance with a Welsh Marcher Lord.

Hugh hadn't cared. He was grateful for any kinship with the formidable knight, and had continued to follow Robert's prescribed training even when he left Court.

When he had seen his friend again Robert had been a changed man, but they'd stayed close.

'I heard you were the last who saw him.' Eldric shook his head. 'Still can't comprehend how the bastards got him.'

'He went off alone,' Hugh supplied. 'And he was just a man.'

'A legend.'

Even more so now in death.

A death that the English mourned, but that Hugh knew was a lie.

Secrets and more secrets.

Robert was still alive, and married into a Scottish family. And if he was found he would be formally executed.

Hugh, who held his secret, would most likely be murdered on some abandoned road, his body left to rot in a forgotten wood.

He had made a vow that day to Robert, on Scottish soil, that he would never tell the King or his fellow man that Robert still lived. A solemn vow. A traitorous one, as well.

Hugh didn't care. The only thing he cared about was his friendship with Robert, and that he'd take to his grave…wherever that was to be.

However, that didn't mean he wanted to die any time soon, and Eldric merely mentioning Robert was a threat.

'What are you doing here, Eldric?' he repeated.

Eldric kicked at the dirt on the floorboards. 'Attending a dinner tonight. It's St Martin's Day.'

Holidays. Celebration. Hugh wasn't in the mood for merriment.

Standing, he signalled to the door. 'I shouldn't keep you, then.'

'I came to take you with me.'

Hugh bit back a telling curse. Wanting no company, he'd purposefully kept quiet about his arrival. He'd wanted one night to wallow in self-pity upon being forced to return here. One night to drink as if copious amounts of ale in this hovel didn't hold bitterness.

But that was not why he wanted to curse. It was because Eldric had been invited to a traditional dinner and he could bring a guest.

'How long have you been here?'

'Weeks.'

'Weeks' meant he had been here before the King had sent *him*. If Eldric was a spy, it didn't have anything to do with him and Alice.

So perhaps it was true that he'd came on a detour. But no detour took that much time in a town the size of Swaffham.

'Weeks' meant something else. Friend or no, Eldric wasn't on any mere detour. Even if it was futile, Edward had sent Hugh here on a mission to find the Half-Thistle Spy, and he didn't like any interference. Eldric being here for weeks was definitely an interference.

Of course Eldric could have lied about his time spent here, and hadn't, which should go in his favour. But there were too many coincidences that Hugh didn't like.

He also didn't like it that his flagon and his cup were empty.

'The fare will be delicious at the mayor's house,' Eldric said.

The mayor's house meant Alice. The one woman he shouldn't see. Not in the state he was in. Not *ever*.

Knowing his going could only be a trap, Hugh answered, 'Why not?'

Chapter Five

'Finally you've arrived!' Elizabeth exclaimed as Alice was ushered into the receiving hall.

'Not soon enough,' Alice said, allowing the servants to remove her heavy cloak, hat and gloves.

'As usual, the November wind is battering this house,' Elizabeth said. 'I had a dreadful time getting the children to bed, but at least it's not raining.'

'It's starting to.'

'All the guests haven't arrived yet!'

'They'll come.' Alice blew on her hands. 'How's the goose?'

Elizabeth let out a rough exhalation. 'You knew about that?'

It was Martinmas—St Martin's Day—and the start of the Christmas season. A busy day for farmers, whose livestock had to be slaughtered and dried for the coming months, a profitable one for beggars knocking on doors for alms, and a gluttonous day for feasting. Lots of food, and even more drink. And at her sister's home Alice would gain invitations to others' homes.

'Esther hasn't been able to talk of anything else for

the last two days.' Alice fluttered her hands in the air and widened her eyes. "'Elizabeth can't find a St Martin's Day goose! What will be done? Something has to be done!'" She rubbed her hands to give them warmth. 'This morning I had to order her to stay at home.'

'*Order* Esther?' Elizabeth strolled into the parlour. 'Who ever heard of such a thing?'

'So true!' Laughing, Alice followed her sister. 'Luckily for us both, Bertrice had heard from three other sources that a goose had been delivered to the mayor's kitchens.'

'Bertrice? How is her ankle?'

'Mending, much to Esther's relief.'

'They always were good friends.'

'Hence the reason why the gossip of no goose for St Martin's Day caused a scandal!'

Elizabeth shook her head ruefully. 'Oh, I know it's been years since you've been to a formal function, dear sister, but it's not that I have a choice.'

Alice stamped her feet, which tingled with the cold. 'Out of the two of us, you made the wiser decision.'

Elizabeth smile widened. 'Yes, I did, didn't I?'

Alice felt a pang in her heart at Elizabeth's happiness. The role of mayor's wife was ideal for her sister's excellent social skills. It was made all the more perfect since she and John adored each other.

But Alice had her own bit of happiness to divulge. 'Today, William needed no instruction with the abacus.'

Elizabeth clapped her hands. 'Oh, I'm so happy for you.'

Another pang. This time of annoyance. 'Not happy for me, for *him*.'

Elizabeth's elated smile dimmed. 'Yes, for him. It's—'

'No more, Elizabeth. This is better for him.'

It was an old argument. William was the only child of Bertrice's friend, Sarah. When she and her husband had drowned, Bertrice took him in. Bertrice hadn't always been able to corral William. As he got older, Alice would find him wandering the Great Hall or other official rooms. It hadn't taken long for Alice to realise how bright and curious he was.

She'd always helped families with food, clothing, tools and sometimes with chickens or goats from her own stocks when her father wasn't looking. But with William, she had given to in other ways by educating him on matters around the house.

Eventually the little tutorials had turned into lessons. And now, William came to the house twice weekly for his studies.

Alice was certain William would make one of the finest stewards in the country, if only someone would take him on.

'Is it better for him?' Elizabeth pursed her lips. 'You know he has to be noble-born to run a household.'

Alice's frustration burned, despite her certainty that her sister was wrong. 'Perhaps I intend to put him in a more…accommodating home.'

'Mary *knew* it!' Elizabeth's smile was triumphant. 'She knew that if you couldn't provide for him in Father's home she'd end up with William in hers.'

Alice wasn't surprised her sisters had talked about her. She also wasn't surprised that they'd guessed her plans. Still, she didn't know how they were feeling.

'And did Mary protest?'

Elizabeth sighed. 'She didn't…*un*protest.'

Alice wanted to smile her own triumphant smile. It

wasn't an agreement, but it was a start. William had many more years before he'd be fully trained. In that time she could wear Mary down.

William would be perfect for Mary's household, and she didn't live that far away. Alice would keep him herself, but knew her father would never allow William to run his home. Her father wanted the best of everything. And that included having people in his employ with only the best connections.

Her father would take on the eighty-eighth cousin of the King even if he was a thief and couldn't count with his fingers.

'Has Father Bernard told William he intends to crown him Boy Bishop?' Elizabeth asked.

Alice did smile then. William—quiet and analytical—would be the best Boy Bishop in all of Swaffham, if not in the whole region.

It was a great honour. Every year a boy was chosen to be a pretend Bishop from the sixth of December to the twenty-eighth. Under the guidance of Father Bernard, William would officiate all the Advent services apart from mass.

There was a part of Alice that thought William would make a great steward for the church but, as much as William was worthy, even *she* knew the church would never accept someone with no royal blood.

'Not yet, but I have no doubts Father Bernard will tell him soon. There's no one more suitable for it.'

'He does have the most beautiful voice in the choir, which will help him secure the post,' Elizabeth said.

'And he has me to make sure it happens,' Alice said.

Elizabeth made a tsking sound. '*This* is why you remain unmarried. All your projects and causes. At least this particular project—making a child, with no connections or blood, steward of a wealthy landholding household—will start and end with William.'

Alice rubbed her hands towards the fire.

'Alice?' Elizabeth said in a warning tone. 'It will end with him? It's fine that you help the families here in Swaffham with other things, but William must be the only one you educate.'

Alice arched her brow. If she could help William, she could help others. Her sister had *her* projects as well, and Mary's household was larger than the entire Fenton family's. Alice had this.

'Why?'

'You are my most frustrating, sister.' Elizabeth glanced through the open doorway. 'But we're here to celebrate Martinmas. The Alistair and the Benson families are in the other room, and no doubt wondering what we're arguing about.'

'We're not arguing.'

'Chatting heavily, then.'

Alice smiled. 'Certainly.'

Elizabeth clasped her hands loudly. 'Don't think we won't chat heavily another day. But right now I need to ensure that Cook hasn't packed her satchel and left the kitchens.'

'Oh, yes! What a tragedy would occur if the precious goose can't be shoved in the oven and the cook, in shame, runs away!'

Elizabeth shook her head in chagrin, and Alice knew she had her sister on her side.

However, even as Alice's heart warmed, unease settled upon her. It was time for her to meet everyone. To laugh even if she didn't feel like it. Even if she disdained the waste and chatter that didn't help her projects. It was time to begin what King Edward had ordered her to do. It was easier arguing with her sister.

'Who else is coming?'

'The Alistairs and Bensons, along with Lyman and Mitchell. Also, a few from the town council and a couple of shopkeepers,' Elizabeth said.

Trust her sister to be supporting her husband. 'Ah, to address cleaning up the streets?'

Elizabeth smiled conspiratorially. 'I intend to ply them with lots of wine until they agree.'

'Lots of wine? That should make the Alistairs and Bensons happy.'

'No doubt the Alistairs more than most.'

Family friends for years, the Alistairs and the Bensons were like uncles and aunts to the Fentons. It would be easy for Alice to procure an invitation into their homes for investigation. They might be practically family, but she couldn't dismiss anyone from being responsible.

Apprehension made her dizzy. But with Elizabeth beaming nothing but goodwill, how could she not do what the King commanded? What wouldn't she do for her family?

'That seems like quite a party for St Martin's Day,' she said.

'Oh, I might have invited one more... Just to help your cause.'

Alice bit her tongue. It was what needed to be done, but the mere thought escalated her apprehension.

'Anyone I know?'

'It's a surprise. I have it on good accord that the gentleman who will be attending this evening is visiting family and hasn't been in town for years.'

Hugh had not been in Swaffham for years.

Alice's heart skipped. There was no reason Hugh should come to Swaffham. No reason at all, except she'd seen him in that garden and he had said he would talk to the King.

'You've gone pale.' Elizabeth's mouth turned down. 'Have you changed your mind?'

Alice tried to stop her spinning thoughts. It couldn't be Hugh. For one, Elizabeth would never have requested Hugh's presence, and two he couldn't be visiting family since he had none here.

'No, no. Merely...nervous, I suppose.'

Her sister's frown eased. 'It's the gentlemen present who should be nervous. That gown is stunning on you.'

The gown she had chosen tonight was one of her favourites. A silvery grey bliant with a purple surcoat. Alice had also adorned herself with a silver belt and the daintiest silver and pearl necklace she owned. She knew what the colours did to her eyes. She'd need every bit of confidence she could get.

'Go in. If not to show off that gown, you must be cold—and the fire in the other room is much larger.' Elizabeth gave a small smile. 'They don't bite, Alice, despite your avoiding them all these years...and I'll be with you soon enough.'

Plastering a smile on her face, Alice followed her sister out of the comfort of the private parlour and into the much larger public room. After some brief pleasantries and a nod to her guests, Elizabeth departed. A servant offered her a drink, and Alice took it gratefully.

She'd need the warmth and the wine's strength—

especially since Lyman and Mitchell turned immediately upon her entering. She knew them well enough. Both single, both with some means. Both of marriageable age, and just the kind of men who were her target.

Alice took a fortifying sip.

Following behind Eldric, Hugh stepped into the mayor's dining room, expecting the reactions of the seated company. In past similar situations, he had revelled in the quiet bite of that moment when complacency turned to outraged surprise or amused curiosity.

Unfortunately, this time he wasn't able to absorb all the surprised reactions on his sudden appearance before their ever-polite host and hostess rose to greet Eldric, who was already by their side.

With barely a glance from Elizabeth, the servants swiftly rearranged the table settings to make room for him. Other servants left to retrieve additional food.

All of it worked like societal clockwork. Even the guests seemed to move with precision as they adjusted their seats. Except for a few people, he didn't recognise anyone. Not a surprise since most of them washed their hands of his entire family.

What was surprising was that Eldric had lied when he'd said he was permitted to bring a guest. The evidence of the servants adding a place for him was all too clear. Hugh would have to pay him back later for this trick.

Far less interesting was the fact that Baldrick Alistair was still alive—and fatter than ever. And his wife was already slurring, despite the early hour of the evening.

But there was alertness from the two single men he instantly recognised. Lyman's eyes had narrowed with unconcealed disgust even as he'd inclined his head. Mitchell had been too young to understand when Hugh had left, but appeared pleased at his return. As if his presence would revive a decidedly dull affair.

Since he, too, had a role to play, Hugh nodded to them both though he was truly aware of only one guest.

Alice—who stayed seated until the moving chairs forced her to rise, whose eyes widened in surprise and then quickly narrowed in anger and something else that flushed her cheeks.

It was a flush he shouldn't have been able to see in the dim light of the room, but he was distinctly attuned to it despite his impoverished childhood and the secrets that would separate them for ever.

When she rose, he wondered if she would step closer to greet him. He wondered, in the state he was in, if he would close the distance.

Too much ale. He needed more control when it came to her and his mission. And surely it was the ale that had made him agree to attend tonight. It couldn't be because Alice was here.

'The seating is prepared.' Elizabeth's voice was serene, though her hands were clenched in front of her. Elizabeth—so obviously a lady. She didn't approve of him being here, but would never insult him or Eldric by saying so.

'Thank you, Elizabeth,' he said, 'for the courtesy of your home this evening.'

The lines of worry around her eyes eased. 'It's St Martin's Day, Hugh, and all are welcome.'

Clever Elizabeth. Welcoming him and letting him know he wasn't special at the same time. When they were young she'd been friendlier to him—but that had been before Alice had been forced into the empty well.

Seating himself at the place she'd indicated was for him, he loosened the tenseness in his shoulders. He was in Swaffham, sitting down to a St Martin's Day feast, not entering unarmed into an enemy-laden field.

Although he had to wonder about that enemy field. Because subtly, strategically, Elizabeth had directed the servants to set him a place...next to Alice.

Before this moment, Alice hadn't known it was possible to freeze with heat. Hugh was a mere hand's breadth away. She felt more shock now than she had when she'd seen him at Court.

She felt more of his presence than ever before, too. Her eyes tracked every bit of his height, the broad sureness of his shoulders in his white tunic, the way his black leather breeches clung to his thighs, the gleam of the belt around his waist and the shine of his fine boots.

No doubt it was the unexpectedness of seeing him in the confines of her sister's home...and realising he would be sitting next to her.

Simply that thought alone made heat suffuse her and froze her to her seat, while anger and frustration coursed jaggedly through her shock. She welcomed those emotions—intended to use them to get through this farce of a celebration.

How dare Hugh show up to her sister's dinner? She'd been clear in the garden that she wanted nothing to do with him. And now she could do nothing to get rid of him—not without causing a scene. And she wouldn't ruin Elizabeth's party with accusations.

So she moved her focus elsewhere. Watched as others

were seated around her and counted each place being occupied. Only then did she realise that though Hugh would sit next to her they wouldn't share a trencher.

She had the honour of doing that with Lyman, who made her very skin crawl. But it wasn't enough to take her attention away from Hugh, whose tall frame slid into the chair to her right like a sword into a sheath.

The ease of it escalated her hostility and awareness of him. More so as she felt the heat of him at her side smelled his unique scent of snow, pine and steel and watched the graceful lethality of his hand reaching for his goblet. Such a simple task, but it gripped her heart in her chest.

She wouldn't make it through this dinner—knew that at some point she'd grab that goblet and pour its contents over him. And the blame wasn't only on this man at her side, but on Elizabeth, who sat serenely next to her husband.

Her sister could have sat Hugh anywhere at the table. Knowing Alice's resolution, she *should* have sat him elsewhere—several chairs down, so she couldn't see him, couldn't hear him, couldn't...*feel* him. But her sister hadn't done that because she was testing her.

So she unclenched her fingers digging into her skirts and straightened her shoulders. When a wrong had been committed, she made it right. To do so here, she wouldn't talk to Hugh. She would persevere through this simple dinner and secure herself invitations to peoples' homes. The King had commanded her. Hugh, who had inveigled himself an invitation, would have no power over her. As for her sister's actions—she had courses of food to get through while she prepared her words.

* * *

Hugh grabbed his goblet, peered into its depths, and knew that the King might easily use Elizabeth as a strategist. There were two scenarios as to why she'd sat him next to Alice. Either Elizabeth had forgiven Hugh for all the perceived wrongs he had done against her sister—which he doubted, or she had done it as an experiment to see how he behaved. But, if so, why?

Hugh chanced a glance to Alice. Her chin was high, her body arched away. She was surprised by his presence, and angered by it, too.

Oh, she'd made it clear she wanted nothing to do with him, but Hugh had requested an audience with the King that day after their argument in the garden.

A request that had been immediately granted…as if the King had expected it. Unfortunately, nothing of Alice's relationship with the King had been revealed.

No, his hope for answers was deterred, and he'd left the royal rooms with only more questions.

Because the King had ordered him to return to Swaffham—a town he despised, and whose people despised him. Return and spy on Alice.

And so, like the spy he was, tonight he would use her anger and surprise to his advantage. He still had too many questions when it came to Alice and her relationship with the King. Too many threatening factors, this town, the Seal, the Fenton family. Factors that needed to be tied…fixed…or at least forgotten.

Yet, all the schemes and factors were nothing when compared to the woman by his side. Even in that brief glance he saw the way her chestnut hair curled in the candle's light, the almost familiar way she had of sitting with her back straight, her shoulders rigid. Pride and determination in her every movement. Traits that were so much *her*, he would have recognised them anywhere.

Alice—whom he longed for and needed as much as air. Alice—who was very neatly ignoring him. And he was letting her…coward that he was.

He had never been good enough for her. And now his own actions made him a traitor to the King. Ignore Alice he must for his own sake, but a King demanded he watch her. He no longer felt like he was choking on the lies and deceit, but drowning in them.

'It seems as if we're sharing tonight.'

Hugh rolled the tenseness in his shoulders and turned to his right. A petite woman was looking expectantly at him. A similarly built man sat to her right. Most likely her husband, who wouldn't be sharing her trencher as was his right.

'It appears I've disrupted the seating arrangements,' he said.

'I don't mind.'

He recognised that light in the woman's eyes. He glanced at her husband, who sat with his new trencher partner. There were no warning glares sent his way. It seemed the husband didn't mind either.

'You don't remember me, do you?'

She was pretty, with dark hair and hazel eyes, her cheeks and chest plump with good food and health. If he *had* known her, he'd forgotten her—as he had everything about this town.

He gave her an appreciative glance and noticed the light flaring in her eyes. 'I'd like to be reminded,' he said.

The arch of a brow, and familiarity flashed through him. It was coming to him now.

'Maybe I won't tell you…to see how you'll tempt the information from me,' she teased.

He kept his expression neutral as he glanced at the feast he was to load the trencher with. 'May I?'

'Of course.'

'Is there anything you don't want?' he asked, as he reached for the serving spoon for the goose, and shifted to give room for the servant to pour the sauce.

'I think I'll take…everything.'

She'd been greedy back then as well, and had taken full advantage of the men who courted her. Even when she'd agreed to Gerald's proposal she had flirted. Now he wondered if it went beyond that.

'*Everything* is the least of what you deserve, Helen.'

'Ah, that didn't take long at all—and I thought it would be a fun way to pass the time. Whatever are we to do now?'

He laid thin slices of goose on the trencher and reached for the vegetable medley. 'About what?'

'About you coaxing other matters from me.'

She was propositioning him, and by the way her husband had turned his back and was whispering with his new companion it was clear this was sanctioned by their marriage vows.

And all of it was occurring under the watchful eye of the serene Elizabeth and her husband, Mayor of Swaffham. Was this evidence of more approval?

He'd thought the Royal Court brimmed with deception and unchecked lust, but this old town was no better.

'You have me at a disadvantage,' he said. 'How am I to know what tempts you?'

There was a slight brush of her hand against his as

she tore off a piece of their trencher. 'You're a clever man; I'm sure you'll figure it out.'

Her lips were at full pout, her eyes knowledgeable, but open to appear guileless, innocent, when she was anything but.

'You have too much faith in me. I'm afraid I'm not that clever.'

He saw the light dim in her eyes before she returned to her food. She took a few more bites before she gave a tap to her husband's arm. Oh, she understood the game well enough. He'd been polite, but had fully declined her proposition.

Still, simply the fact that it had happened made him feel sick. She had taken holy vows before God with the man on her right. If *he* was ever so lucky as to earn a wife, he would fight God and the Devil to keep her faith in him. Naive beliefs, he knew, but nonetheless true for him.

He was a man grown, who had travelled, fought and killed. He shouldn't be surprised that Swaffham now reflected the insidiousness prevailing over the rest of the country.

He was a twice-made fool. First with the lingering thought that Alice remained untouched, and second that this town he hated had remained the same as well.

He had drunk so much ale before he came here, and now he imbibed the wine. None of it was softening his thoughts. He was on that most hated plain of not being sober and yet not drunk enough.

Eyeing his goblet, but not taking a drink, he signalled to a servant to serve the rest of the feast laid out before them.

Knowing that nothing could make him forget his

restless thoughts, he would be better keeping sober in order to perform his futile mission. Fake though it was, the King had ordered him here, and he knew he had to go through the motions.

Appearances were everything in this game.

But by all that was holy, he wanted only one night to forget where and who he was.

Chapter Six

Forcing another smile, Alice worried that she wouldn't make it through dessert. Her sister never did anything in half-measures and, while Alice would rather give to those more in need of food, Elizabeth, the consummate hostess, would have several desserts set out in an order to highlight the wealth and orderly labour of her kitchens.

Alice wouldn't normally be ungracious about the role Elizabeth must play as lady of the mayor's household, but this one time she resented it. Only because by sitting here she was about to break one of God's commandments. If Lyman pressed his thigh to hers one more time she'd take her knife and stab him with it.

Her duties to the King and her family wouldn't allow her even to frown at him. Any sign of displeasure at being here would have her sister's all too observant eyes noticing it. Likely then Elizabeth wouldn't invite her to any of the upcoming festivities, and she wouldn't be able to do what she had come to do.

To catch the eye of Lyman and Mitchell and garner invitations to their homes.

Which, it seemed, would occur sooner than she liked. She didn't know what her sister had said to Lyman and Mitchell, but they were certainly paying her attention. All she had to do was smile and answer every one of their questions.

Unfortunately, the longer she spent in Lyman's company, the more she wanted to leave, but Mitchell was affable enough.

Invitations hadn't yet occurred, but perhaps they were waiting till it was more appropriate, or more private. Any woman in her situation would be honoured. After all, she wasn't young, and they knew of her various charities and projects in the town.

For her potential suitors, she knew her family connections were important, but they were not her only attraction. So she feigned the appropriate flattery she had learned to mimic at Court, and wished Lyman would quit glancing at her chest.

How could she endure any more of this?

A glance to her sister confirmed that she'd endure it to the ends of time. Any of the people around this table could possess the Half-Thistle Seal—could be committing treason.

Even Hugh...

What was he doing here? If he'd talked to the King that day, had the King sent him here? And if so, why? Did it have to do with the Seal? Or, if the King had denied his presence, was he here because of *her*? That made no sense. He had rejected her that day long ago. Because of her vow to marry him, he had avoided her even before that.

No, he couldn't be here because he'd wondered about her. It had to do with the King. And yet...

Every bite and drink she took, every question she gave and answered—through all of it she thought of Hugh sitting next to her. It didn't matter that she kept her eyes away from him. His very presence enveloped her. Even if he hadn't been there, she'd have been thinking of him. Either comparing his height to Lyman's, or the colour of his eyes to Mitchell's.

All her life she'd felt as if some thread bound them together. That they were at the whim of an unseen distaff and spindle. At the mercy of a master spinner who twisted the thread, tightened the edges. Made something sublime or frayed. For it had always been him.

Unlike what her sister thought, it had nothing to do with the vow she had made when she was six. If he hadn't embodied everything she'd ever wanted, how could such a flimsy childish vow ever have sustained the years of loneliness she'd had?

No, when he had rescued her she had instinctually known the man he was. So much more than his family. Determined, kind. Respectful. And his haunted eyes had clenched her heart and sealed it from opening for anyone else.

But he had changed since she saw him last. He was hardened. Cynical. And he thought her a whore. She would have nothing to do with a man who could so easily—

'Enjoying your meal?' Hugh said, his voice low, but not melodious. As if he'd forced the words to sound pleasant.

Alice glanced to Hugh. His eyes were intent, and there was a slight frown to his mouth as if he was determining something. His hair was still wet from the snow outside, but it looked as if it had been brutally combed with his fingers to tame the waves there. His clothes were rumpled, as if they'd been pulled out of a travelling sack. His jaw was unshaven, his demeanour worse than wear.

He had been drinking much during dinner, and if she was right, quite a lot before. And yet… And yet none of it mattered. She wanted to run her hand across the roughness of his jaw, to kiss the frown from his lips.

She also wanted to throw the contents of her goblet at him. She was a woman grown. Her musings were pathetic. More so now, since he had revealed the man he had become.

Alice forcefully stabbed at her meat and it almost skidded off her trencher. 'Of course,' she answered. 'I have such lovely company surrounding me.' She pointed to Lyman and Mitchell.

Hugh's eyes darkened as he acknowledged that she didn't point in his direction. 'It seems you enjoy your company quite a bit.'

His jibe against her innocence immediately erased her feeling of vulnerability. 'What isn't there to enjoy?' Alice said. 'And I see you're enjoying yours.'

She signalled to Helen, who had surprisingly turned her conversation to her husband. Helen *never* talked to her husband.

'I'm certainly enjoying this feast,' he said, dragging his meat through the sauce. 'But this food can't be as good as at the King's table.'

And so their conversation returned to the King. She had never sat at the King's private table; her feasts had been taken at the public banquets. However, perhaps she could have answers to her own questions.

'The food at the Tower was…exceptional.'

'Did you have much time to eat?'

That was *all* she had done. She wasn't nobility—only a wealthy merchant's daughter. It had bought her the attention of the Court, but didn't rank her in any standing. Until the game, she had been ignored, without even Esther to keep her company. But that wasn't for this conversation.

'Why are you talking to me?' she said, low to ensure her words weren't overheard. Already she could feel her sister's eyes on her and knew she had talked too long with Hugh...and yet her sister had sat them together.

'Is a lowly knight not worth talking, too?' he said.

Hugh's fingers danced over the trencher he shared with Helen. That slight movement sent an ache through her that she tried to hide as his eyes caught with hers. His were dark, as if childhood pain and anguish had seeped deep within him. As if he was now wrapped with a malevolence she didn't know or understand.

He was an enigma to her. There was cruelty to the curl of his lips, a blade-like cynicism in the way he held his body. The tilt of his head silently mocked everyone sitting around him.

Especially her.

'That's ridiculous,' she answered.

'Is it when evidence of your attendance at Court belies otherwise?'

She was a twice-born fool. She ached even while he insulted her. And this wasn't how she'd gain suitors or a traitor.

'If you're simply going to insult me, then why start any pleasantries?'

Why indeed? Hugh had no idea what he had wanted to say to Alice when he'd turned to her, but insulting her wasn't it. Yet as the meal progressed, he seethed inside; wanted to prevent the conversations she engaged in. Jealousy? When he had never felt it before?

Of course he'd feel it with Alice. Even so, the King had demanded he stay close to this family because of the Half-Thistle Seal, and it wouldn't do to insult her.

It also wouldn't do to apologise. That would be admitting to feelings. He could have *no* feelings when it came to her.

'Insults? I'm merely commenting on the food, and the differences of the fare laid before us.'

Alice's eyes lit with fire. He still hadn't been careful enough with his words. He didn't want to be careful. Simply hearing her talk to the other men burned in his heart, when he shouldn't feel anything for her at all. Not after all these years—not after his past or his present deeds.

'What I eat and with whom is hardly an interesting topic of conversation,' she said.

'Oh, I disagree.' He lowered his voice, leaned in, caught the warmth of her skin, the scent of rosemary and wool. 'Is this how it has been?'

'How what has been?'

'Since that day when you tried to kiss me? You holding court like this…garnering the attention of men.'

She opened her mouth, closed it. Started to speak again. 'And for what purpose do you think I garner the attention of men?'

Stop. He should stop. And yet his conscience, his heart, prodded him to continue.

'You were in the King's private chambers over long. I'm surprised you deign to consider these men worthy of you.'

'And you say you do not trade insults?'

He did, and he was, and he was a bastard for it, too. He only knew that no man was worthy of her—especially himself. Yet he relished the knife-prick of the words. He didn't like Alice laughing with other men. *Had* she turned to another after he had denied their kiss, or was the King her first?

'I merely reflect on the facts before me,' he said.

She frowned. 'This conversation isn't appropriate for the St Martin's Day feast.'

They shouldn't be having this conversation at all. Yet he couldn't help it. For some reason, she continued to face him too. *Why* was she acknowledging him?

She wasn't merely acknowledging him. She was studying him. His insults...his reminders of the past. Words laced with bitterness and truth. Not held back because he was here. Because he had drunk before he'd come, and that Alice was sitting next to him.

The various shades of grey in her eyes, the cadence of her words, her scent...all were too achingly familiar.

'What are you doing here, Hugh?'

'Having dinner,' he said quickly, to hide his surprise that she'd asked the question. She should have turned away from him by now, and yet she held his gaze.

God, he loved her eyes.

'In Swaffham?' she said.

'It is the start of the Christmas season, isn't that a good time to be home?'

Her eyes narrowed. 'When you never have come before?'

Suspicion and frustration laced her words, but there was something else too, like worry or fear. He scanned the company around them. Everyone was busy with their trenchers or their conversations.

He had expected her surprise at his arrival. And anger, perhaps, because of their conversation in the garden. He hadn't expected the apprehension underlying her words.

It was his turn to lower his voice, and he bowed his head to whisper in her ear. 'Why are you so concerned, Alice?'

She darted her eyes around—perhaps, as he had, to see if anyone was listening.

'Concerned? I'm merely pointing out the facts. Isn't that what you did with me? I see no point to this conversation.'

Crisp and direct, with no hint of unease. Perhaps he had imagined her unease. If so, what *was* his point in talking with her?

Because a king demanded it. But a monarch didn't require him to notice the light flashing in her eyes. To see some glimmer of the Alice he'd used to know. Not the one who held court in her sister's house or garnered the attention of a king.

He wasn't here to feel the knife-tip of jealousy either. He only needed to find useful information for the King. It clearly couldn't be the true owner of the Seal. So he needed to provide something else to appease his silver-hungry sovereign.

While he was here he'd do what he was good at: spy.

Raising his voice just enough to be overhead, and to plant the seeds so he could report half-truths to the King, he said, 'Tell me—how is your family business? Is it as profitable after the heavy rains that have occurred over the last year?'

Alice frowned, her eyes casually sweeping over the dinner company. She'd always been clever, and probably didn't want this conversation overhead.

'As well as ever, I assure you.'

Now he needed to solidify for her the fact that someone around this table was desperate enough to be a traitor. 'That is good to hear. I've heard there are many who have suffered, and have become almost desperate to do anything to make ends meet.'

She nodded, as if in concern, but her grey eyes spoke only of retribution. If they'd been alone, other words would have been exchanged. *This* was the Alice he remembered—the one who fought for causes. Who righted wrongs.

But what or whose cause was she fighting for? Other families' or her own? He gave no regard to the King's request for him to find the spy who bore the Seal; he gave even less in watching the Fenton family, since it never did his soul any good to torture himself with Alice's presence. But there *had* been rains here, and he knew at least one family around this table had suffered. When he returned to Court without the Seal, perhaps his king would be satisfied with information.

'Yes, the weather has been hard on most families,' she said. 'It is good that those in Swaffham stand together as an industry.'

This would be of interest to the King, whose need for coin almost outpaced his need for power. 'Work together? Doesn't it help that your family owns most of the lands and almost all of the sheep?'

'Having sheep and land is useless without someone to spin the wool and put it through a loom.'

But working together was something different. He

was here to pretend, to find information for his King, but what she said interested him, too. What changes had taken place here since he left?

'Lamb could be used for many purposes, but the spinners and weavers have no other purpose.'

'Only those who have been gone too long would have such a view.'

'Or those not born here?' he said, and almost bit his tongue. This wasn't about *him*.

'I never thought that mattered,' she answered softly, for his ears only.

Fool. He didn't need her words—didn't need confirmation or reminders of his past or hers. Talking of his belonging to this town wasn't the way the conversation should be going.

He kept quiet and watched her lift her goblet and take a sip. The rose of the wine coloured her full bottom lip until she licked the drop there.

Despite his knowing better, his body reacted.

He lowered his head, perhaps to exchange further words for her ears alone, perhaps to kiss her. When it came to Alice, he constantly fought the battle in him to stay away.

Her eyes widened taking in his response, his closeness. Suddenly bitterness scraped across his heart. He'd seen women do such things at Court. Alice must have picked up the habit there.

He straightened. 'No, apparently not. John wasn't born in Swaffham, and yet he's now Mayor. Of course he *is* married to your sister. Very convenient for your father.'

She shifted her seat. 'My father stepped down as mayor.'

'Recently?' He raised a brow. 'During the rains, perhaps?'

'He is older now, and too tired to work. The council voted for John.'

Her father had never liked to work, and it wouldn't hurt her family to have a member still privy to the town's secrets. He'd seen it more times than he could count. Those in power liked to stay in power. He had nothing against it—except now the King wanted him to find a traitor…and being the focus of the King didn't sit well with him. He needed the King's focus elsewhere.

'An unbiased vote of the council, I'm sure. John is clearly up to the position of Mayor.'

'I believe you've spent too much time at Court.'

'Why is that?'

'You talk of nothing and are very good at it. I find this conversation neither interesting nor useful.' She tilted her head and turned neatly away.

He had his answer. She knew she was being insulted and wouldn't stand for it, and she would defend to the end anyone she cared about. Despite what he had seen at Court, and what she wouldn't deny, there was still some of the Alice of old in her.

But he had another answer as well. There truly *could* be some financial concern in this corner of profitable England. Her father had made a terrible mayor, but the council changing to John could mean something else. The King depended on the taxes here. Perhaps he could find some information regarding financial woes that would appease his sovereign. If not, he'd plant seeds of financial desperation, enough to deflect from his own traitorous deeds.

Would the King let him get away without a suggested

name? Probably not. He glanced around the table, noticed Lyman looking down Alice's gown again, and knew it wouldn't be difficult at all to drop a few lies.

Distasteful, but necessary in order to protect Robert. He had given a vow to his friend to keep his secret and help protect the Colquhoun Clan against King Edward. He would live with the consequences of upholding it.

Alice tried to unclench her jaw. A few words with Hugh and her thought of tossing wine at him was no longer enough. She wanted to stab a knitting needle into him. He knew perfectly well that he insulted her. He had also neatly avoided answering her question. Why was he here?

Whatever the reason, Hugh's presence *did* concern her. If he was truly loyal, then perhaps he knew that she spied. Perhaps the King had asked something of him as well. If he wasn't loyal, then at the least he was a distraction, and at the most a hindrance.

Turning her back on Hugh was easier, and it suited her purpose and the King's as well.

So she smiled at Mitchell, who sat across from her. It was easier to forget Hugh when she talked to Mitchell. She had always liked him. He'd moved away a few years ago and only recently returned. His family business of weaving had suffered significant losses, and he was the only child who had returned to help save it.

'How long will you be in town?' she asked.

Mitchell's eyes lit up. He was delighted that she'd asked a question meant for him alone. 'For the winter. My father hasn't been well, and needs my help.'

His mother was a spinner, and they also held a small weaving and spinning business. They had done much trade with her family's wool over the years.

'I have heard that. I'm sorry.'

'He is a stout man; we expect him to recover. Until then I'll ensure the cloth is tended as it should be.'

He mentioned nothing of his father's poor business choices and their lack of disposable income.

'It has been a while since you have done such work,' she said.

'True, but I have returned, and it is good to be home regardless of the circumstances.'

A pang of guilt hit her heart. He was devoted to his family...but that didn't mean he hadn't committed treasonous acts. *She* was testament to what someone would do for their family.

'If I may ask,' she said, knowing full well the reason she was prying, 'what have you been doing in the years you've been away?'

'As you know, I left with my brothers to gain our fortune. I spent some time in London, where both my brothers happily settled, but I found that cloth was somehow still in my blood. So I travelled some more, and when I discovered a different thread-making procedure on the coast, I knew it was the way forward for me and my family.'

If he'd been to the coast he'd been to the docks. Such a convenient location to trade secrets.

'Usually when I talk of business, women's eyes glaze over,' he said, smiling.

Her eyes normally would have glazed a little by now, but she needed access to his home, and it was easy to talk to Mitchell. 'Given my own family business, is it so strange that I would have an interest, too?'

'Maybe not strange, but I can vow it makes for very pleasant company.'

Alice smiled. 'Do you have samples of this different thread-making?'

'Not samples. It has something to do with the spinning itself. It is something I want to show you and your family.'

'This week? I could come to your home?'

Mitchell opened his mouth... and closed it.

Lyman, who'd been sitting quietly chewing his food, spluttered over his wine.

'I think my sister has the same enthusiasm for wool as do you, Mitchell,' Elizabeth interjected. 'But, since I, too, am interested, I wonder if I could come along?'

Alice glanced across at her sister, who pointedly didn't look at her. Her sister had many telling looks, and the not-looking-at-you one was the look her and Mary feared.

It meant she'd done something wrong...

Ah. A lady should wait for an invitation. But she was no mere lady; she was attempting to be a spy and there was very little time. Clearly she'd have to learn to balance these things.

She turned to Mitchell to apologise, but it seemed he had regained his composure and his confidence because a look of wonder lit his face.

'I'd be delighted,' he said, 'to have you and your sister to my home. I will make arrangements.'

'Well,' Elizabeth said, too brightly, 'that's a day settled then.'

'What were you *thinking*?' Elizabeth whispered, after she'd bade goodnight to the Bensons and the Alistairs.

Gelsey Alistair had needed help from not one but two

servants to get her into her waiting carriage. Baldrick, her husband, hardly better, had at least been gracious enough to leave early.

Unlike Hugh and Eldric who, along with Mitchell and Lyman, remained in the dining room.

Alice fervently wished they had left ahead of the Alistairs.

'Inviting yourself to his house when he hadn't invited you!' Elizabeth continued. 'I thought Lyman would have a heart attack—or, worse, call out your virtue!'

Hugh had questioned her virtue—had *he* heard the way she'd invited herself to Mitchell's home?

'It's winter.' Alice clasped her hands, preparing for her sister's verbal storm. 'His father is poorly. You know they haven't many resources. I thought it easier on him.'

Elizabeth gave an exasperated sound. 'You've been with children too long. You can dictate to *them* your go-ings and comings, but not to your own peers. And you certainly can't go to a gentleman's house by yourself.'

'What can't she do by herself?' Eldric beamed at her and her sister.

Hugh stood behind him. His eyes focused solely on Elizabeth.

Alice didn't want to talk of this in front of anyone, let alone Hugh, but her sister simply waved her hand and said, 'Alice intends to discuss textiles with Mitchell.'

Alice didn't know if Hugh was purposely not looking at her, or simply didn't care enough to do so. At what point would she stop caring?

'Seems harmless enough,' Eldric said.

'But you know her.' Elizabeth laughed daintily, heedless of Alice's warning look. 'She never does *anything* harmless.'

Eldric laughed. 'Ah, yes. The back of my leg still hasn't recovered from that spirited mount of hers the other day.'

'I thought you had only recently returned?' Hugh interjected.

Eldric raised his brow at Hugh. 'As you know, you don't need to be in Alice's company for long before suffering some sort of injury.'

Alice clenched her hands at Eldric's seemingly friendly but cutting words. If she had a sensible bone in her body, like Elizabeth, she'd leave well enough alone. But she didn't—and she wouldn't. If he thought her a whore, she'd play that part, too.

Smiling broadly, she playfully tapped Eldric's arm. 'Your being behind my mount was entirely your own fault, and you know it.'

Eldric's smile returned. 'And *that's* why you had me ride outside the town's border to bring sacks of bread to those families?'

'It was the only way to get you away from me.' She pointed her finger. 'Why are you everywhere I am? You're even here. I believe you are following me.'

Hugh's studying eyes were on her now. For some reason it made her feel reckless. Being around him made her feel reckless. Feeling his gaze, being reminded of his words in the garden, made her angry all over again.

'It's dangerous to follow you,' Eldric said. 'Why, the next day you had me cleaning the church.'

Elizabeth laughed. 'The church? You didn't!'

'He's making that one up,' Alice said.

'Am I? And for what purpose?'

'What reason does *any* man have for displaying his good deeds? So he can be doted on.'

'Ah, I'm caught out. *Would* you dote on me?'

Eldric was definitely flirting with her. While he might not live in Swaffham, he did have a residence here. Therefore he was as much a target for her spying as any other in the town.

Tapping her chin, she answered, 'No...'

'You wound me.' Eldric put his hand on his heart. 'If you did, I would probably carry on with more of your good deeds.'

Alice gave a true smile then. The more they talked, the more Hugh's inscrutable mien turned to a scowl. She was provoking him, yes, but he'd come to Swaffham, to her family's house. If he didn't like what he saw it was *his* issue, not hers. She had a traitor to catch. Eldric was a target—as was everyone else in this town.

Elizabeth laid a hand on Eldric's elbow. 'My sister will be busy with other projects. Soon she'll be inspecting Mitchell's new thread-making methods.'

'That gives me all the more reason,' Eldric replied. 'If only to warn Mitchell about getting too close to you. What evil good deeds will you demand of *that* poor man?'

'I'm retiring for the evening,' Hugh interjected. The cold tone of his voice was a marked contrast to Eldric's warm one. 'I'll be in the carriage, Eldric.'

With a curt nod to Elizabeth, Hugh turned on his heal.

Eldric's warm eyes dimmed. When he turned to smile, it didn't reach his eyes as it had before. 'I suppose that's a signal for me to retire as well. Thank you, Elizabeth, for allowing him to come.'

'Of course,' Elizabeth replied. 'He was welcome. Yet perhaps not so very welcome over the next month.'

Alice hadn't expected her sister to announce her intention of marrying, but her statement couldn't be taken for anything differently.

'I don't follow,' Eldric replied.

'She means,' Alice said, taking charge of this conversation, 'that I have agreed to accept a wedding suit. She believes Hugh might disrupt that plan.'

'Ah, yes, I did notice the seating arrangement.'

'St Martin's Day seating is always planned,' Elizabeth said.

Eldric's eyes narrowed. 'Does Hugh know?'

Alice felt like throwing her hands in the air or hurting someone. Preferably Hugh. 'It is none of his concern. And if his knowledge is a concern to you, your conversation has certainly proved otherwise.'

'Yes, but had I known…' Eldric glanced behind him, and then gave a formal nod. 'This will be an interesting time that I look forward to very much. Now I should see to the carriage.'

'The night seems milder, so I hope the roads fare you well tonight,' Elizabeth said.

When Eldric was out of earshot, Elizabeth raised one imperial brow.

'*That* didn't look like anything was over.'

'This dinner certainly is, and the goose was delicious.'

'Alice, what is going on?'

'Other than my eating entirely too much and wanting to sleep for three days, I don't know what you mean.'

'You do know what I mean because you did two things this evening—'

'Only two?'

'You have certainly never spent time with wool merchants or spinners before. Your projects have always involved the poor and less fortunate.'

But those poor and less fortunate wouldn't get her into the home of a possible traitor.

'I know that's our sister Mary's passion, but it's not that I don't *like* the business. It's difficult not to have some concern—especially with Father's severe lack of care.' Alice lifted a shoulder. 'Anyway, doesn't my interest only confirm my dedication for possible suitors?'

Elizabeth tapped her chin. 'As to those suitors... I noticed you ignoring someone the entire night.'

'I thought you'd chastised me for giving Mitchell too much attention.'

'You know who I mean.'

If she ignored her sister the conversation would only get worse. 'Hugh? Of course I ignored him. I told you I am looking for a husband, and Hugh hardly suits.'

Elizabeth frowned. 'You didn't look at him once. You purposely avoided him. No one does that unless they want to talk to them.'

'Your argument makes no sense,' Alice scoffed, though she knew exactly what her sister meant. Every moment sitting next to Hugh had made her feel like wool on a distaff just waiting for the spindle to twirl and pull. 'And I did talk to him once.'

'Then quickly turned around,' Elizabeth pointed out.

She had—like a dangling spindle with too much weight. 'Don't you have any duties other than spying on me?'

Alice immediately regretted her words. It wasn't only the use of the word spy, it was because—

'I know you too well, sister,' Elizabeth interrupted. 'When you prevaricate, you're on the defensive. So what is it that you're hiding?'

Chapter Seven

The morning air was crisp and cold with a heavy mist. Hugh didn't care about the bite of the air or the swirls of icy wind that brushed against his tunic. What he did care about was the weight of his sword and the terrain around him as he faced Eldric.

It was madness, being out here at this time of day, in this kind of weather. The mud and frost-crusted earth made for dangerous footwork. But he revelled in the fact that Eldric hadn't hesitated when he'd suggested it. He owed his friend retribution for last night.

He made a swift raising of his sword as Eldric swung down. The clatter was nothing to the reverberation arcing up his arms and stabbing down his back.

'Quit!' Eldric gasped.

Hugh shook his head. Eldric was a taller and broader man and, given the terrain today, Hugh was taking the full brunt of every blow. His shoulders ached as if he carried one hundred shields, the slightest weight had become excruciating.

Eldric was faring no better. His sword visibly pulled

on his strength, its tip lowering with each of his breaths. Hugh knew he simply had to outlast him, and quickly.

He swiped his sword low, and Eldric missed the tip by stumbling back. Hugh took advantage by digging in his toes and swiping again.

He'd been a stumbling fool last night. A night at a dinner he never would have accepted if not for the amount of alcohol drowning out all his reason. In the light of day he could excuse himself, tell himself that he'd needed to keep up the facade of searching for the Seal.

But his ego shouldn't have been anywhere near Alice last night.

On a surge of strength he thrust forward again, and again.

'Enough!' Eldric spread his unsteady arms wide and bowed his head to take gasps of breath.

Hugh clutched his sword's hilt in both hands and dipped the tip into the hard earth, so he could lean on it. Stupid, when he knew how to treat his weapons—knew he'd have to clean and sharpen it again. But if he didn't his buckling legs would give away how close Eldric had come to defeating him.

He'd won, but didn't feel like a victor. Hugh's body quaked, and he could barely breathe, but that restlessness underneath it all was barely quenched.

'Let's swim,' he declared.

'Are you joking? It's mostly frozen.' Eldric pointed to the small lake.

'And I'm mostly mud, thanks to you who led us to this delightful patch of ground.'

'I did, didn't I?' Eldric smiled as he wiped the hair off his face. 'Since it was you who suggested such a folly, I thought to give myself as much advantage as possible.'

It had worked, but not enough. Hugh pulled off his tunic, his arm shuddering at the full stretch.

'Good God, you're serious. I can barely stand up, and I know you are no better.'

'The cool water will wake us up.'

Eldric yanked off his boots. '*Cool?* There is ice floating along the edges!'

'We'll be quick.'

'I'm not competing in this, too,' Eldric said, but he was quicker to the water, his large frame diving under before rising to the surface.

Hugh shouted when the water hit him, but he welcomed the numbing flow against his skin as he swum out to Eldric's depth.

Despite the cold, both men trod water, letting the mud and the blood swirl away.

'Don't care if I win or lose this round—I'm heading back before my ballocks is smaller than berries,' Eldric said.

Hugh followed, noticing for the first time the markings on Eldric's right arm.

'I didn't take you for the decorating sort,' Hugh gasped through the water.

Eldric's stopped mid-stroke, surprise lighting the determined look on his face. 'Decorating?'

'On your arm.'

Eldric lunged abruptly ahead again. When he suddenly stood, Hugh, breathing hard, pulled up next to him. Still in the water, still surrounded by ice, he was ready to return to the shore. His friend looked ready to swim to France.

Despite Eldric's countenance being suddenly blacker than the water they swam in, Hugh prodded. 'There are three stripes evenly spaced on your left arm. What's the anger about? Are you embarrassed? You wouldn't be the first to hold still while someone sliced your arm. If you wanted to look fierce, you should have practised your sword skills.'

'Do they *look* like clean knife-cuts?' Eldric bit out.

They didn't. But then he didn't expect Eldric had got purposely tribal cut. 'So you got drunk, and the man who did it had a few more cups than you.'

'They're slices from *arrows*. I got them in battle. Two battles.'

Hugh sluiced the water off his face. 'Are you saying those were done by some bowman…on purpose?'

Eldric cursed and surged forward again. Hugh followed. Fast and sure strokes until he reached the shore and heaved himself to the dry hard ground.

Hugh battled his thundering heart and shaking limbs. The restlessness in him was appeased. He didn't know if it was the exercise or his friend's tumultuousness.

'Yes,' Eldric said, pulling himself up. 'And by the same archer.'

Winter air slashed against his bare skin, and Hugh scrambled for his clothes. Eldric seethed with emotions he recognised, but didn't understand.

'Not a very good archer. He missed you three times.'

Eldric yanked his clothes from the ground, the fabric spilling over his clenched fist. 'He did not miss.'

Hopping, almost stumbling on Eldric's words and their import, Hugh tugged his breeches over his wet legs.

'He did not miss,' Eldric repeated, wrapping his

braies around his waist, 'because as he sliced my arm he killed the men who had watched my back. These—' Eldric pointed to the top two slices '—were in the first battle. I hardly paid attention to the first—a mere scratch compared to Thomas's death. Then the second happened, and it burned across my arm that was already throbbing from the first hit. Already consumed with Thomas's death, I had to face Michael's. I looked at my arm, and at my friend with an arrow through his throat, and I called for retreat. We fled, but I looked for that bastard. I burned with retribution even as I feared for every man who ran beside me.'

With hands shaking as he tied his belt, Hugh understood what Eldric wasn't saying. Fear in battle for yourself and others made you reckless, or hesitate. Men died because of fear.

'This one—' Eldric pointed to the wound directly underneath the other two '—I earned later. It, too, preceded the killing of a man who was watching my left flank.'

'By the same archer? How is that possible?'

'Do you doubt it?'

He would, if not for his friend's certainty. 'How could he know it was you?'

'One of the questions I have been asking myself, and on that day I almost got an answer.'

'You saw him?'

Eldric nodded. 'He was at a distance, but I'd noticed men falling with unerring accuracy. Maddened, I searched everywhere. I looked in places he couldn't possibly be. And then there he was: up in the trees. In the *trees*!' Eldric shook his head as if he still couldn't believe it. 'I was running for him. Full out. In the battle

I dodged and weaved through men. As I did so he aimed
and let loose another arrow. *This* arrow.'

Hugh gaped. He had to. Eldric was not heavy-footed.
When he ran, a man would be hard pressed to catch him,
let alone cut him accurately. 'The skill...'

'The revenge,' Eldric whispered. 'That bastard knew
who I was as I ran for him, and still he marked me.
When it happened I looked behind me. To this day I
wonder whether, if I had simply left well enough alone,
Philip would still have died.'

'What happened?'

'An arrow struck Philip. I had to stop—had to see if I
could...' Eldric shook his head. 'When I turned around
again the archer was gone. I never saw him again.'

'Personal *and* business,' Hugh whispered, now fully
understanding.

'That's why I'm here. I've been tracking him ever
since. When I get close he disappears. That's because
he never *appears*.'

'You think he's here?'

'I can't imagine him hiding in Swaffham, but he's
near. I know nothing except that he's small. Almost tiny.
But that and his bow skill have been enough information to allow me to track him.'

'A Scotsman?'

'I don't think so. He's too well versed with the English garrisons. He is either part of them or a spy.'

'One of our own shooting at you?'

Eldric ran a hand over his face. 'As you said—personal and business.'

The day had changed. Hugh's restlessness had come
to this. A stalemate of discord.

'You win,' Hugh said. 'I know for certain that I've

nothing but the bitterest of winter berries between my legs now. I'm for ale and a hot fire.'

The grief in Eldric's eyes eased. 'I *knew* you were getting soft.'

25th November

The afternoon's insidious wind snaked up Alice's skirts until even her shivers had shivers. The market didn't hold the usual cacophony of animal sounds, but different distractions filled the void. Celebratory notes sounded as entertainers delighted children and the smells of warm bread and spiced ale wafted in the crisp damp air.

Alice had never liked the market's delights. Still, she painstakingly walked through every row of stalls, careful to feign interest in each ware. More careful to ask questions of each vendor.

She'd been doing this since she'd arrived home. Markets and vendors and sellers were a font of information as easily for sale as their loaves and jars. Most were the same vendors, but sometimes there was someone new.

She was getting desperate for new ones. Since she'd begun she'd asked hundreds of questions, but most of the answers didn't further anything of what she had already gained from her own household.

Lately she'd sensed that the vendors had become less open and friendly to talk with her. With every shrug and non-answer, she felt the bars closing in on her family.

At least now she had a reason to be here.

Twelfth night would come soon, the time to exchange gifts, and though she needed information far more than baubles and frivolity, she also needed to shop. She loved her family's warmth and generosity, but could never appreciate their need for presents when there were families worse off.

But it was easy enough to find the ribbon Elizabeth had mentioned. It was a beautiful weave of blue and green that would be perfect for her sister. Perfect, but not good enough.

It wasn't the market making her maudlin, it was merely her work on the project she and Mitchell had planned with the spinners. It was merely that morning with William, who had complained and moaned in frustration because he had not been able to do his sums. It was the fact that for the first time she had lost her patience with him.

Her slamming of the abacus on the table had shocked him—*and* herself—and he'd scrambled off the bench and out of the room. His eyes had held tears of frustration at himself more than hurt, but she felt terrible. She'd always had patience with him before. *Always.* She would apologise to him as soon as she'd finished her shopping.

Her heart eased a little, but not enough. She had to face the truth.

It wasn't this morning with William that was weighing on her, nor the fact she was shopping when she'd rather be helping with the spinning project. Nor even the fact that Hugh had returned to Swaffham or that it'd been a fortnight since she'd talked to him.

Her feeling out of sorts had everything to do with the fact it'd been weeks, and she no closer to finding the Seal.

The King had been specific on the size of the Seal, which was quite small, but other than that she had no idea if it was made of metal or wood…if it came with a handle or not. So she had to search everywhere, for anything. She was blind—searching for something she'd never seen.

He had said he wanted the information as soon as she knew it, but how long would the King give for her search? It was winter now, and freezing, which made travelling almost impossible. Would that be a valid excuse for her delay—?

'Isn't it a bit early for shopping?'

Alice didn't need to turn to know it was Hugh. But she did pause to brace herself. Every meeting they had was full of confrontation when she needed matters to be *easier*.

Glancing over her shoulder, she arched her brow. 'It's almost noon—hardly early.'

Whereas she knew the crisp air did nothing for her but make her skin hurt and her nose red, Hugh stood proud, strong, and as unfailingly beautiful to her as always. The harsh winter air had coloured his skin, accentuating his jaw, his nose and brow. The wind had ruffled his short blond hair, loosening the curls she had thought lost. The sun highlighted the depth of the eyelashes that framed his blue eyes.

His cold, unreadable blue eyes.

He stepped until he faced her. 'True, but in the past when it came to Twelfth Night you always shopped the day before.'

She didn't want to be reminded of those times when she had begged Hugh to shop in the market with her. She also didn't want to talk about herself. Not when it seemed Hugh was always underfoot.

'Is that why you're here?' she said. 'To shop?'

'Why else would anyone be here?'

Again, he hadn't answered her question. 'When it comes to you—'

'Are you paying for that?' The vendor's reedy voice interrupted them.

Alice looked at the ribbon tightly wound in her hand. Sighing, she nodded to Cranley, who followed her today, and he released the coin the vendor asked for. Though it was customary, she didn't negotiate. She'd already crushed the merchandise. She also didn't want to play games with Hugh. Not when she had work to be done.

'We should continue,' she said to Cranley.

'Allow me to accompany you?' Hugh said, as if she wasn't pointedly ignoring him.

She opened her mouth to disagree, but then realised she'd tried to ignore him on St Martin's Day and every day since then. He was still here.

Why was he?

She could not shake the feeling that it had to do with her. Or that the King had sent him here because of the Seal.

The Seal... She had distracted Elizabeth from making further enquiries, but despite her best efforts to hide what she was doing, her sister was suspicious.

Hugh inclined his head. 'Your endeavours with gifts could help me.'

His words were laced with cynicism, displaying more differences from the way she had known him to be. All through his childhood he'd tried to curb his father's drinking, had worked tirelessly to save what little land they owned. He had come to her rescue when those boys had lowered her into the empty well.

Despite his efforts, his father had died from drink

and his land had been sold to her father. From the proceeds he had purchased armour and paid for his travel to Edward's Court.

Over those years while he'd trained, he had returned for only a few days or weeks to Swaffham. During those times, she had noticed him achieving a warrior's build and assurance with the sword. Had watched him train with Eldric, who would often return with him. Her childish hero-worship had quickly turned to admiration. And a sort of ache as she'd watched him train as if he still had something to prove.

It was the memory of one of those times...that last time she'd seen him...that made her ache all the more. With embarrassment, with her own shame, with anger...

It had been her own fault. She'd approached him as he was slicing his sword against nothing. But she'd strode too close. She hadn't been thinking about the sword—only him. It might have meant his sword slicing through her, but his training had required control, precision. He had stopped, the tip skimming her belt.

But he hadn't controlled his temper when he'd stopped the lethality of the sword and exploded towards her.

She didn't remember the words he'd used as he cursed. Only remembered his anger—his anger and his incredulousness because he hadn't known she was spying on him. The mutinous embarrassment in his expression.

But that wasn't what had caused her to ask the question. That wasn't what had brought her steps closer to him. No, it was the emotion Hugh had displayed that had made her take those steps, had made her ask him to kiss her. It had been terror. He'd almost killed her and it had terrified him. He'd felt something—for her.

So she had asked him to kiss her. And Hugh, who had always protected her, had looked as if he wished his sword had struck true. Until, upon a shudder, he'd taken that last step, put his leg between hers, one hand cradled her jaw and his eyes locked on her lips.

The warmth of his hand, the living, breathing hardness of his body had contrasted with the cold, unyielding sword he'd still clutched in his hand. And then it had been only Hugh, his head lowering, and her standing on tiptoe to meet him before...

Before Hugh had raised his eyes to hers and stopped. Hugh had stopped. And it hadn't been anger or worry or terror in his eyes. He had simply...gone from her.

When he'd stepped away she hadn't needed his words. She'd already heard them in the impassiveness of his gaze. 'Run to your home, Alice, before you do something you'll regret.'

To her shame, she had.

He had left days after that confrontation. She had hid on her family's estate and helped with the residents. And had vowed she'd never run again.

Yet here she was, standing in the town square and trying to avoid Hugh. No more.

Inclining her head, she addressed Cranley. 'I should be safe if you want to return home now.' She met Hugh's steady gaze. 'Shop with me if you like.'

'Then it will truly be like old times.'

'Some things should not be repeated.' She watched Cranley's retreating back and hoped she wasn't making a mistake.

'If we aren't to repeat the past,' Hugh said, interrupting her thoughts, 'then why allow me to walk with you? You're not even looking at the merchandise surrounding you.'

She stopped between stalls and the heavily laden bystanders bumped along beside them. 'Because I have no interest in the merchandise, but I *do* have an interest in why you are here.'

'Bertrice insists on cleaning my home. Since I was unable to sit by a roaring fire, I found myself at a loss for anything to do this afternoon. The market provides entertainment.'

Again, he hadn't divulged an answer.

'Is it the King again? Is that why you're here with me now?'

He raised a brow. 'The King?'

'That day in the garden you said you'd talk to the King. Was the conversation not to your liking?'

There was a knowing curve to his lips. 'You remember that day very well.'

So did he—and she was tired of his games. 'The talk didn't go well, then?'

Crossing his arms, he widened his stance. She felt the market crowd at her back, and she avoided their enquiring eyes.

'What makes you so sure?' he said.

So many questions he asked, and she had too many unanswered. But there was one certainty. He wasn't who he had once been.

It wasn't only in the years that had hardened his body and in the brutal way his hair was cut, so close to his head, the light blond almost destroyed. It was also in the harshness of his blue stormy gaze, the cynical tilt to his lips. The knowing way he held himself. He was a man, a warrior. One who had seen the world…and found it unworthy.

'Because you didn't stop what was started there and because you're here,' she said.

Still the same casual stance, but she sensed an alertness in him.

'What didn't I stop?' he said, his tone still conversational. 'Your status as his mistress obviously had come to an end. You are here, and he is elsewhere. I assumed the King tired of you as he did the others.'

She ignored his words and listened to their meaning. 'Yet you still hound me with it, which serves no apparent purpose. Just as your presence here makes no sense. You don't shop; you don't ever visit Swaffham. I can only conclude that you're here because the King sent you.'

He glanced around. 'And why would the King send me here?'

Alice almost stumbled into answering him. If it was possible he didn't know she spied, then she would be revealing too much. Even now people might be listening.

'What would I know of the ways of kings and knights. I'm only a wool merchant's daughter.'

He released his arms. 'Why do you think the King sent me here?'

Cold sweat slid down Hugh's back. He could never remain detached when it came to Alice. All the more a fool him, to think he ever could. And losing his composure in front of Alice in the middle of the town square on market day was hardly the behaviour of an accomplished spy.

On the surface, his mission was simple. All he'd been ordered to do was to keep an eye on the Fenton family and find the traitor who sold sovereign secrets. He assumed the King thought the Fentons had something to do with the Seal, even though he knew they didn't. He merely kept watch so he could report honestly and give an accounting of what they did. He had learned long ago to keep more truths in his tales than lies.

Now, however, Alice acted as if there was something more. As if the King had talked to her about stately matters and lies and schemes. In truth, there had been the opportunity when she'd spent time in the King's chambers, but he had dismissed that notion. He'd never met a woman spy.

And she hadn't denied she was the King's mistress. *She hadn't denied it.*

Despite his having no right, he felt jealousy burn through him. Even now he could not quell the frustration and need. Especially not this morning, with the bright sunlight revealing all the colours hidden in her hair and the depth of grey in her eyes.

All his life he had compared other women to her, and now a king had had her. Under the heat of another man's caresses did her cheeks flush red as beautifully as they did now? Did her curling hair fan across the bed linens as wildly as it blew in the winter wind?

How many nights, days, years had he tortured himself with thoughts of the way her lips would part, the way her breath would taste before his lips claimed hers? How many nights, alone, had he wrapped himself and given in to imagining the softness of her skin, the give of her generous hips. Even now he craved to know the way she would meet him. Finally to know, from the very way she held herself, how she would change as she rode him.

Alice…a king's mistress tossed away as all the others had been since Eleanor. But every hair on the back of his neck warned him. Alice, King's mistress or not, wasn't safe. Her actions today were not merely those of a lady shopping. Her questions to him were not simple enquiries.

'What did the King want of *you* that day?' he asked. 'Why do you have interest in my being here?'

Abruptly, she strolled on, her eyes observing the wares in the market stalls. 'It's been a long time since you were here. Surely others have asked you the same?'

He kept pace with her, kept his voice low, but his heart hammered in his chest and his mind raced at the possibilities. Maybe he had thought wrong that day at the Tower.

'You refused him, didn't you? Despite his being the King.'

'What would I refuse?'

He went to grab her, but she turned too swiftly for that. They had stepped away from the thickest crowd of shoppers and it was time to lay this conversation to rest.

Alice's heart thumped in her chest and her breath caught. This walk had been a mistake. She hadn't uncovered anything about Hugh, but she had revealed too much regarding herself.

Now they stood in the quieter part of the market, away from the stalls around the fountain. Now it seemed as if Hugh would not let her run.

Not when he stepped closer, his posture mimicking that time six years ago when she had recklessly asked for his kiss. Why could she not forget that day? Why was she plagued with memories of this man she could never have?

'Don't. No more. Whatever is between us—' he began.

'Whatever's *between* us…?' she asked.

He looked away, shook his head. 'There's nothing that can be done about that. Not now. Not ever. But this—' He waved his hand. 'Your shopping early for Twelfth Night. Your asking questions of the vendors. If there's something more going on, I need to know.'

Alice could not think beyond his words. His eyes roiled with emotions she could almost catch. Regret. Embarrassment at words he hadn't meant to say. Words that were an acknowledgement of his feelings for her.

Equally alarming—he knew she'd questioned the vendors. It was as if she had been picked up and placed somewhere else in the world. She couldn't make sense of it.

She didn't have time to make sense of it now. She thought she'd been careful, believed she could lie and no one would notice. Hugh had noticed.

'How long have you been following me?'

'Answer me,' he said.

She had given a vow to the King. 'There's nothing going on.'

Anger. Menace. Whatever confusion or roiling emotion there had been in his eyes after his revealing words was gone. Now he looked every stitch a knight—and one who would cut her down.

'Is it true, then? You slept with the King?' He lowered his voice, deadly soft. 'Or is it false and you're protecting something…someone? Tell me. Is it you or the King?'

What did she care for the King? She wouldn't risk her family. 'Wasn't it made clear to you that day in the garden? I was in the King's private chambers. Why else would a woman be in his chambers?'

He shook his head, as if warning himself against thoughts or words, before he bit out, 'No matter what you are doing for him, he won't take you back to his bed. He never does.'

Humiliation scored through her, but she didn't hold back her taunt. 'Maybe it's another's bed I'm wanting.'

'Enough! There's more going on here.'

She agreed—and she could be as angry about it as him. Again he leaned over her, as he had all those years ago. This time, he accused her of being a whore. She had enough of his confrontations. Instead of standing on tiptoes, she ground her heels into the earth, ready to tell him to step away, but there were more words.

'Tell me this,' Hugh continued, 'when you were there in the King's bed, while you were under him, what did he command you to do?'

Her first instinct was to slap him. Her second was to deny.

Instead she gave a mere twitch of her lips as she replied, 'When I'm in the King's bed it's I who command him.'

Chapter Eight

❧∼∽∾∿❧

Words. Only words. But they ripped through Hugh's defences so quickly he knew he couldn't erect them properly again.

Alice turned then and walked away. He let her.

Too much at risk. Too much at stake. How much was true and what could he believe?

He breathed in raggedly, watched her retreating back, her steps quick but short given the crowds. Her skirts were swinging around her hips, her back straight. Pride. Determination. But at that pace she wouldn't get far.

She needed to get far. At least until he'd reined in his emotions.

Think.

The King knew of the Half-Thistle Seal and believed it to be in Swaffham; he had also demanded Hugh to spy on his mistress. Was it possible those two orders weren't connected?

No, otherwise nothing made sense. Edward had never spied on his mistresses before because he'd never kept his mistresses for long. So he had to take the information Edward had given him. Such wrong information.

Hugh was the spy, and the Half-Thistle Seal hadn't been in Swaffham until Edward had sent him here.

Could Edward suspect him and be setting him up?

It was possible Edward did suspect. So why send him here to pay close attention to his former mistress?

Alice…a mistress, who commanded men? He could see it even now. Her petite curves free of her clothes' restraint, her eyes heavy-lidded with desire. Her lips plush and wet from kisses.

He'd held her against him only a few times in his life. Still he was seared with the memories of how she had felt.

And other men had known her thus?

Breathe. Look away.

Jealousy's blade pricked at his heart and he longed to stab back. Never worthy—neither in the present time nor in the past.

Now she bedded the King. Edward had been devoted to his wife Eleanor, but he was a man and had had a few discreet mistresses since her death. Alice held no title, held no country—she would be quickly dismissed if she hadn't been already.

So why request that Hugh spy on her?

Too many questions. He had people to protect in the schemes he played. Though everything in him told him to walk away, he needed more information.

'What are you doing?' Alice asked when he came up beside her.

'Following you,' he said.

After what she had just said she'd expected more scornful words, and for him to allow her to walk away. 'Why?'

'You dismissed your servant, so I'll accompany you.'

She wanted to ask on his reasoning again, but stopped herself. He had been angry mere moments before, and she had given him cause to leave. Or at least to be shocked.

She'd been shocked at what she'd said. She'd never even been kissed, and now she'd practically told him she'd lain with legions.

Anger spiked through her confusion. So what if she *had* been with legions? He had rejected her; had no claim on her.

But all that didn't matter. Because now it was as if Hugh was another man altogether. His eyes were unreadable, the muscles in his jaws were relaxed. Everything about him was relaxed. He was up to something. This wasn't right.

'I don't want you here.'

'You want privacy? Perhaps because you were intending to buy a present for me?'

Aggravating man.

'Come, we don't even need to talk,' he said. 'A lady shouldn't be unaccompanied in town.'

She *needed* to be unaccompanied. It was exactly what she wanted to be. 'I'm finished in the town.'

'Will you be returning home?'

'Yes.' *Lie.*

'I'll take you there.'

It was too early for her to return home. Hours would be wasted if she did, and she didn't have time for this. If she'd had an abacus to slam down, she would have.

'Perhaps I'll go to Mitchell's.'

Hugh tensed beside her. Just a little—just enough for her to notice. Why was she noticing?

'Then I'll accompany you,' he said.

She stopped walking and looked at him. It was her turn to raise her brows.

His brows were drawn, chin lowered. His eyes almost unreadable, that storm inside him brewing.

'I'll accompany you there,' he repeated.

There was no getting rid of him. She'd have to occupy herself with the project, when she'd meant to go by the property tomorrow. It would be late by the time she arrived, and she'd hardly be useful.

Yet with Hugh by her side there would be no more questioning of vendors either—another day lost in helping her family. And she didn't like it.

'Then you'll leave?' she said, walking again.

He kept pace with her. 'Why do you go to Mitchell's?'

He was stubbornly by her side, and unhelpful with his answers. She needed Hugh gone.

'I am not going to Mitchell's.'

He placed his hand on his chest. 'Come, Alice, I'm weary, and I only wish to be a gentleman.'

'You wished to be something else.'

His expression darkened before she realised what she'd said, and she wondered where this boldness had come from when she had no experience with it. Probably from frustration and worry. She had no patience because the King would have no patience, because William was worried about his Boy Bishop duties, because winter storms would soon arrive and families needed work and shelter.

She closed her eyes, rephrased. 'I mean, you are up to something else.'

'What could I possibly be up to?'

Everything. Nothing.

She hurried her pace. She was more than suspecting now that his presence had to do with the King, but if he wasn't telling neither was she. And he still wasn't leaving her side.

'I'm going to the south-west corner of our land,' she said. 'I'll need to stop at the house for supplies first. After that, if you insist, ride with me there.'

Her family's land was vast, with thousands of sheep. Hugh had never been privy to surveying it before. The old horse his father had kept was used only for the most necessary trips. But there were days when he didn't want to return home, and on those days his feet had taken him almost out of Swaffham.

'There was a barn there...falling apart.'

'If you come, you have to help.' She stopped, stared at him the way she had in the garden. Assessing. *Commanding.* 'You *will* help.'

'With what?'

'You'll see.'

He tilted his head. 'Is Mitchell there?'

She waved her hand at him and sped up her footsteps. Even if she hadn't gone silent he would have known her patience was gone.

So was his.

'Secrets?' he said. 'I'll know them all, Alice, no matter how fast you walk away.'

Hugh heard the commotion before they turned the bend in the road. Pounding against metal, shouts, smells of burning coal and wood. Fires and smoke clashing with the winter wind.

Whatever he had been expecting by following Alice here, this industry was not it. It was already late afternoon. Delay had been caused by the retrieval of two horses, the saddling of two more.

The winter light was dimming. They had no more than a few hours' daylight left, but everyone worked as if the day had just begun.

When others spotted their arrival, there were more shouts. Children and their mothers strode forward. Alice's two horses carried large sacks and baskets. Food, blankets, supplies. Now he knew why.

As Alice alighted she was greeted warmly and with much chatter. He shook his head at the sight before him.

All morning in her presence there'd been suspicion between them. Since he had insisted on accompanying her, she'd kept a stony silence. Though he'd burned for information, he had gathered his patience to wait until they arrived. He had thought this trip would be useless—until now.

Alice was surrounded by people. The worry in her eyes had eased, a smile curved her lips. She held the hand of one small child.

The stares coming his way were merely curious, and he dismounted. He recognised no one. They could be from Swaffham, but he saw the tents, the many fires. These people were living here in the dead of winter on her family's land.

From the staples she had brought, from the questions and answers she gave, he concluded that she was assisting them.

All the years he'd stayed away from her, from Swaffham, this was what he'd dreamed of when he had dared think of her. Her and her beloved projects; her helping others. Her care and kindness.

Seeing it gave him no ease, only more questions. As did the industry here.

He began a tour of the grounds. He had been gone many years, and none of this was recognisable. No sheep in sight, the landscape was dominated by what had once been a decrepit barn and at least one hundred people.

The barn was larger than he remembered it, even with the roof and one wall completely torn down. Not for long. Men were already measuring and cutting wood for posts and braces. Older children and women were weaving branches for the wattle. Large barrels nearby were full of the daub mixture that would be made into large balls to fill in the walls.

Numerous fire pits surrounded everything to provide warmth for the workers and to cook their food. Whenever he got close to one he reached out his hands, as all the others were doing. Large pots of soup, bread, onions and potatoes were being passed around. Not cooking, but keeping warm. Ready for when it was time to rest.

Whatever he had been expecting here, this wasn't it. Alice had said she wanted to visit Mitchell, but this wasn't Mitchell's land and building barns wasn't his industry.

It wasn't the usual kind of project for Alice either. Her past endeavours had been focused on more intimate care.

At first it had been patching up injured animals, then small children. Then bringing food for families in need, or tending someone who had fallen sick.

That Alice could be seen here, as she crouched, circled by dozens of children with eager hands, reaching for the bits of fruit she'd brought. Her smiles were at ease now, her brows arched in gentle warning. She was handing out apples to the younger children. No doubt to share with the older ones. Giving them power when they usually had none.

Handing over the last treat, she stood and wiped her hands on her skirts. As the last of her supplies were carted away, and the last child left her heels, he walked over to her.

'What *is* all this?'

Alice looked around her. Despite the weather, the work was going faster than she'd expected. Her talking to the women and children had helped greatly to ease her other concerns, but not all.

Regardless of his demand to accompany her, she had brought Hugh here. His presence in Swaffham only complicated her tasks, but since he insisted on being here she would use him for her own purposes.

'I'm working with Mitchell to help the spinners here.'

'How?'

'He's travelled recently to Italy. Seen the making of the Great Spinning Wheels—have you seen them?' At his nod, she continued. 'He knows how to improve them, with tables so a spinner can sit and produce more thread, but they need space. The foundations of this building are still good, and most of the walls. It seemed a solution.'

Hugh's brows were drawn, but she didn't know what to make of that.

'It's more than a solution,' he said.

Was it? She'd never concerned herself with the family wool business—not as her sister, Mary, had—but Alice realised she could love it too. Because it helped people. And in that Alice understood how she could contribute. After all, there were many spinners in Swaffham who would gain more income with Mitchell's tables if they had the space to put them.

'Who are these people?'

'Mostly from Swaffham, but a few are from other towns. They were staying in the barn until we had to take off the roof.'

'All this in *winter*?'

'Shearing season is in the spring. In order to be ready, we needed to move quickly. It'll be too cold soon, and they will return to their homes, but I'd hoped we'd get the roof on.'

It would be a slow process. 'Many of these people aren't builders.'

'The women are spinners. With Mitchell's tables and chairs these women would be able to share work and help each other as they worked.'

'Where did you get this idea?'

'I've been forced to sit in circles and do needlework. Talking passes the time more quickly. Spinning requires space, and Great Spinning Wheels even more. This will allow them to be more comfortable.'

Hugh went silent again, looking over her shoulder, watching the chaos.

She found herself watching for his response. She shouldn't care what he thought; he said he'd help, and in that she believed him. She might not trust him now, and he might think her a whore for the King, but she did need help. That was her only concern.

'This is different from what you used to do,' he said. 'I thought your sister was more interested in the efficiency of the industry.'

'She is, and I can't wait to share this information with her so she can start something on her own land, but I have realised I can look at it from my point of view as well—from the views of the spinners and their families. This might be a solution for them to earn more, too.'

'So you're helping people.'

She nodded.

He exhaled, his expression easing. 'I'll help today and over the next week. The weather's changing already. I'll see if Eldric can spare some time.'

Despite herself she said, 'This wasn't what you expected when you followed me here.'

He opened his mouth, closed it. Started to speak. 'I think, when it comes to you, I'll keep my thoughts to myself.'

He smiled a little then, as if in jest. She knew otherwise. He had been expecting something, and it hadn't been answered here.

'Do you intend to keep following me?'

'We met by happenstance in the market, Alice. You were unaccompanied.' He tilted his head. 'I merely fitted a role.'

Not one that she wanted him to. He wanted something from her, and he would keep following her until he had his answer. She didn't need him around, not when she had other tasks to do, but it wouldn't be terrible if she could get Hugh out of her way *and* the extra hands she needed.

'Well, your role today is hard labour.'

'Scaring me away with work? You'll have to do better than that.'

She knew too much of him to believe anything she said would turn him away. He might carry a storm in his eyes, but it was as if that storm was in his life as well. He had been relentless in achieving knighthood. Tireless in helping his father.

No, she didn't want to scare him; she simply wanted his questioning, calculating gaze to be gone.

'Why are you here?'

He looked away, shrugged. 'I think you need me.'

And there was the reason she wanted him gone— because while it was true his extra hands were needed, his words seemed laden with other meanings.

And he was wrong; she didn't need him. Not any more. She'd made a life for herself here, and the King threatened it. She didn't need Hugh to complicate matters.

'I need to find Mitchell now,' she said. 'He must be on the other side of the barn.'

Hugh's countenance darkened, but she turned before he could answer. She was eager to get to work. To accomplish something this day so that all was not lost.

The sun was setting, the fires were blazing and there wasn't enough light to work any more. Instead of readying for the night, Hugh and the others were cleaning their tools and preparing for the next day.

Wrapping the last of the hammers with heavy linen, he stood to roll his shoulders and knew his blistered hands would give Eldric the advantage in training tomorrow.

But the wall was mounted, the eaves were assembled for placement, and most of the thatch was ready to apply. A couple more days and there would be a roof. Which was good, because the mist was heavy, the clouds dark. Soon the heavy rain and the snow would bury the ground.

It was madness to build in weather such as this. But it was inspiring too. Many of these people looked as if they couldn't afford tools; they needed this work *now*. They also needed the work that would come from this kind of production.

Alice was changing people's lives here. She'd done it before—by saving puppies, by giving food where needed—but this…this was providing a way forward. Not merely for these people in Swaffham, but for the wool business, too.

Who *was* she?

I command the King.

The years had strengthened her. Always compassionate, always kind, but now there was fortitude in her.

It wasn't only in the way she directed the builders. It was in the way she was side by side with the other women—how, when she could, she pointed out ways of improvement. He watched her learn as well.

All his life he had longed for her. A sort of heart's wish. Now her strength drew her to him. She had become…a man's wish.

Was she the King's mistress? She had never denied it. And yet seeing her like this, seeing her strength, he was wondering if it mattered.

A mistress was a woman, who needed a man for protection. Alice displayed none of those traits. She was complete.

And yet, she was in a King's chamber. Had the King been drawn to Alice's resolve and kindness? Maybe she hadn't gone to the King because she was forced. Perhaps instead of the pleasure being coerced from her she had taken instead.

And there he felt and understood the source of his jealousy. Because she hadn't taken from *him*. His body tightened at the mere thought and unbidden his gaze fell on her.

She was bent over one of the fires, sitting next to the children, and like them she was skewering meat onto sticks to cook. Her face was animated as she listened to the little girl sitting next to her. The fire's light played along the fine features of her face. Her upturned nose, the plump fullness of her bottom lip. The colour of her skin shone gold. He wanted to touch it to see if it was as warm as it looked.

All his life he'd cursed himself for comparing other women to her, but now he knew he had no choice. Unworthy though he was, everything about her called to him.

Done for the day, and knowing he was to accompany her home, he felt a certain lightness enter his chest. He felt himself almost smiling—before he saw Mitchell striding towards Alice.

Over the last several hours he had watched them engage together. Noticed their ease of conversation, their gestures. It was clear that Mitchell's family hadn't fared as well as Alice's. Still, he was one of the established spinning families who had been there for generations. Privileged. Those who were invited to and accepted at the best dinners and festivities.

It seemed their friendship hadn't waned in their years apart, or in their differences of income.

Bypassing three men carrying large stacks, he walked slowly towards them. They might have grown up childhood friends, but Mitchell's time abroad had changed that. He was looking at Alice now as a man would a woman.

Alice seemed oblivious. Maybe she didn't know— was innocent and therefore didn't understand that she shouldn't be standing so close, or laying her hand on Mitchell's sleeve.

Or maybe she did know.

Stamping through a deep puddle, Hugh hurried his pace.

Alice was listening to Mitchell bemoaning the lack of sufficient wattle when she saw Hugh storming towards them.

At first she almost ignored him, as she'd tried to do all day, but the certainty of his step, the steadiness of his gaze, warned her otherwise.

Knowing Mitchell didn't need to hear a confrontation between her and Hugh, she excused herself and walked to meet Hugh.

There had been no argument or calamity to account for Hugh's darkened demeanour. After his insistence that he accompany her here, he'd ignored her since their arrival.

But now she watched him as he walked around the production and wondered what his thoughts could be; if he approved of what was happening here.

When he stood in front of her she quickly dismissed that thought. She didn't have to seek approval from anyone—especially him.

'Are you ready to leave?' she asked, though she saw Hugh was peering avidly over her shoulder.

She turned around and glimpsed Mitchell's retreating back.

When she turned to Hugh again, his expression had eased. Was he *jealous*?

'You want me to leave?' he said.

'No, I meant—'

'Does your father know what is happening here?' he asked.

She shrugged. 'No more than he has ever concerned himself with these affairs.'

'Does the King?'

Always back to the King, and that explained his blackened expression—not jealousy.

'Why would the King care?'

'You will increase productivity here.'

'I hope so.'

'You'll increase income for him as well. There is some secret here, Alice.'

At the word 'secret' she turned her gaze away. Perhaps if all was as it should be, this *would* be a secret. She hadn't even thought to tell the King. Would it soften him towards her if she brought him more taxes? She doubted it.

'You've been all over this camp; I can hardly hide secrets here.'

He raised a brow. 'But elsewhere…?'

Was this just his cynicism or something else? There had been times today, as he'd heaved cut wood over his shoulders, as he'd conversed with others, when she'd glimpsed the Hugh of old—the one she'd fallen in love with.

And, try as she might, even with his past rejection and his current mockery, she found parts of her wanting to know... If he hadn't left, if he had stayed, would it have been like this? Would they be side by side, working together?

Madness to think that. Foolishness. But he had helped today as he had said he would. Despite his cutting words, despite his watching her too closely.

And she couldn't even ask why—couldn't answer his questions regarding secrets. Because she'd have to lie...and right now she wasn't sure what her lies would be.

He stepped forward. 'Are there other secrets, Alice? Because—' He shook his head, looked away and exhaled.

'Because what?'

'Have you been doing this since I left?' he said. 'Have you been helping people?'

He wasn't entitled to *any* of her secrets—and yet she'd seen him carry the extra sacks when a child had stumbled.

She didn't owe him anything, but his expression seemed troubled. And she needed to answer him with some truths, or else continue her lies.

'Not like this. But there's a boy, William, who thrives with numbers... And Bertrice's ankle is still healing, so I've been ensuring she doesn't overwork it. And, of course, there's always—'

A curve of his lips stopped her. She remembered her family's disapproval of her projects; how the townspeople accepted her help but didn't understand it.

'Don't stop,' he said. 'It's good to hear this. It's good to know that you've been here doing this.'

'Now that you know, you can stop following me.'

He didn't blink. 'I *wasn't* following you, remember? But I am curious why you were at Court.'

'I was invited there...just as my father has been for years.'

Another step.

Alice was aware of the children settling down, and the families eating. Aware, too, that Mitchell had left and it was time for them to go.

And yet she didn't want to leave. This moment was somehow different from all the others with Hugh. There was tension, but not so much confrontation. She didn't know why, but something had changed over the last few hours. A few moments spent together...a few stolen looks. His frequent gaze...

He was looking at her differently now too. Standing closer.

Too close.

Was it her words to him about commanding the King? Was it because there was a delicate truce after the day's labours?

She didn't need this—didn't want it.

Stepping back, she said, 'It's time to return home.'

His eyes rested on her as if he was reading more into her words. The moment stretched, felt taut. As if a master spinner was twisting the thread that bound them.

This close, she noticed the length of his lashes, the depth of colour in his eyes, his broad jaw, roughened by the beginnings of a beard that she knew would be gone by tomorrow. His lips, blushed bright from the cold, looked soft, vulnerable on such a masculine face. She suddenly felt like resting her fingers there, to protect them from the cold wind.

The longer she looked at his lips, the more her heart

felt lopsided in her chest, like a spinning wheel about to break its axis.

Her eyes glanced to his again, looking for answers, seeing if he could see her thoughts.

She could make no sense of his expression, and no sense of his next words.

'It is time,' he whispered.

And she had to wonder... Time for what?

Chapter Nine

'I can't do it,' William said in despair. 'I'm sorry, I shouldn't be taking your time with this, but I can't be Boy Bishop.'

Alice's heart ached for him. He was a mere child, and on this chilly December morning was his first sermon. It was time for him to go to the pulpit. Except he was hiding back here, and Father Bernard had come to her for help. The church was already filling, and she could hear the din of voices and many feet shuffling against the flagstones.

If this was the only heartache in her life she'd take it. She would do anything for William. But even now, when he needed her, her thoughts still jumped to other moments, other heartaches.

That market day with Hugh, and her reply to him. As if she could command the King. Oh, why had she replied to him as she had? She never would have with anyone else. It had to be because of her time at Court and her projects. It was the frustration of being at the whim of her monarch, and her family held in the balance. All her anger she'd felt and used against Hugh.

She'd used it, and taken satisfaction in it. How the shock had widened his eyes; the fact he'd followed her and demanded to accompany her. The way he had watched her all that day. His assessing gaze burning with familiarity and heat before she could turn away.

More troubling than that, it was the way Hugh helped that day at the barn, the feeling of some accord between them. His eyes softening, telling her it was time, when she still couldn't comprehend what he truly meant.

Weeks had gone by since then, and she was still searching for the Seal. Wary now, because Hugh could be following her, she'd been more careful while she walked through the Alistairs' corridors. She'd asked more open-ended questions while visiting the Bensons' kitchens, sculleries, and cellars.

No matter where she went, or how often she looked over her shoulder, she felt as if there were shadows following her. No doubt the shadows were her own dark thoughts that kept her up at night. The King thought the Seal was here, so *why* couldn't she find it?

Alice crouched down so she could look William in the eye. 'Of course, you can be Boy Bishop. Father Bernard has watched you study, he's rehearsed with you— he believes you to be more than ready.'

'Father Bernard is merely being kind.'

'Because you sing so well?' she teased.

William blushed. He *did* sing well, but it wasn't that that had made Father Bernard choose him for Boy Bishop. It was William's care for others. Even now he was doing it—caring about spoiling her day, about ruining Father Bernard's service.

'You do sing well,' she repeated. 'And you work hard; it's why you were chosen.'

The Boy Bishop position was meant to be fun, but William had taken his studies in earnest…as if he belonged.

'What if I hesitate or can't remember my words?'

'If you hesitate it'll simply give us time to settle into our pews. If you forget your words only you and Father Bernard will know. In the end, remember Esther won't notice because she'll be asleep.'

William almost smiled, but quickly wobbled again. 'Maybe the sermon is too short. Father Bernard's sermons are much longer.'

'Shorter is better. Then we can all get on with eating and talking. That's the best bit about church anyway.'

He looked at her sideways, as if judging her words. 'You're only saying that because you've helped me all this time.'

He didn't know how much he meant to her, or how much she'd fought for him over the years. Now—today—despite his fears, she realised he had other people fighting for him, too.

When Father Bernard had caught him reading the Bible left on the pulpit, she had explained she was helping him to become a steward. Expecting reproach, she had been surprised when Father Bernard had allowed William access to the precious words. Now he was Boy Bishop, and Father Bernard had helped with that as well.

'And why have I helped you?' she said.

'Because I was in trouble for turning the pages of your books that day?'

'Is that what this feels like? Being in trouble?'

'Well, doing sums is trouble.'

She pressed her lips to avoid laughing. 'But *you're* not trouble, William, you could never be that to me.'

William's face screwed up, as if he were holding in emotion, before he turned his head away so she wouldn't see. But she did. And she was glad she did. He was always holding things in. Not unlike—

It wouldn't do to think of Hugh now.

'You have a gift, William, for understanding words and numbers. I enjoy our time together and I am very proud of you.'

He turned his head then, surprised. Probably because no adult would usually dare talk to a child this way. But William wasn't a normal child—he was too intuitive for that.

'I love discovering how your mind works. With that, and your diligence, you'll soon be far beyond *my* capabilities.'

A darkness flitted across his eyes and she kicked herself for her choice of words. He was an intuitive child, but still a child. He needed care, not her clumsy attempts at comfort.

'There's more?' William played with the fringe on his belt.

'There's so much more for you to learn, and your being Boy Bishop is merely another step. Perhaps some day Father Bernard could show you more books.'

Wonder erasing his worries, he asked, 'Have *you* seen more?'

'Not as many as I wanted to, but once the monks in London hadn't yet closed a door and I glanced into a room full of scrolls.'

'Full? How big was the room?'

'As big as this church.' She exaggerated, but only a little, and it was worth it to see the lingering darkness in his eyes disappear completely.

Oh, to see his eyes shine. She wanted to see more of it.

But even at that thought, she didn't know how to give him more. To have access to such a wealth of knowledge, he would need a suitable donation and noble blood. As generous as Father Bernard was, there was no circumventing the Church's requirements—and, as wealthy as her family was, how was she, one of several daughters, to get such a sum from her father?

Maybe her family was right and she *was* setting William up to have more heartache than he'd already suffered.

'But we'll keep on taking steps for now, and the more steps you take, the more treasures and knowledge you will discover.'

'So this...' he looked around, as if seeing everything for the first time '...is another step?'

'Simply one step. You've done that before.'

He was nodding eagerly when Father Bernard appeared in the doorway. Smiling, she gave William a fierce hug and wished him all the best.

As she walked along the corridor, she sent a private prayer to God, who surely would be listening, that if anything should happen to her, either Elizabeth or Mary would provide for William—that what hopes she'd given him wouldn't be lost.

The church was full to bursting when she entered the aisle alongside the nave from the north transept. From this vantage point she saw John and Elizabeth, who was covering her mouth to hide her laugh. John's humour was legendary in Swaffham.

Her father, to John's left, was craning his neck to see if anyone of importance was around. He spotted her first and gave a welcoming smile. Even now she was grateful for her family. If her prayer was heard or not, she knew they'd help her. Elizabeth might point out the weaknesses of her projects, and her father might continually be baffled by them, but in the end they stood together.

She walked further along the aisle and saw Eldric standing in the shadows of the narthex. His face was grim, his eyes focused on someone already sitting. She followed his line of sight to Hugh, who was sitting to the far left. Unlike the rest of the parishioners he wasn't talking or looking around. Instead, his head was bowed.

Was he praying? She'd never seen him like this.

Seemingly pulled by the thread that bound them, she stopped behind a pillar to watch him.

He looked almost pained. His eyes were closed, his jaw tight. He looked as he had when he had insulted her for being in the King's bed. If so light a word could be applied to their conversation. His words had lit a shock in her so fast, she had only been able to react in kind.

But weeks had gone since that market day when he'd helped her with the barn. Nights had passed, too, and her body was no longer sixteen years old but a woman's, full grown.

She compared his stance then to that moment when she had demanded his kiss. That day was faded. But the market day was fresh.

Over every insult and heated word they had exchanged, over every kindness he had shown that day, somehow she must have been taking in the way his body had almost been against hers. His unique scent of snow, pine and steel. The way his cloak's collar had brushed against the roughness of his jaw, the dip of his lower lip.

Because that was what she had replayed during the subsequent nights...that and his words. He thought her a whore, and had said so with a bite of anger, but it was another heat that flashed through her body since then—and now as she watched him.

The slanted light from the windows showed dust floating in the air, but also the broadness of his shoulders, the strong slant of his jaw, his fingers splayed on his muscular thighs.

Since that day at the market it hadn't been the King she'd imagined in the bed over her. It had been—

Blue eyes opened, unerringly finding her. His brow furrowed, his eyes changed... She pressed against the pillar, but could not look away. The soft light that revealed his form to her hid half his face in shadow.

Hugh. Here in Swaffham. In her church.

His expression changed from puzzlement to something she shouldn't recognise but somehow did. Something unholy and necessary. Something reflected and repeated inside her. Want. Desire.

No, she hadn't dreamed of any king in her bed. She had dreamed of this man. And now, with fervency, she took in the reality of him. Watched his fingers clench into his thighs and his back straighten as if taking a blow. His lips parted as if he were pulling in a breath he'd forgotten to take. She felt her own part with them.

Hugh's eyes were sheened with emotions that weren't unreadable, empty or cold. There was more there, so much more, and she couldn't look away.

When she had first seen him in the hall at Edward's Court, she'd thought his eyes like a storm about to break. But she knew better now. Hugh's eyes were a storm that never ceased. And it felt as if those emotions were crashing towards her.

There was a settling of the townspeople; a loud murmuring of appreciation. A different noise broke through her restless need.

Alice swung her gaze to the left. William was cautiously approaching the pulpit. *William.* Grabbing her skirts, releasing her breath, she hurried to her seat—but not before glancing to Hugh, who disappeared.

When she searched the narthex shadows, Eldric was gone as well.

Chapter Ten

'I don't think I've ever seen Father in so fine a spirit.'
Elizabeth signalled towards the banqueting table groan-
ing with food.

The apples were studded with cloves and the mead
flowed from shallow flagons like a waterfall. The tiers
of cheese and bread that had been arranged to look like
a wild boar had been applauded as they entered the
room and were now almost unrecognisable. The boar
itself had received a standing ovation.

'Of course he's happy.' Alice adjusted her mask.
'We're surrounded by a lavish affair that doesn't de-
plete his coffers.'

Elizabeth laughed. 'True.'

Her father was easy to spot, with his hands full of
food and his cheeks red from the candles and the people
around him. He was always happy. Even their mother's
death hadn't deterred him for long, but that was to be
expected given their arranged marriage.

Being reminded of that part of her childhood only
darkened Alice's restless mood. 'Although when *hasn't*
Father been happy at a party?'

'No, this time it's something else. I think he's been happier since he's begun spending so much time in London.'

London and her father and his mistresses. Always his mistresses. 'I haven't seen anything different. He's the same as he's always been.'

She was a wealthy wool merchant's daughter and the King wanted gold and silver. So, though her father hadn't quite forgiven King Edward for increasing his wool tax, her father was flighty enough to still be impressed by royalty.

The King, seeing an easy way of appeasing at least one rich merchant, often asked him to Court. And so Father's mistresses had begun. Alice had been surrounded by them during her brief stay. She hadn't liked that any more than playing the game for a seal in the Tower's darkened passageways. She shivered just thinking of the dark.

'No, there are rumours—' Elizabeth said.

'Can we not talk about Father?' Alice couldn't take any more. She'd been back for months already, and the Christmas festivities were truly starting now. She'd thought there would be a lead or something she could follow regarding the Seal, but there was nothing. Nothing…and her family was at risk.

This was something she could not fail at.

'What is wrong?' Elizabeth asked. 'Your foot is beating like a hummingbird's heart.'

She stilled her foot, but it didn't help her restlessness. 'Nothing's the matter.'

Tonight there would be plenty of distractions and she could search Lyman's private rooms. With any luck during the mummers' dance she could search *all* the rooms.

'Well, you are certainly in a foul mood of late, and tonight, it's worse. If you mean to find a proper suitor—'

'Don't. Not tonight.'

'Why not tonight? That *is* why you're here. Lyman is throwing the largest party of the season, he's got us wearing masks, and he can't stop staring at you.'

Lyman was no doubt looking at her breasts.

'Although why you're interested in him is beyond me.'

She was interested if he was a traitor. What if he asked her to dance? She didn't know what was worse. That any one of the men she danced with could be a traitor. Or that after she'd risked her reputation by searching their private rooms she could be forced to marry one of them. How could she ever marry *Lyman*?

'I believe he may be misunderstood.'

'Speaking of which—I think our father has changed.'

Her father was currently eating himself into a stupor. 'I thought we had finished that subject.'

Elizabeth rested her hand against her arm and Alice stopped scanning the room. 'I'm trying to tell you there's someone special for him. He's been seeing only her.'

Her father had been supposed to see only their mother, but that hadn't stopped him from being with others. Still, it was hard to be angry with her father. He was always so happy, and her mother had not been miserable. In fact, she'd adored their father. Her father, from all she could see, only cared for himself.

Alice had never understood their relationship. Maybe that was why she took things too seriously. Why she tried to help others. Because her father never thought of anyone but himself. But if she sometimes thought of others...she *always* thought of Hugh.

'Where is Mary?' she asked instead.

'Being doted upon, as always. Her having married an even wealthier landowner has made her quite popular. She's sitting in the other room.'

The smaller room was much warmer, with plenty of cushions and sofas. Alice had looked at it longingly before heading to the hall. She needed to find a traitor, not rest in comfort.

'Why are we dressed for a masquerade when everyone can guess who we are anyway?'

'There are a few who look unfamiliar,' Elizabeth said.

'Oh, you mean the Alistairs? Truly, no one can guess *them* when already she is weaving around.'

Elizabeth covered her laugh. 'All right, maybe not those two.'

Alice sighed. 'I can't believe Mary's here. She's due any day.'

'Nothing will stop her from visiting home during Christmas season—you know that. Although her husband is certainly trying to keep her off her feet.'

'And where's John?'

'Talking with the burghers even now. He's constantly working.'

Elizabeth sounded all too proud of that fact. As the most prosperous wool merchant and landowner, it should have been up to her father to be mayor of Swaffham, and he had played at it several years ago. Played at it poorly. When it had been suggested that John become mayor instead, her father had readily agreed. He got the power of his wealth and John got to do all the work.

Yes, the Fenton family had all the power in Swaffham. Both her sisters had married well.

And then there was her. A spy.

'Mitchell is looking quite handsome tonight,' Elizabeth pointed out.

Alice forced herself to concentrate on those around her. Wearing a mask, but still recognisable, Mitchell was laughing with other merchants. There was a sense of pride about him again. She was all too happy to see it.

'He should be looking tired,' she said teasingly.

'Oh, you're not turning into a tyrant, are you? You know you are lucky Mitchell has the temperament he has. Not many men would allow such industry with a woman.'

Mitchell was gracious, but he was also desperate. She and her sisters knew they were lucky that their father cared for no industry at all. Mary most of all, because she thrived on it when she lived at home. But Elizabeth and she also had an understanding, since they'd grown up with the farms and the sheep.

Although Alice cared more for helping those less fortunate, she couldn't help but be excited by the project. Despite the weather and the season, they had been able to get more carpenters and tradesmen. The barn restoration was coming along nicely, and supplies for the Great Spinning Wheels were soon to be delivered.

'I'm surprised you're not exhausted,' Elizabeth said.

She *was* exhausted—which didn't help with her restlessness or her anxiety. She wanted to spend time with William, with the barn and the families it would help.

Instead she was scanning a Great Hall, with anxiety fraying her every nerve.

'I *am* tired,' she said. 'But thrilled. You should see the barn. They are repairing the west wall and adding a fireplace, and I'm thinking we need another fireplace on the other side, too.'

'With all that wool and wood? I can't imagine the damage if a spark is let loose!'

'But in the winter the women may argue on who sits near the fire.'

'Why will the spinners argue?' Mitchell said, joining them.

Alice moved to make room and gave him a smile. 'In the winter, with only one fireplace, they'll all have to take turns to sit near it.'

'You want more fires in the building?' Mitchell shook his head. 'The workers have several fires lit and the supplies are lying near. Already we've had near misses. Can't imagine what that would do inside a closed building.'

'Is there something you can put between the sparks and the spinners?' Elizabeth asked.

'I'll see if it's possible,' Mitchell said. 'But these men have been gathered hastily, and most haven't worked together before. Their differing opinions only increase in the worsening weather. Something happened today I've been wanting to tell you about.'

As Mitchell launched into a surprisingly humorous story, Alice couldn't help laughing. Elizabeth was right. He was looking handsome tonight; he was also quite charming. How easy it would be to fall in love with him. They would have moments like these to share. They both knew the wool trade, and with his ideas and partnership, they could be successful.

Except, as handsome as he was, her heart didn't stop at the mere thought of him. He wasn't, nor could he ever be, Hugh.

Over the din and overly bright laughter, the sight of Alice stunned him. Hugh stood thawing from the cold in Lyman's Great Hall, but it wasn't the fires or candles warming him—it was her.

He had expected the crowds to hide Alice's petite form, or her mask to cover her turned up nose, but his eyes unfailingly found her.

Her golden-brown hair gleamed in the candlelight. Some elaborate confection that curled and framed the face that he had never forgotten, but which had changed since he'd left. She was even more exquisitely beautiful to him than before. Tonight it was painful.

The heat of the crowd and the room had brought a flush to the creaminess of her cheeks. Her grey eyes danced behind the light blue mask more brightly than the flickering candles.

The gown she wore was a blistering bright yellow that skimmed over curves that shouldn't be noticeable under the acres of cloth covering her, and yet the style and ties of her surcoat tightened the blue chemise beneath, accentuating what every man coveted.

There was no denying her form, no stopping his body tightening in recognising it. And he wasn't even close to her. God, he needed to be close to her.

Ever since their meeting at the market, lust, need and raw want had haunted his days. It wasn't because of her words, or the fact she could be the King's mistress, but how she was with the children and workers. He'd tried to look at her as only a pawn in this game he played, but couldn't. With her so lovely, and knowing her heart was still kind, he could barely breathe.

'It's hasn't changed, has it?' Eldric said.

He pretended to look around, though he didn't want to see any of it. Too much reminded him of a past he wanted to forget. The fact that the town of Swaffham had become wealthier since he'd left did little to improve his mood.

'It's prospered since I left,' he said.

He had some wealth in his own right and he was a knight. Any lineage he had now was his own. But returning to this town only reminded him of the time when he had been helpless against the disparity between his own life and that of Alice's family. Of a time when he had known he wasn't good enough for her.

Coin he might have now, but he still wasn't good enough for her.

'Lyman's hall has had many improvements...' Eldric interrupted his thoughts '...but we both know you were looking at her.'

'You wouldn't be much of a spy if you hadn't noticed.'

'You watch her quite a bit.'

'Something you wouldn't notice unless you are watching *me*. And is there a reason I *shouldn't* watch her? Perhaps you don't like the injuries she gives to you?'

'Are we to talk about St Martin's dinner again? Because I thought I'd explained my interest in her is harmless.'

'Yet you showed it anyway.'

Hugh still didn't know why Eldric, who had ignored Alice since then, had flirted with her that night. Had

Eldric been testing his regard when it came to her? Hugh was always either near or with Alice. No doubt Eldric had his answer regarding Hugh's feelings by now.

'Her sister says she intends to marry. Best get used to it if you won't pursue her.'

Hugh adjusted his shoulders. 'Tell me again why you are here?'

'I have told you,' Eldric said.

He was trying to find the archer who had marked him.

'I haven't seen you making enquiries.'

'Perhaps it is *you* who watch *me*?' Eldric suggested. 'Remember, I was here before you arrived. Maybe I should be making enquiries of you.' Eldric took a drink and waved his goblet. 'Anyway, it's winter now, and I'm for warmth. The King knows where to reach me.'

And Edward knew how to reach *him*…and Alice. All here in Swaffham.

He knew Eldric's duties, and he knew his own. What he still hadn't figured out were Alice's. Days now of watching her, and still he couldn't come up with any answers. Who *was* she?

Time did change people, but her lively behaviour… her provocative words…were beyond what he'd expected. It was as if she had become someone else.

And he couldn't accept such a change.

Naïve, perhaps, but in all the corrupted world he had hoped she remained constant. Many a dark night, after many a dark deed when he had blackened his own soul, he had thought of her. As if simply knowing her made him a better person.

Yet she was more beautiful than she had ever been.

Though he wanted her more, needed her more, she *had* changed.

Her overly bright laughter, her extravagant gowns, her attendance at parties. Her private meeting with the King, her blunt words to him. This woman who attended tonight could command a king. She commanded *him* though they'd never touched.

But even so… It was too much of a change. He refused to believe her to have changed so much.

Especially in the ways she remained the same. The restoration of the barn, her laughing with that little girl, her kindness to the boy William. *That* was the Alice he recognised.

The other one who sparkled too brightly made him suspicious. Something was not as it should be.

As the Boar's Head festivities spun around him, and distractions and drink flowed freely, he wondered if tonight he would find the truth.

'The music's good, at least,' Eldric said. 'The perfect opportunity to dance.'

Bemused, Hugh turned to his friend. 'You *dance*?'

Eldric shrugged. 'I've been known for it. Plus, there was this woman as we walked in. Did you see her?'

He had noticed no woman except Alice. He couldn't stop thinking of what she had said to him at the market. Words that he had forced inside him, so he could do his duty, and follow her.

But he had forced them in and he couldn't forget. They haunted him all day at the barn. Then in church there had been a flush to her cheeks, a curiosity and a hunger in her eyes that had burned through him. He had expected to see her there, but hadn't expected—

'Are you certain you did not see her? She came to

about here.' Eldric pointed to his lower chest. 'And was about this big around.'

Hugh shook himself. He'd lose his head if he let his guard down. 'It was a child.'

'None of the children have masks,' Eldric said. 'And she had this look in her eyes... You didn't see her? I would like to dance with her.'

Who he *did* see was Mitchell, his eyes roving over Alice as they laughed. Mitchell stepping closer to whisper in her ear.

'Dancing's not the reason why I'm here.'

Eldric's brow rose. 'There's a *reason* you're here?'

Distracted. Too comfortable. He truly would lose his head. A mere slip of his concentration and he had alluded to his orders. To watch Alice and all the Fentons, as he had told the King he would. At the same time to find some hint of a reason why Lyman would be the traitor with the Half-Thistle Seal. To at least point doubt so the King wouldn't look too closely at *him*.

Hugh smiled. 'Of course, there's a reason. I can only supply so much ale when *you're* drinking it.'

Eldric lifted his shoulder. 'I've had enough of ale. I'm finding that woman.'

Hugh raised his glass as Eldric walked away. He didn't want to move at all. From this vantage point he could watch every detail of Alice, but she hadn't yet seen him.

What would it be like to dance with her? Had he been a spy for the King so long that all he could do was watch?

A carol had started. Groups of people were gathering in a circle, their right arms raised, their left clasping their partners. Grand circles of people that would become smaller. He knew this dance well. It was one of the few that allowed touch.

Soon either Lyman or Mitchell would ask Alice to dance. Would hold her hand as they circled each other and her skirts brushed their legs.

Like hell.

He wasn't about to stand by watching another man... any man...hold her. Not while he had breath in his body.

Alice freely tapped her foot to release her restlessness. Elizabeth was busy talking to Mitchell and now Lyman had joined them, and she didn't think either of them would notice.

Lyman came to tell them the mummers' dance would soon begin. It would be the Wedding Dance this year. It was one of her favourites, but she would miss it. Because when the mummers were dancing she'd make her excuses to search his rooms.

She was getting good at excusing herself. All she needed to indicate was her need for the garderobe and then simply go somewhere else. To forage through desks, wardrobes and purses if she was lucky.

Most often there wouldn't be enough time. At least tonight there'd be entertainment. If the dances didn't provide enough distraction, the food and talk would.

She truly did need time tonight, since she'd been unlucky in other homes she'd searched. Part of it was the lack of time she had, the other was her lack of information. The King had provided no insight as to whether the Seal was wood or metal. If it was the size of a man's hand or as tiny as a thumb. All she knew was that the impression it made was not very big. Which meant she looked for something possibly easily hidden.

How was she supposed to find it?

What would happen if she didn't?

'Do you want to dance?'

Alice stopped tapping her foot and turned to Hugh, who had caught her unawares.

And he continued to catch her unawares: his appearance was startling to her every sense. It seemed impossible that he had returned to Swaffham. And after all this time it should have been impossible for her to be so affected by him. And yet she was.

Tonight his clothes were as fine as any nobleman's. The burgundy lines of his tunic framed his lithe build and were trimmed in velvet. The silver around his belt and boots glinted. During his time here his hair had grown, curling now around his collar. None of which softened the hard slant of his jaw or his piercing storm-filled gaze.

'Which dance?' Her eyes strayed to the lock of hair that fell loose and soft over his forehead.

There was a quirk to his lips. 'The one that's beginning right now.'

Aware of eyes on their exchange, Alice carefully chose her words as she looked to Lyman and Mitchell, hoping they would get her hint. 'Yes, I would like a dance.'

'Then let's begin,' Hugh said, taking her hand in a sure grip.

His hand shouldn't have felt possessive, nor familiar, and she almost yanked it away. It wasn't that she wasn't above making a scene when it came to Hugh. She had done so many times in the past. However, tonight was her only chance to search Lyman's house, and she couldn't argue or have more delays.

So she allowed his hand to stay, and it held hers longer than the dance provided. The dance that she knew well, but for the first time somehow didn't know at all.

It was because Hugh was holding her hand. His palm pressed to hers, their fingers tangling, his callused fingertips brushing her wrist. The fact that he drew her closer as they joined the other dancers.

It was a polite dance, with simple steps, but the revelry had started long ago and drinking had blurred the lines of formality. Already the dancers were bumping into each other, and parts of the circle were too tight. But Hugh arranged them in a space, and Alice attempted to concentrate on the other dancers and not the man still holding her hand.

But for every step she took he was there beside her. For every nod and smile to the dancer on her left, she had to give a nod to Hugh. And while one movement was mere polite formality, the other felt like something else. A dance, surely, but one she didn't know the steps to.

And with every precise turn of the bodies within their large circle she became all the more aware of every precise step that she took with him. As if she did two dances. One with the circle of people around her, and one that encompassed only him.

'You talk much with Mitchell,' Hugh said, inclining his head in order to be heard without shouting.

'As you know, there is much for us to talk about.'

Alice turned, released Hugh's grip, turned again and he took her hand.

'The barn restoration is on your property.' Hugh stepped forward again. 'And yet you spend a lot of time in each other's homes.'

They kept their voices low, and this wasn't a conversation she wanted heard by anyone. It seemed the dance agreed with her, for the music and the circles changed.

Hugh released his hand and crooked his arm with hers. Locked as they were, their swaying brought them closer. She felt the pull of his sleeves against hers, his scent, the warmth of his body. The pressure and strength of his arm linked with hers. With the raising of their right arms, his left tightened to hold her for the turn. She knew the deadly strength in his arms, felt the keening need to know more.

The turn was successful, and she released her breath and her arm.

He had sounded almost jealous—but he'd sounded like that before, in the garden. When he'd followed her there to find information regarding the King.

'You are following me.'

'It's a small town,' he said.

Which made her all the more suspicious.

'One you've returned to though you have no ties here.'

He locked his arm with hers again, tensing it more than required by the dance steps. It brought her closer to him.

'No, I wouldn't have ties to the *merchants* here, now would I?'

What did the merchants have anything to do with anything? He was from nobility, and far above her station.

'Your father was a knight.'

This time he purposely brought her closer. 'Do you think I'm an outcast and should have remained one? I wasn't born here, so therefore don't belong?' A quick turn of their bodies and their backs were to each other before he was at her side again. 'Sorry to disappoint you, but I have a right to be here as much as you.'

She stumbled. His arm linked with hers and supported her until she matched his step again. He didn't say any more and neither did she.

She couldn't. It hadn't mattered to her that he wasn't born here. But it was clear it mattered to him.

All those years he'd helped his father, fought the boys in the town who had made fun of his poverty, of his father's drunkenness.

She had only seen it as heroic, had only ever seen the decency and the goodness in him. Never had she seen his childhood and his actions as a source of shame. And yet his words cut with embarrassment, with pain.

Run away, Alice, before you do something you'll regret.

She had run away, only thinking of his rejection, never thinking of the meaning behind his words that day. Yet now, here, with him in this dance, whirling around with the candles happily lit, and laughter and cheer surrounding her, she saw his past in a darker light. As something filled with anguish and shame. Did he think she would regret *him*?

Another step and he was beside her. His face implacable, his jaw tense. His arms held her at just the right angle, holding her assuredly, but no longer possessively. They kept circling…circling.

Her life with him might have always been this way but those few words had revealed something else. Something in the heat of anger, in the sweep of the dance, that he hadn't meant to say.

The dance sped up and no words could be said. It brought their bodies closer together as they stepped in and out. Her full gown and sleeves trailed in the sweeping movements, looking like waves crashing to shore.

She felt like those waves, and Hugh was her shore. She vowed she wouldn't run away again. She was only now realising where she should run *to*.

When the dance ended, they parted without words. The mummers' dance would start soon, and she would begin her duties to the King.

She watched as Hugh walked away, saw the breadth of his shoulders, the assuredness of the way he held himself, parting the crowds as if it was his due.

He didn't look back, almost as if he hadn't asked her to dance, as if he hadn't commented about her being with other men or whoring with the King.

That day in the market, in the heat of his words, he had let slip that there was something between them. Was it possible? Was it true? She was beginning to believe it wasn't only her. But if so, he held himself away still. As if it was he who was running.

Circling. Circling. She felt no more or less than wool on a Great Wheel.

But tonight she could do no more.

Frustration, anger, and need warred within him. Hugh stormed through the Great Hall, looking for a reprieve or a distraction. Eldric was nowhere in sight.

Why had he danced with Alice? It could never be simply a dance with her. Stupid to think otherwise, but he'd been consumed with jealousy.

He'd had no right, and yet he'd taken it. Given her

no choice although she had noticeably tried to escape his request.

Instead he had taken her hand, which had held some of the strength he ached to feel. Taken her hand, brought her as close as the dance allowed. Brought her closer when even that was too far away. Had seen her eyes display every emotion in their short exchange. Umbrage. Pride. And the last. The last...

Why had he said the words he had? They revealed too much about himself to her. And he had seen every aching awareness and understanding flaring in her steady gaze.

He had just laid every hurt he'd ever felt at her feet as if she would care. She *couldn't* care.

And yet...her grey eyes had watched him carefully, so he hadn't dared to speak again. She fixed things. If she saw a wrong, she set it to rights. She'd done so all her life.

The one shining light in his life was that she had never tried to fix *him*. Never pitied him. When all the others in Swaffham had given him handouts or disdained him, she had acted as if he was unflawed.

That fact was the one untarnished part of him. Now he had revealed the shame from his past as if...as if begging for her to remedy him.

Angry at himself, he grabbed a flagon that was thankfully still full of ale and looked for a goblet.

The moment the King had ordered him to spy on the Fenton family he'd dreaded it. He'd avoided even thoughts of Alice since that day in the field when he had almost killed her...kissed her. He *should* have kissed her. Maybe then the ache of those years away would have been less.

There was only one remedy tonight, and that was what was in his hands. The King's orders be damned. There would be no spying tonight, no more observation. He would steal this drink and return to his own home.

Who *was* he to her? He had the wrong background, the wrong family. Her father, delighted with nobility, completely ignored Hugh's lineage. His father had seen to that disgrace.

He should ignore Alice now. He didn't know her, there were questions with her involvement with the King, with her asking questions, her projects, and kindness to others.

Too many questions, and too many traps to be caught in. Eldric did watch him regardless of his glib remarks. And yet...

Almost out of the room, he turned as if unable to help himself. One last glance saw Alice approach her sister, Mitchell and Lyman. Others were there as well, but his eyes were only on Alice as he looked for some trace of pity still lingering. Some glint in her eye to show that she intended to arrive at his door tomorrow to remedy a wrong.

None of that was there. Instead Alice craned her neck around her would-be suitors. She tapped her foot impatiently as Mitchell laughed.

This wasn't the woman he had observed earlier in the evening. The one who had laughed too brightly. This wasn't the woman he'd observed over the last month, partaking of all the festivities and wearing ribbons in her hair.

Right now there was a hint that she was the Alice who didn't care for such lavish banquets because it didn't help those less fortunate. His lips curved at her impatience and disapproval.

Maybe when this was all over and he returned to the King, he could forget the Alice at Court who laughed too loud and wore extravagant dresses. Maybe he could continue to remember her as he had always done. Helping children, and frowning at banquet waste.

She gave another glance over her sister's shoulder. He saw her more clearly now. Her eyes were wide, with a line deeply drawn between her brows. Her mouth was downturned, her bottom lip clamped by her teeth. This wasn't impatience…it was something like worry or…*fear.*

He shook his head and put the goblet down. This wasn't right. Her tapping foot no longer looked impatient. It looked restless with nerves.

This wasn't the Alice with her projects either.

Alice was not as she should be, or what he thought she should be.

Maybe…she put on a facade. Perhaps he saw the contrasts with her because one wasn't *her.* But which one, and why the contrasts?

He had nothing to go on but her conversations regarding the King in the garden and at the market. Her questions regarding his presence and neatly not answering his own. Her disappearing at every party and in every home they attended together.

He had dismissed all those moments because he hadn't seen her in six years. Dismissed their connection, his awareness of her, because he hadn't wanted to look too closely. Hadn't wanted to feel the ache. Because he had been jealous when he had no right to be.

But now he did. Now he saw her nervousness, the façade slip. Now he saw her craning her neck to observe the mummers approaching the stage.

When she slipped away he couldn't dismiss anything.

She was up to something, and he aimed to find out what it was.

Chapter Eleven

'I thought I'd find you here,' he said.

'Spindles!' Alice jumped, the candle in her hand sputtering, sputtering. She watched in horror as the flame bent again and went out.

Utter darkness.

'What are you doing here?'

Hugh's voice…coming from the far corner. The one behind the desk she had momentarily and gratefully spied when she'd entered the room before closing the door behind her.

Hugh was here, in a room where he had no right to be. But then neither did she.

'I was looking for…'

'Yes?'

'I was looking for the garderobe.'

'When you poked your head in here and raised your candle you knew it wasn't the garderobe because you entered it and closed the door behind you.'

And then the light went out, and she couldn't see.

Don't think about the darkness.

'You've been caught, Alice, it's best to be truthful

now,' he said silkily. 'What did the King say to you that day?'

'Why are you asking me about the King now?'

'Because you never answered my question.'

Don't talk about the King... Don't think about the darkness. What was she left with? Hugh and his voice which seemed closer.

'There was never anything to answer.'

'Enough games,' he said, low and no longer from the corner.

She found her voice. 'I could say the same to you.'

'It isn't safe to go into other people's rooms when you're not invited.'

She knew it wasn't, but she'd gotten this far without getting caught. She wasn't caught now, since she had said nothing and she could leave.

Except it was dark, and somehow she'd lost the direction of the door. Already she could feel her heart racing, the spent candle in her hands slipping.

Don't think about the darkness. She had to distract herself.

'How do you know that?'

'How do I know what?'

'That my being here isn't safe,' she said, swallowing against the tightening her voice.

If she could keep talking maybe he would too. Then the darkness wouldn't matter.

'I'm merely a guest,' she continued. 'and I wandered in here by accident. You wouldn't know it's not safe. Not unless you know something. Who exactly is playing games here? Tell me, how do you know?'

Absolute silence. Darkness closing in.

'I'm the one asking questions...'

Strong arms grabbed her. Alice gasped. The candle fell to the floor. The familiar scent of pine, snow and steel enveloped her. A moment of struggle before she realised it was futile. When she stilled, he let out a sound—half-surprise, half-satisfaction.

'You're trembling. Scared? Good—you should be. So which is the true you? Are you about the dresses now or helping the children?'

Not these questions. Not lies. Not in this darkness. 'Let go of me.'

'All those parties you've attended, all the times you disappeared—is this what you've been doing?'

'Let go of me!' She lashed out until he did—easily, as if he had never held her—then stepped back.

Without Hugh's arms, without his hands on hers, the darkness surrounded her. She bit her lip, held back a cry, reached out in the direction he was. To find some safety from the darkness.

Alice's hand suddenly gripped his tunic sleeve. Her fingers, like daggers, felt the full length of his arm, and pulled him towards her. Her gasps were nothing more than desperate pants for air. Her trembles were now shudders. Hugh pulled her in tighter and felt the fast thumping of her heart. She was terrified—but not of him.

'My God, Alice. After all this time?'

Hugh cradled Alice in his arms and her trembling body shook him. He hadn't thought at all about the darkness when she'd entered the room. When he'd laid the trap, and said the words. He never would have done so if he'd known the candle would go out.

Then as he'd talked to her, he heard the fear at the edge of her voice. The stridency of her tone as she gathered herself. He had encouraged her fear. Those who were afraid often confessed.

Had he made it worse for her? He held her, but it wasn't enough. Her body was rigid with fright, her trembles turning to shivers and back again. He heard her sniffle, give a great hiccupping gasp.

He held her closer. Held her as he had always meant to hold her. With all his body, his arms tightly wound around her back.

'I've got you,' he whispered against her hair. 'You're safe.'

He brushed at her hair, her cheeks, felt the evidence of her tears. He brushed them away too.

'There's light here, Alice. See it between the slats of the floorboards? There under the door?'

He felt her move her head, her breath hitching softly as she made each discovery.

'You see it?' he repeated.

'Yes,' she whispered.

She gave a ragged sigh and rested against him. And in that way, he felt Alice as he had always dreamed he would. *Her*—her body. His defences gone.

He'd never held her like this. And in the dark, he was conscience of the way her legs tangled with his, the curve of her hips just under the sweep of his fingers, the give of her breasts, the tenderness of her hands clutching his tunic.

He shouldn't feel the relief and satisfaction that he did, but he felt it down to his very marrow. More so because by wrapping his arms around her, he had eased her trembles.

'Still?' he said.

She rubbed her face, her tears, against his tunic,

somewhere near where his heart lay. 'Afraid of the dark?' she whispered. 'Yes…ridiculous for a grown woman.'

'Not ridiculous when you suffered the way you did.'

'It *is* foolish since I've been scared of the dark for longer than I was stuck in that well.'

As he looked back over the years, the memory of her shrieks that day still broke him. He didn't even remember why he had been in that part of town. But he remembered seeing Allen and his friends laughing and patting each other on the backs and shoulders.

Their camaraderie hadn't made him pause. In fact, he usually did everything he could to ignore them. But their self-satisfied expressions had stopped him cold that day. They were pleased with themselves. And he knew Allen, the largest of the boys, tormented those weaker than him.

Sometimes he taunted Hugh with snide comments regarding his father or his threadbare clothes. Most times he preyed on someone younger or smaller than him. If Allen was happy, he and his friends were up to no good.

So Hugh had changed direction and walked towards the well. He didn't know what he'd been thinking. He hadn't needed to get involved. He'd had enough to do; his own burdens to carry. But his steps had steadily brought him closer.

It was then that he'd heard her bitter cries for help. The pleading, the words, the shrieking.

Alice's helplessness had snapped his pent-up rage. His fists curled; he'd lengthened his strides into a run before he'd given it a thought.

He hadn't shouted out as he'd ploughed into Allen. It had been as if Allen's cruelty was the manifestation of all the years he'd fought against his father. Against the town. Against his peers, who were supposed to be his friends but who heaped only more torment upon him.

With the first swing he'd felt the satisfying crunch of breaking Allen's cheekbone. Then he'd taken on the rest until they'd run.

He'd never felt anger like that—neither before nor since. He had still been angry when he'd lowered a rope to pull Alice up. So angry he hadn't explained that it was *him*. So up had come the shrieking child, her arms and legs swinging.

She'd broken his nose…and made it worse when she'd tried to fix it.

He rubbed his hands down her back, soothing her, soothing his memories. It was only the two of them in the dark, their past remembered through her fear and his actions.

'I'm sorry,' he said again.

'I'm the one who broke your nose.'

He huffed out a breath. 'It looks better this way.'

She had said that to him at the time. 'You remember that?'

'How could anyone forget how you attacked me? I was in agony, but you wrenched my nose to the left.'

Her small hands on either side of his bloody nose… his eyes streaming… He had held her then, though he'd wanted to fling her away. Held her until her trembles and fears had eased. Like now. He rubbed her back. Felt the warmth, the curves, her strength—felt her hands grip his tunic in answer.

'You could have stopped me.'

'I tried.'

No, he hadn't. Not really. He had been comforting her and drying her tears.

'I made it worse. What did your father think when you got home?'

Alice regretted her question the moment he tensed against her.

'As I'm sure you remember, my father didn't say much at all—let alone have an opinion about my nose,' he said.

Pressing her hand upon his chest, she pulled away to see his expression. Her eyes had adjusted to the darkness, but the light coming through the slats wasn't enough for her to see what was in his eyes. Still she tried to tell him he had it wrong—about his past, about that day.

'I want you to—'

'What are you doing in here?' he interrupted.

Another change of subject, and she felt no relief. Neither talking of their past or her present was easy. Especially since she needed to lie to him. But he'd seen her come in here, and close the door. She couldn't pretend she was in the wrong room.

'The dance will end and we'll have to leave soon,' he said.

Affected by the dark, by his comfort, a part of her didn't want to lie to him. If she said something—if she confessed what she truly had been doing—what would the King do? Yet right now, in the dark with Hugh holding her, the King felt very far away.

'I was looking for something.'

Exhaling, he turned his face away. 'It's time, isn't it?'

He'd said that to her once before after the barn restoration. After they worked together and had some accord. It felt like that now with his arms around her. With his comfort in the dark. It felt like they were coming to some understanding, but she didn't know what. 'It's time?'

'For the truth. For some answers to the questions I've had. Because here, now, I'm beginning to comprehend what is real, and don't know if I...' He shook his head. 'Please tell me this has nothing to do with the King.' He took a step away, but his hands remained on her shoulders. 'That you're not in here because the King sent you.'

She didn't want to lie to him. 'Why would the King send me into Lyman's room?'

'Then this has nothing to do with that day in the King's chambers?'

She didn't know what to say, and then she heard a sound from him. Swallowing—as if he was suddenly afraid.

'If it is, be careful what you say to me.'

'Why should I be careful?'

Absolute silence—as if she'd shocked him. As if he held a thousand words back. And then she knew—from his silence, from his actions, from the few words he'd already said.

She knew because this was Hugh. She knew the calibre of man he had been, and she'd already glimpsed the man he still was.

And right now he was soothing her in the dark. He was protecting her because he knew... He knew she was in danger.

'You said...' she began. 'You said I'd been caught. You said it isn't safe. You're a spy, too.'

His hands tightened on her arms before they released her. Her trembles were almost gone now.

'Are you spying on me? Did the King send you here to make sure I followed his orders? Or…are you here to stop me?'

'Too many questions,' he said curtly. 'You won't get confessions that way.'

It wasn't the dark making her ramble; it was the enormity of her realisation. 'It's true, then?'

'What is?'

Now there was his cynicism again. 'All of it. The King *did* send you here to spy on me. You *are* like me.'

'You can't be a spy,' he said. 'You're a woman.'

His words sounded as if he was trying to convince himself. 'The fact that I'm a woman didn't bother the King when he commanded me. He didn't tell you this when you requested his counsel?'

'You're here because of your project with Mitchell, Alice. You *have* to be.'

His words were short, brisk, as if he was forcing them to be true.

'You know that's not true,' she said.

'It's enough,' he whispered.

It should be enough. Christmas season…the rains flooding the fields…Mitchell's inspiration for the spinning wheels. But the King had demanded more of her. Everything. Her family was at risk. And now Hugh was here in Swaffham. Asking questions, following her. Being cruel and then revealing kindness.

Maybe he was so adamant about her keeping secrets because he kept a few himself.

'As you know, what is and isn't enough doesn't matter when it comes to the King's command.'

She wanted to step back, move, think through all of this. She could hear the revellers below. The entertainment was still in full swing. Even so, she didn't have much time. And she hadn't had time to look yet.

Hugh's presence be damned—she had to look. She wouldn't get another chance like this.

Forcing her eyes to follow the lighted slats, she walked to the desk and felt along its corners.

'What does the King command?' His voice drew out each word in cold lethality.

She couldn't see anything, and was worried she'd knock something over. 'Why would the King send two spies to this town?' she replied.

She had known it was foolish to bring a candle into the room, when she could be easily caught. But her fears had battled with her duties, and it was simply easier to see. Now everything was murky dark with the only light from the covered windows, and the thin light between the floorboards and under the door.

Where to start?

When she'd opened the door, all she'd taken in was the desk. She hadn't seen if there were other places to search.

'Are you here to ensure I complete my assignment? Because I haven't found it yet.'

He was silent. Remained silent. She realised it was a good tactic, because in the dark she wanted to make confessions. She also wanted to mourn her lost opportunity.

'What is it you're to find?' he said, but his voice sounded far away—as if he could barely get the words out.

'Did you see anywhere else to search in here? I've

got the desk, but this is a large room—there could be other places to look.'

'There's a cabinet under the window.'

She heard him step closer.

'What is it you're looking for?'

She disrupted a couple of scrolls. 'Hopefully Lyman's not observant.'

'Tell me it's not true—that you're not a spy.'

'Why are you acting so angry? Remember all those talks of secrets and kings, and your following me? This is it. I'm showing you; I'm answering your questions.'

'It's not safe—he couldn't have asked you to do such a thing.'

'No, it's not safe—for my family is threatened. So here I am.'

Silence again. She glanced up, could barely see his outline for he didn't move. He looked as if he hardly breathed.

She knew the feeling.

'He has threatened you and your family?' he said.

She righted a candlestick. 'Why else would I be doing this?'

'I thought—'

'You thought I was his mistress.'

'Stop—just stop.'

'We don't have much time. If you're here to make sure I accomplish what he asked me to do, then you can see me doing it. If you intend to stop me, you should probably start.'

'Why are you doing this in front of me? Why are you showing me this?'

'You are a spy, like me. I know you are, so you can't pretend.'

'Then, if so, you are betraying secrets.'

'I don't have a choice.' She paused. 'I trust you.'

He cursed. 'Never trust anyone.'

She did stop then, as he moved towards her. There was no light at all, but she could see the rigidity of his shoulders, his clenched fists, the jut of his chin.

'I trust you,' she repeated. 'You saved me from the dark. You won't harm me.'

'I could.'

Hugh's voice helped her concentrate, to not think about the darkness, but his tone prickled unease up her wandering hands.

He wasn't pleased about their exchange.

Well, neither was she.

Was it the fact that the King had made her a spy? Was it her, a woman risking her reputation in a man's private chambers?

Too many questions and no time to waste.

'You're going to help me. I've delayed already and I haven't any time left. You wouldn't let something happen to my family.'

'It's been six years, Alice. You don't know me at all.'

She didn't. But she was realising that time had passed for both of them.

'You don't know *me* if you think I could be the King's mistress... Or *anyone's* mistress.'

Hugh pinched the bridge of his nose, felt the bump there. She had punched him when she'd thought he was one of her tormentors. A part of him...down to his very bones...recognised that she wouldn't capitulate to her monarch's demands. 'I know.'

'And yet you made those comments?'

Her words shamed him. 'Foolishly. Heatedly. But I

realised that it only mattered because it wasn't with—'
He bit back the words he, a traitor, should never say to
her. Instead, he said, 'I need to apologise.'

Her lips parted, as if she was going to say something
else, but she shook her head. 'You can apologise by
searching that cabinet you saw by the window.'

He had expected more anger. He'd insulted her—
and not only once. But there was something more here.
Something he needed the answers to, but didn't want
to ask. Still...

'I need to understand first. The King sent you back
to Swaffham to look for something in Lyman's house?'

The King had sent him to look for the Half-Thistle
Seal, to pay close attention to the Fenton family. Could
it be that the King suspected Lyman as well as the Fentons? That might be the break he needed in this night-
mare he was embroiled in. Him returning to Swaffham,
facing his past, facing Alice. If he could place the blame
on this man who stared at Alice too lasciviously then
something good would come of it.

Except it didn't matter if it was Lyman's house or
all the houses of Swaffham. The real trouble was if the
King had sent her to look for the Seal, that only meant
she looked for *him*.

'It isn't necessarily Lyman's house I need to search,'
Alice continued. 'It's all the houses. After I played his
game of finding a seal—'

'A seal—?'

Denying the truth didn't stop the words. His body
shook, shuddered, and he exhaled his held breath. The
Seal. If the King had sent her to find it, that meant he
didn't trust Hugh. It was possible that the King sus-

pected him. But that couldn't be true. He'd been careful. Lives were at stake.

He'd been *careful*.

Before he knew what he was doing he took steps to be next to her, to touch her. By placing his hand on her arm he could solidify whatever words they would now exchange. Not the stuff of nightmares, but reality.

'It was only a game—or so I thought.'

He didn't want to discuss games. 'What seal?'

'The game at the Tower of London was a test to find a fake seal. When I was the winner the King deemed me worthy of finding a true seal.'

There would be no coming back from what she was about to say—no remedy. He wouldn't be able to hide his thoughts or reactions from her. If she looked for the Seal she would find *him*. He couldn't lie or hide the truth from her. Either way he would be found out for the traitor he was.

His past separated him from her; his present made it all the more unbearable. His lineage had been forced upon him, but the Seal was his own inspiration. His own blackened deed.

Alice, who was always so determined to right wrongs, to fix misdeeds, had been commanded—threatened—by the King to find a traitor. If she found the Seal—if she found him—she would know him as a traitor. And the only way for the King to right the wrong would be to execute him.

It wasn't his death he worried about. It was the loss of that unreserved admiration in her eyes when she looked at him. She'd never tried to fix *him* before. Now she would see him as an enemy.

He had thought himself, if not safe, at least secure

that the King had sent only him. But he hadn't. And right now he didn't want to think about the King not trusting him. He only wanted to think of what Alice was about to say and how he would react.

'What seal?' he repeated.

'A small one with a half thistle,' she said in the dark. Hugh kissed her.

Chapter Twelve

Arms that formed a cage embraced her. A male body that exuded the smell of snow and pine and steel and heat slammed against her own. Jarring her hip against the desk she searched.

Hugh.

Hugh holding her tightly, holding her as if she would fly away on the storm he held in his eyes. The scratch of his jaw, the intent of his lips demanding against hers.

Until she held him just as tightly, her fingers linking at his nape, entwining with his curls and the velvet of his collar.

She thrust her body up to meet his. So there was no dark, no desk, no room. Only him.

And there were no more demands but only coaxing as her lips softened against his and she opened for him. Opened as she had wanted to that day long ago. But she knew that it wouldn't have happened like this then. It was the dark, the circumstances, the fact that they'd waited.

It was worth the wait. There was a sound—his, hers—as he pulled her more to him, as she pulled back.

He yanked his lips away, slid them along her jaw, behind her ear. Her fingers kneaded him, bringing him closer, tighter. Wanting more.

And then there were words.

'Alice...'

'Please,' she said, rubbing her cheek along his more abrasive one, moving her fingers along his shoulders, feeling his muscles tense along his arms, his back.

There was a hitch of his breath when she slid them along his lower back and up—up until she was fully pressed against him.

'All this time...' he said, his lips trailing down to her neck. 'All my imaginings... I couldn't know... I wouldn't.'

She arched and gave him more access, and shivered as his kiss became harsher, hungrier at her collar. She hated her clothes then—hated his as her fingers clenched in the fine weave of his tunic. He was restless too as he yanked her to the other side, as if his lips, his hands, could have more access on her left than her right.

He gave a growl of need when his hands pressed down her back, down until he was cupping her, lifting her.

She gasped then, lost her grip on his tunic. Her weight fully upon him as he stepped forward to find the desk behind them.

Stumbling. A curse. The hold broken.

Alice couldn't catch her breath. Heard the harshness of Hugh's. Felt it against her cheeks before he pulled away from her.

The cool air of the room between them was unwanted, his hand on her hip not enough, so she pressed her weight against the desk to steady herself.

Why had they stopped?

The darkness held no answer for her. She couldn't see what was in his eyes. Her thumping heart came to its own conclusion. Fear that Hugh was gone from her again. As he had left that day in the field, before he kissed her.

If he had truly left her, it would be worse. So this time, no matter what was said, she wouldn't run. She'd face him.

'You kissed me,' she said. 'You stopped.'

With effort, Hugh released his hand from her hip. What had he done? He had jeopardized everything for a kiss. For what he craved.

'I did. The music changed.'

'I didn't hear.'

Neither had he. It was the shock of pain in his shin from hitting the desk that had jarred him away from what he wanted to do. Sweep the desk's contents to the floor and unlace Alice's surcoat.

'We need to go; we'll be caught.'

She drew in a shaky breath. The sounds of need she'd made still echoed in her ears.

'I didn't search the room or the cupboard,' she said, her voice faint. 'The candle's on the floor.'

'I'll get it; we'll search the cupboard later,' he said.

Straightening, she released her hands from the desk, and he stepped back to give her space. To give himself room so he didn't take her again.

He wanted to take her again.

'We'll be back?' she said.

An idea forming, he nodded. 'I'll help you search for this seal. I'm invited to the same parties as you. With both of us searching, we'll find it.'

'Is that what the King sent you to do? To help me?'

He couldn't answer her. Too dangerous. Too much risk. All of it.

'We have to go—the music's stopped,' he said, though he heard nothing but the roaring in his veins.

Chapter Thirteen

December 26th

'So how are we to do this?' Alice said.

'We do this as planned.'

Hugh looked around. The day was clear, crisp, and an icy wind shivered through the trees. People were gathered in the square. It was St Stephen's Day, and the wren hunting would soon begin. There was always chaos on Wren Day—mostly because the young boys scrambled to be the first to catch a wren in its nest.

When caught, the wrens would be skewered on a long pole decorated with holly, so that they could be paraded around with music and drink before the burial. It was a good time for the boys to boast, to show their prowess—and to teach the wren not to chirp the next time St Stephen attempted to escape his execution.

The irony of the tradition wasn't lost on him. Hugh had a wren in his own life, and her name was Alice. One word from her to the King, and he'd be sent to execution as well.

So he had made more plans, devised more lies. All to

keep one vow to his friend Robert. To protect him and his family. Never to let King Edward know he was alive.

So he would keep Alice close and pretend. If he could when it came to her.

Alice a spy. To this moment he still tried to deny it, but he knew she spoke the truth.

The King truly had made Alice a spy, had sent her to Swaffham to search for the Half-Thistle Seal. To search for *him*.

For the last few days he'd paced his tiny house. There were too many consequences of the truths before him.

One theory was that the King didn't trust him to find the traitor on his own and therefore had enlisted Alice to help him. There were several problems with this theory. As a spy, he had been involved with numerous missions; Alice had never done this before. The King had never sent anyone to assist him before, and he rarely worked with others. Thus, there were too many holes in that theory for it to be true.

The other theory was that the King truly did suspect the Fentons as deceivers, so he had orchestrated some way for Hugh to work with Alice. Convoluted. Far-fetched. If the King suspected Alice's family then he wouldn't notify her that he was looking for the Half-Thistle Seal.

So that left him with the King not trusting him. Because if Edward had sent Alice here to search for the same seal it meant he didn't trust Hugh to find it. Perhaps because he already believed Hugh had the Half-Thistle Seal. It also meant that the King knew of his relationship with Alice, or at least had guessed there would be a relationship.

And, relationship or not, it came down to his own

life and Robert's versus Alice's. He knew the King, and knew he would kill or imprison Alice's family if she didn't return with the Seal.

Hugh was in a trap. The only saving grace was time. Alice didn't suspect Hugh of being a traitor. He could keep her close, pretend to assist her, all the while thwarting any ability for her to find it.

If, however, he couldn't think his way out, he would soon be heading to his execution—as the wrens were today.

'But I don't like what you planned. I don't like any of it.'

'As you've been saying.'

He had been arguing the opposite. Clever Alice—of course she would ask questions.

'I had a perfectly good plan to find it. With you by my side I won't gain as much access to people's homes. How could I have a suitor—?'

'If I'm one?' he interrupted. 'Well, I'm not.'

If only his body would remember that fact, and not recall with utmost accuracy how sweetly she felt in his arms. When she briefly told him of her plan, to gain access into homes by gaining suitors, he almost kissed her again – a *claiming* kiss.

'They don't know you're not a suitor since we have to spend time together and collaborate.'

'If you keep acting cross with me, they would think we don't suit.'

'It is easy to stay cross with you.'

He relished every moment that she was. In spite of the deception that he played, there were moments that were sincere between them. Moments when they could discuss topics with ease. He could see how much she had stayed the same and yet how different she was now. How much he regretted losing these years without her, but how much he delighted in her...like now, as she tapped her toe.

These moments were only a brief reprieve from his darker thoughts, from his feeling that he was neatly snared and the guillotine was about to drop. And yet, a resolution out of the trap continued to elude him. 'I think William looks worried,' Alice said. 'He keeps looking at his pole and then at the other boys. Do you think perhaps he's worried he won't catch anything?'

'Are you asking me about parenting skills?' Hugh said.

'I think I am.'

Even if this was a trap, these snippets, these moments when Alice asked him questions on everyday life, made Hugh's last days worth every sacrifice. Even though it was an illusion, it was life he had never thought he'd get a chance to live with her.

'William's inspecting the sharpness of the tip. He won't be catching the wrens on the pole like fish. The wrens are tiny—he'll have to catch them with his hands. However, if the pole is too thick, or not sharp enough, he won't be able to tie the wren or the holly to it for the parade later on.'

She pursed her lips. 'Do we *have* to talk about the birds?'

'Would you feel better if I scared them all away?'

'Yes.'

For her, he already intended to do so. The wrens were important to the tradition, but not essential. Some tying of wren feathers to the poles would work as well. It was the parading, the music, the reason to drink at the end that was the true sport.

Wrens were even too small for food so there was no necessary purpose to catching them either. And he'd never forget Alice and her puppies. He knew this wouldn't be her favourite tradition.

'We'll see what happens,' he said instead.

She gave him a scowl, and then her frown turned contemplative. 'They're moving.'

Hugh brandished his own pole. 'And so will I.'

'I don't know how this will work.'

He wasn't worried that she wasn't clever enough to do the job of spy, he was worried that Alice would be too perceptive.

'There will be a parade. Bump into people—feel their purses if necessary.'

'I can't believe we're doing this. That this is what has brought us together.'

He tried not to read too much into the meaning of her words. 'We're not together, remember? We can't discourage your true suitors. Plus, I'm the one having to scramble on my knees to catch the tiny creatures.' He darted a look at her scandalised face. 'Or not. You merely have to worry about the parade.'

'I was doing fine before, when I couldn't share my worries with anyone, but now I seem to be useless. Fretting. I'm *never* like this.'

She never had been before, but now her family was threatened. If he could gut the King for putting this burden on her, he would.

'Don't worry. We'll see it through. And you're not fretting. You're thinking of all the things you have to do and all the ways you might get caught. All spies have those concerns.'

She smiled up at him, her hands clenched within her fur-lined cloak for warmth and her feet quickly dancing on the soft dirt to hold back the cold.

He felt like smiling back. Here they were together and, at least to outward appearances, looking as if they celebrated a tradition.

Alice was not the King's mistress. Merely trying to save her family from ruin and hanging. And here he was, trying to protect her soft heart by saving birds. When in truth he'd shatter it, because *he* was the true threat to her family.

He had days still—weeks if the weather turned foul. There was time to find a solution, and protect his friend. He had given a vow, a traitorous one, but he would keep it or die.

He'd faced adversities his entire life. He would prevail against this one as well.

'Your pole looks splendid!' Alice exclaimed.

'I didn't catch any wrens,' replied William.

'None of the other men or boys did either.' She pointed to the top. 'I think you have the most wren feathers and holly, and your pole looks the heaviest.'

'It isn't heavy.'

Alice hid her smile. She could see William's arms shaking.

'Of course it's heavy—just not heavy for you because you're strong.' She nodded to the other boys. 'It would be heavy for *them*, though.'

William's grin widened. 'I'm going to make them lift it!'

Alice waved as William stumbled ahead to his friends and the rest of the revellers. Somehow she and Hugh were the last in the parade that wound through the town.

'Thank you.'

'For what?' he said. 'We found no seal today.'

But for the first time since the King had commanded her she felt a glimmer of hope. If nothing else, she was trying everything she could to find the traitor. She wasn't good at bumping into people, or feeling the purses around their waists. But at least there was ale being drunk, and her clumsiness was taken as a consequence of the crowds and the drink.

'For saving the wrens.'

'You never saw a thing.'

No, she hadn't. He'd been subtle. If she hadn't been looking she wouldn't have caught him. A knight, a warrior—but with such an underhanded and subtle skill for scaring wrens. He must have learned it as a spy.

'William certainly has the most feathers tied to his bow. I've never seen wrens moult so many before. It's almost as if someone had plucked them from the birds, or stolen some from other nests.'

'Fanciful thoughts!'

She glanced at Hugh, caught the teasing light in his eyes that he allowed her to see, but his face was inscrutable.

He was good at being duplicitous—even in something so simple as a Christmas tradition.

Had he lived this way since he'd left? When he left Swaffham, he'd been determined, single-minded. He'd pulled himself up with hard work and skill. Not with lies or flattering words.

Where along the way did his cynicism come from? He'd been so *angry* when he'd arrived. His manners had been smug, suspicious, spiteful. But since then he'd changed. It was more than his helpfulness with the barn restoration. Now he was almost *attentive*.

She should be more cautious when it came to him, but he'd shown other sides to him, and she needed his help. And she knew, somehow against all evidence, that she could trust him.

What a strange connection of events to bring them here now. Both of them spies. Both celebrating a winter tradition with a comfortableness she'd never had with him before.

'Tell me something of your spying.'

His brow rose. 'It isn't wise.'

'Then tell me something else.'

'That isn't wise either.'

He slowed his pace. They were out in the open, their conversation could be heard, and yet there was no other time.

'Pretend we're at dinner and we're exchanging idle pleasantries.'

He gazed at her, taking in all her features. A brief glance...a warming glance, before he looked away, his brows drawn.

He took a few more steps while she walked beside him.

'Well?'

'Anything between us is hardly "idle", Alice.'

His comment, spoken so calmly and in a low voice startled her, and she missed her step. He grasped her elbow and brought her close.

Rain, steel... Hugh. She felt off kilter, like a distaff

with lopsided wool, like she'd slammed into him again as she did at the Tower.

He released her suddenly. 'Tell me something of *your* life.'

She shook her head, gathered herself, and continued to walk. Her legs were feeling more unsteady than that brief touch warranted.

'Other than that one fateful trip to London, I've been in Swaffham all my life. Except for the upcoming journey when I tell my monarch if I have succeeded or failed, I don't plan to leave again. Not much else has happened to me.'

'I doubt that.'

Another glance. It wasn't his gaze that warmed her, but his words. Attentive. She truly needed to be cautious with him.

'Tell me of those years,' he said. 'Tell me what projects you've been doing.'

'I have had no projects.'

'You *always* have a project, or a cause, or someone to fix.'

His words scraped uncomfortably. Didn't anyone understand her need to help? If she didn't help, what else was left for her? She'd thought he understood since he had worked, if not beside her, at least with her.

'You know of the barn restoration with Mitchell.'

'Yes…' Hugh turned his face away.

Silence as they took slower steps, falling further behind the crowd, the children and their poles. Away from the revelry and happiness.

What did she have at this moment? Questions…a tentative trust between her and Hugh. Threats against her family. And yet she wouldn't choose to be anywhere else.

Because of her vow or her childhood infatuation? No. Because *this* Hugh—the one with his silence and suspicions and cynicism—she wanted to know more of.

'I know you say it isn't wise, but—'

He looked at her then. 'Do you know why?'

Blue eyes, their storm never ceasing. She'd thought she knew the Hugh from her past, and though she'd seen glimpses of him, she knew he had changed. But the years apart had changed her as well. She would withstand the King threatening her family. She wouldn't run away again.

'Would you have me share my life and give me nothing in return?'

'It's safer that way.'

'I have my monarch after me—I'm far from safe.'

Hugh tilted his head, as if contemplating her words. 'I went to Edward's Court to train as a knight. It wasn't until many years later, and quite recently, that he asked me to find information for him.'

'Why?'

'It's trying times for him. There is much deceit and many secrets. I'm constantly needed.'

'It's dangerous.'

'Almost always.' Hugh shrugged. 'He doesn't ask every knight under him to do such tasks. Most knights come from royal lineage and have families to return to, or families of their own making. I have none of those. Therefore, I can travel to where he requires me to be.'

To most, it would be exciting. To her, it sounded lonely.

'Can you ever decline the tasks?'

He smiled, but it didn't reach his eyes. 'You have met him—can you imagine such a scenario?'

She shook her head. At first she'd been overawed at the power emanating from Edward, but then there had been that moment with the horn. When he had reflected on the importance of kings versus lovers.

'When he asked me he didn't need to threaten my family. I... I wanted to help him.'

'He's the King—he has his flaws, but he is a good man.'

Kings, spies, traitors...and walking with Hugh in Swaffham during Wren Day. Far different from the way she had expected this time of year to be. Far more than she'd hoped for.

'It's never been this way before.'

Hugh could feel Alice glancing his way as they walked. Luckily it was easy to avoid her questioning gaze as he manoeuvred them around the town, kept them far enough away from the others, but not too far that they would look suspicious or cause Alice's reputation to suffer.

'What hasn't?' he said.

'You and I. We've never talked like this.'

Because he had avoided her since the time he'd seen her with those puppies. When he hadn't been able to avoid her she'd been breaking his nose or asking for a kiss.

That kiss.

Clumsy with desire for her—that was all that had stopped him in Lyman's house. His arms had been full of her, of her responses to his touch, to his lips. He'd been blind to the room, to the danger, to everything except her. He wanted to sweep everything off that desk, and take her as he'd dreamed a thousand times before.

And then what? Then he'd be tortured at the memory of it. Just like now. Probably worse.

He deserved worse. But he'd take these snippets of time until then.

Purposely keeping his pace slow, he let them fall further away from the revellers. He soaked up every moment of her walking beside him. The fact that she came no higher than his chest, but her steps were quick. Her cheeks were red from the cold, but the extra colour highlighted the ivory of her skin, the brightness of her grey eyes. Eyes gazing at him warmly.

'No, we've never talked like this.'

Most likely because he didn't have many pleasantries to talk about. More snippets of time like this and she'd begin to glimpse the darker side to him. He couldn't keep it from her. He struggled to do so now. They already talked of the King and his spying.

'And yet nothing's ever idle between us, Alice,' he repeated.

'Do you want it to be?'

He closed his eyes on that, shook his head.

'I'm glad we can talk this way,' she said. '*Be* this way.'

When she slowed even more he could almost hear her weighing words. He didn't know if he could take any more closeness to her.

'Why? Because of your vow?'

He'd tried to keep his tone light—knew he missed it when he saw her frown.

'You won't tease me on that, will you? You never

have before. Even when I asked you to kiss… Well, you were there.'

He stopped then—didn't want anyone to hear this part of their conversation. 'I could never tease nor could I ever forget.'

'I haven't either,' she whispered.

Her words were a sweet balm that also stung his heart. So many years lost between them. What had happened in the years he'd been away; why was she alone? 'You must have had many suitors since I left.'

'Are you asking me if I turned them all away because of you?'

Foolish words, of course she would have many, and it wasn't as if he lived like a monk since he left. 'I have no right to know.'

Silence from her. Silence he didn't want. 'I'm sorry. I shouldn't have mentioned them.'

She started walking again. 'My projects, as everyone calls them, kept me busy from…proposals. It's probably why my plan to find the Seal has been so difficult.'

'Why'd you do it then?'

'I needed suitors for distraction from what I have to do to find the Seal. I knew if they thought I liked them they'd be more open with words and conversations. Secrets. I'd also have access to rooms and conversations I wouldn't have normally.'

Now that he knew the details, he understood the cleverness of her plan—and he shouldn't be talking to her. She was close to the truth now. He wanted to be her suitor. He wanted to hold her and kiss her again. To spill his secrets and lose his life. Just for these moments.

'They'd never stand a chance if you were after them in truth.'

Alice took a breath, braced herself for whatever would happen next. 'I was after *you* in truth.'

He paused. 'Too much honesty you give me.'

She was now realising she hadn't given enough. 'Why not? Holding things in secret hasn't worked for us.'

'There is no "us".'

'There is—why deny it? You kissed me.'

They stopped walking before they reached the town square. Boys blew whistles and banged drums. Off-key singing and raucous laughter indicated that ale was being poured. It was early afternoon, but the temperature was dropping fast. The day had started off with blue skies, but now it was darkening with heavy clouds rolling in.

Alice was freezing, but nothing would stop her from standing out here in the cold with Hugh.

Since they'd been in Lyman's house she had felt the pull to him stretch and tighten, like wool to a spinning spindle. He was right. Nothing had ever been idle between them, and with his comment she knew he felt the pull as well, though he denied it.

Yet there were still so many questions. Why had the King sent him here? Why hadn't he said something about the Seal earlier? And, more troubling, why had he seemed so angry when she'd mentioned it?

The room at Lyman's house had been dark; she had been able to gauge nothing from his expression, from his eyes.

Not like now.

The winter sky highlighted his every beautiful asset to her. His almost white-blond hair, tousled with curls and the wind. The cleft to his chin, his nose that crooked just a little to the left. His clear blue eyes.

'You kissed me,' she repeated. 'You held me close when we were dancing. You're looking at me…have been looking at me all this time…like—'

'Don't say it.'

His tone was full of censorship.

She wouldn't stand for it. 'Like you want me.'

He closed his eyes and she saw his body shudder. They were out in the open, and yet she wasn't looking to see if someone watched or listened to them. She didn't care. She had a monarch who threatened her. If now was the only time they had, she was going to take it.

She couldn't get any more vulnerable with Hugh. When it came to this man her pride had been lost since she was six. As a woman, she would fight with her heart.

'Maybe I did make a childish vow, but it was the truth. Maybe I did ask for kiss as a girl asks for a kiss, but I meant it then, too. Here's another truth: I'm not a child nor a young girl now, and I still want that kiss. I still want that life with you.'

'We have a traitor to catch. You're not thinking.'

'I'm thinking more clearly than you. The fact there's a traitor in Swaffham, that the King has demanded I catch him, seems insignificant now. It will happen or not, but now there is the two of us and there's a better chance we'll be successful.'

'I'm no hero,' he said, with a curl to his lips.

'I always thought you were.' She said the words softly, teasingly, but they were the truth.

And Hugh looked stunned.

'Because of the well?' he said.

'Long before and after that.'

'Why?'

'Because of the way you faced the town, your father, the way you always bettered yourself.'

He looked to the sky, as if there were answers there, then back to her. 'Is that why you never helped me?'

'What do you mean?'

'You never made me a project of yours. Never swooped in with baskets of food.'

'You never needed them.'

'I was starving.'

She had known that. But it was the way he'd stood, it was his pride. 'You would never have accepted it.'

'No, I would never have accepted your help.'

'Because you didn't need it.'

'You were the only one to think so.'

'Why keep bringing up the past? I don't care about your past.'

'It's not the past you have to worry about,' he bit out, then cursed and spun away.

She waited for him to say more. Waited while she watched his broad shoulders lift and fall with a heavy breath, saw his body held rigid with some anger she knew nothing about.

'If it's not the past, then what is it?'

His back to her still, he answered, 'Can't you accept there can be no "us"?'

'No.' With all the certainty in her heart, no. He'd already alluded to it despite his denials. 'Maybe this is the wrong time, but this is all the time we have. All the time we've ever been given. If it isn't the past, then it must be something now…or in the future.'

He looked over his shoulder. There was no storm in

his eyes now, but she sensed it was there, just under the surface. And she wanted to rage and batter at it. She wanted to break it.

'There is no future.'

Chapter Fourteen

'This storm will never let up,' Esther grumbled.

It had hit with the fierceness of all it had promised. Walking down the stairs, Alice shivered at the wind swirling through her home, despite the servants draping tapestries along the walls and fur along every crack.

Fires blazed, and sputtered against the wind battering against the tiny flues. They made the entire house bright with flame and dark with smoke. It stung her eyes, but she'd take that if it meant warmth.

'At least this time we knew it was coming.'

Every day since the Boar's Head Feast the weather had worsened. After Wren Day it had become unbearable.

'But it's Holy Innocents' Day and we can't eat, and we can't take our mind off our hunger with work.'

'Any work done today will fail, and any new project will end badly. The storm is merely reminding us of our duties.'

'The storm is making Bertrice think her ankle is divine.'

'Her ankle is simply healing.'

Esther shoved straw around the fireplace. 'She says it aches with the storm. I'll never hear the end of it.'

Alice smiled, though she knew she wouldn't hear the end of it either. 'At least she's no longer a burden on you.'

Esther let out huff as she walked to the door leading to the long hallway to the outside kitchens. 'Don't think I don't know what you're up to.'

Alice's smile faded. If only *she* knew what she was up to. After weeks of searching for the Seal, she was no closer to the truth.

No, she was closer—because she was beginning to question everything.

Alice pulled her shawl around her and sat in a chair by the fire. There were shouts from the servants who continued to tighten the shutters. Her father was bemoaning the chill more than his empty stomach. She wouldn't be left alone for long, and would need to help soon.

Hugh had said he'd help her, and it appeared as if he was. And yet, they'd found nothing during Wren Day nor during their riding of horses the day after.

Nothing.

And amongst her fears of not finding the Seal were questions about why she hadn't. Of course whoever had the Seal wouldn't be careless, but there didn't seem to be a trace of it. She'd received no messages from the King on how to proceed either.

There was a part of her that felt she'd been sent here to look for nothing. And yet why would the monarch engage in games that meant nothing?

She still reeled at the fact that there were spies, that subterfuge and intrigue occurred here. Swaffham was a bustling town, but it wasn't London, and yet she believed a traitor was here simply because one man, one king, had told her there was.

She was questioning everything...everyone. Mostly Hugh...and herself.

Hugh.

He was a spy, though why he was in Swaffham she still didn't know. It wasn't to stop her. Instead there was a certain camaraderie between them now. She trusted him—she had to. But everything in her was still cautious.

There were too many questions. Hugh was right when he said nothing was ever idle between them. Whether it be the tumultuousness of her thoughts when it came to him, or how she craved his nearness.

What had happened at Lyman's house? He had guessed what she was, demanded to know what she was doing. When she'd told him he'd kissed her.

She wanted to kiss him again. To finally explore what was between them. Not to run away as she had in the past. She'd braved things enough during the Wren Day parade, but again he'd shut her out.

But the questions kept coming. The question of why then and not now. She knew he felt it, too. Because when she turned too fast, when she glanced at him when he wasn't expecting it, she saw the heat in his blue gaze, felt it linger on her lips.

Wind blasted the house and made the wood creak. The fire before her sputtered and flared and she pushed herself deeper into the chair.

Nothing she did or said had made Hugh repeat what he'd done. She didn't dare approach him again. She had laid out what she wanted. If he didn't want her, then...

Yet he had kissed her. There were feelings there. She knew it now. She was certain, too, that he'd rejected her all those years ago because he'd felt unworthy of her.

He couldn't be more wrong.

Hearing pounding and shouts at the door, Alice leapt from the chair and hurried towards the entrance just as it swung open.

Ice and snow pelted the two boy servants, the floor, herself and Esther, who had shuffled to her side. Freezing wind shoved in a stumbling man, his cloak buried in snow. A visitor unrecognisable until the door was shut and he raised his face.

Father Bernard.

'What's happened?' Alice asked.

Father Bernard pulled back his cowl. His lips were blue, his cheeks burnt from cold.

It was none of those things that stabbed fear through her. It was the stark hope in Father's Bernard's eyes as he asked, 'Is William here?'

'No, he's at home...at Bertrice's.'

The servants rushed to disrobe him of his cloak, his boots.

'He wanted to ensure the town observed the day, but I sent him home,' he said. 'Bertrice came to me when he didn't return. Already searching for him, she was freezing, her ankle swollen, and I left her at the church. I then came here.'

Alice ushered him into the hall, to the chair where she'd been sitting. Blankets and hot broth were brought. He looked at it, and shook his head. His hands were shaking so badly, he couldn't hold it. Alice knelt and steadied it for him.

'It's for tomorrow, and the only thing heated. Tell me what happened.'

He nodded; held the cup tightly. 'It's Holy Innocents' Day. He's gone out to ensure no work is being done. If he's not here, he's out there.'

Out in the storm.

Alice own legs almost gave then, even as she pushed herself away and ran to her room for warmer clothes. Father Bernard and Bertrice were already frozen and weak. It was up to her.

Hugh was freezing to death in his own home. It didn't matter that he had enough timber to heat a hundred homes. His hearth was too small to warm his toes even though he had them shoved next to the embers.

At least before Bertrice had returned to her home she had prepared food for after the fast and hot water in case he wanted a bath. Already hot stones warmed his bed. Months in Swaffham and he was still being pampered. When he returned to London, he would be able to slip right back into his lavish lifestyle there.

If he returned.

What did the King want of him? After he had seen Alice emerge from the royal chambers, after he'd returned from the garden the next day, he had requested the King's counsel. He'd thought it spontaneous.

Now he had to wonder if it had all been planned. But the King couldn't know what Alice meant to him—couldn't know it was he who carried the Half-Thistle Seal. Well trained, all too careful, he'd watched his back.

His obligations, his vows, were dangerous but necessary. Life-saving for Robert and his family. Whether the King was speculating or not, he needed to be more careful.

The same went when it came to Alice. Alice who was far more noble and brave than he. Not only in her wanting to help others, not only in her stalwart attempts to keep her family from the King's wrath. Because she had the courage to walk beside him. To tell him of her feelings, her wants.

She wanted him. Still. Traitor that he was.

Coward that she knew him to be.

Only a coward would avoid a woman declaring herself so sweetly, so resolutely.

He reeled from her words. She didn't care about his past—she wanted him, his touch. She wanted to pledge herself before this town, and God, to him.

A traitor.

He could never have her. Poor, from a dishonoured family. He had never deserved her.

Yet, fiercely, he wanted to be selfish for once in his life. Hadn't he paid enough debts already? Hadn't he earned some happiness as he's taken the jibes of the townsfolk, as he'd fed his father to sober him up?

He wanted simply to hold her hand. Never for himself. If he did, he'd be sentencing Robert's happiness. If he did, he'd be damning her and her family.

Still he sought a solution. He hoped it wasn't in vain.

He looked at his cup—empty, never filled. There were days when he knew to drink deep, and nights when he didn't dare. This was one of them. At least the weather was as foul as his mood and no one would disturb him.

He hadn't drunk since the Boar's Head Feast. He

might never drink again. But he needed a drink, needed to free himself from this town, and his memories.

He had nowhere to go.

This house—tidied because of Bertrice, was repaired enough to withstand a storm. He wanted to demolish it all. Because no matter how many days or weeks went by he couldn't solve the dilemma that was right before him. How to save Robert...how to save Alice.

And why was Eldric pounding on the door?

No, too light to be his friend, too insistent to be polite.

He yanked it open. A boy was shoved through, tripping over his feet and falling to the ground.

'Hugh!' a woman yelled.

Alice.

He pulled her in.

She was cold...so cold. The wind and ice were no longer stabbing her, but she felt no relief. 'Where's William?'

'I've got him. He's safe,' Hugh said.

Her eyes stinging, she watched Hugh pull William onto his lap and press his cheek to the boy's lips. Hurriedly, he yanked off his shoes and stripped off his clothes.

'Get out of your clothes.'

Her teeth chattering, she shook her head. 'Him first.'

'I've got him. I can't take care of both of you. Alice, get your cloak off. I'll get the rest.'

Her bones were frozen, her arms no longer her own. 'I can't. I carried him... I can't lift them.'

'I can't save him *and* you,' he called. 'You can do it—you must. He'll need you.'

He wrapped a blanket around the boy and dragged a tub towards the fire.

Alice looked at William, her relief at finding safety turning to concern at the boy's pale colouring, and the bluish tint of his lips. His eyes were still closed.

'I carried him from the well in the square. What's happening to him?'

He yanked a steaming cauldron of water from the fire and poured it into the tub. 'He's alive, but not waking. I'll put him in water, bring his temperature up.'

Her body trembled more at the thought of a bath. 'Hot?'

'Not hot. His body heat has dropped too much. Yours has probably, too. I can't tell if his hands and feet are frostbitten yet. I won't know until he wakes.'

'Please—just save him.'

William called out as Hugh set him in the water.

'Careful,' Hugh soothed. 'It's water to warm you. Keep your hands and feet in. Lean down.'

More water was poured.

Her cheeks were warming. From tears? Alice raised her shaking arms as Hugh crouched by her side and ripped off her cloak, flung it to the floor.

He cursed.

'What were you thinking? What have you done? I only have one tub, and you need to get out of these clothes.'

Alice kept her eyes on William, terrified now of him drowning.

'Both of you could die!' He unlaced her surcoat, her dress. Her chemise was saturated. Her arms went up.

'You take it off. I've got to get back to the boy.' He

shoved a large tunic and blanket at her, grabbed the second cauldron and poured it into the tub.

William's eyes opened just after she pulled the tunic over her head and wrapped the blanket around her. 'Can you see me?'

Nodding, he gave her a small smile.

'What happened?' Hugh said, wringing out the clothes in the corner.

'He was lost in the snow.'

'And you went out to find him? By yourself?' Hugh shook the cloak and hung it up. 'It didn't occur to you to get help?'

'Bertrice and Father Bernard had already been out in the storm.'

'There was me.'

'I thought I'd find him before I got this far.'

'I'm sorry,' William called out.

Hugh's heart pounded as if there was danger all around him. Instead there was merely a woman and a boy, safe and warming at his weak fire. They would live. Still, his heart would not stop its erratic beat.

'This will take long. You need to come to the fire.'

He left the room, returned with stones and pushed them into the flames.

When he turned, Alice was bent over the tub, and cradling William. Her tiny body hovering over William's gangly one. Everything about Alice was wrapped around William despite the tub, the water, the blanket.

The boy's arms clung just as tightly around Alice.

He knew he was witnessing something not often found. Before it could get hold of him, before he could put words to it, he placed his hand on her shoulder and felt their combined shudders resonate through him.

This wasn't a snippet of time with Alice, or a shared moment. It was so much more and he didn't want to see it—not now. Not when he still hadn't found a resolution.

Ignoring the heaviness in his chest, Hugh continued with the tasks ahead. The boy's eyes were closing again, and he prayed it was only exhaustion and not something worse.

He flexed his fingers into Alice's shoulder to gain her attention. When she looked up, he said, 'We need to keep pouring the water, and you can't get your blanket wet. I don't have any spares.'

Hours spent heating the water and adding it to the tub. Hugh constantly checked the temperature, and threw more logs on the fire. Entertained William, and made sure he stayed awake.

Alice huddled nearby. Hot stones under her feet, a cup of steaming water in her hands, she listened as Hugh tirelessly told his stories and patiently answered William's questions.

Hugh was sharing his life with this boy he didn't know. Since he had to know she was listening, he was sharing it with her as well. These were the stories she'd wanted to hear on Wren Day. Tales of his childhood in Swaffham that she'd never known before. What had happened when he'd arrived at Court, his befriending Eldric and another knight she knew nothing of.

Even knowing that Hugh was carefully cultivating the stories for William, she got lost in them. Enough to finally feel the warmth of the room and know the fact William was truly safe.

She hadn't gone out alone in the storm. Not at first. Cranley had gone with her. When they'd found others trapped, animals as well, and no sign of William, they'd separated.

At first Cranley had refused, but then they'd found Bertrice in the church and they'd talked about what would be done. Alice would carry on to the town square, no more. She'd find shelter.

Only after several assurances had they let her go.

Back into the howling winds, with the sleet slashing against every bit of her as she forced her feet forward. She'd had a shawl wrapped around her face, but she hadn't been able to protect her eyes as she'd scanned for any sign of life or unusual shape. Difficult when the snow had already masked so many landmarks.

It had been against the town's square well that she'd found William huddled. Almost frozen, almost asleep. She'd grabbed his hands before he'd cried out and then lost consciousness. Then she hadn't known what else to do but carry him just as he was.

She had seen the smoke from Hugh's chimney, and forced herself to make the distance.

And now, in the comfort of his home, she was finally believing they were safe. That with Hugh's care William would keep his hands and feet. She clutched her warm cup and realised she could have lost her own.

She had expected more accusations from Hugh about her carelessness, about William's foolhardiness, but he only talked of his own conflicts and tribulations. Grand stories made grander for the boy, but underneath she heard the rest. The pain and conflict of his training, his continual feeling of being an outsider.

And with his actions, with his words, her love could not be contained. What had been said during Wren Day wasn't enough. What she had said all her life to him wasn't enough. She knew that now because he had never denied the truth of her words, he had just walked away.

So foolishly, recklessly, she would approach him again. She wouldn't run away.

As they lifted William from the tub and carefully dried him off, as they laid him down on the bed with multiple covers, Alice didn't hide what she felt for Hugh. She couldn't contain the love she felt. She wanted to know him more.

He had said it wasn't the past that stopped him, but she didn't know what it was that did. She had vowed at the dance that she would explore what he had said in haste about his childhood, about whatever was between them.

A part of herself questioned her actions, heard her sister's warnings when it came to Hugh. But her family had never seen him as she did. This wasn't about some childish vow.

And she knew it wasn't only her with feelings. Hugh had admitted as much. She saw it, felt it in his anger that she'd gone out in the storm, that she spied for the King. He worried for *her*.

And she felt something else now. In his home the distance between them insignificant. All there was was *them*.

It seemed Hugh was aware of it as well. His eyes were darting around the room, maybe trying to see it through her eyes, perhaps looking for distraction. She didn't welcome the fear of almost losing William to the storm, but she *did* welcome this moment.

'You care for him,' Hugh said suddenly, his voice gruff as if he hadn't used it for a while. As if she hadn't heard him give comfort to a child he barely knew.

Alice adjusted some of the stones at her feet. 'He's very precious to me. So much—all of this—has been keeping me away from him. I should have seen his concern, been there for his worry.'

She stopped her words, knowing they were fruitless. The King had commanded her, and if she didn't obey more hurt would occur.

'What is he to you?'

'He's an orphan Bertrice has been raising with her own children, but I've been there for him, too.'

'And so you took him under your wing?'

'I think we all have. Father Bernard has been teaching him the scriptures... I've been teaching him about the Fenton household.'

'Were his parents noble?' he asked.

She didn't understand these pointed questions, but they were easy to answer and they had time. 'The mother was Bertrice's friend. His parents drowned when William was an infant.'

'So...what is the point of your care and your educating him?'

Hugh leaned against the wall—a relaxed pose, but she knew better. Setting the cup of water on the floor, she prepared herself for words. She was used to this from Elizabeth, from Mary, her father. All of them lectured her on her projects. But it would be wrong of her not to help William.

'There doesn't have to be a point to it. We're simply there for him.'

'However—'

'What was *your* point in telling him those stories?' she interrupted. 'You could have told him something else. But you talked about your childhood, your mistakes. That was to help him, was it not?'

Hugh was silent. A muscle in his jaw flexed.

She swept the blanket around her. 'William made a mistake in going out into the snow. You knew there was no point in lecturing him. He's learned his lesson because he almost *died*, so you talked of your mistakes. You talked of Robert, who helped you. Who is he?'

Hugh's chest expanded and he suddenly turned, intent on adjusting the fire's logs. They popped and cracked as he spoke. 'He's the famed Robert of Dent. Even here in Swaffham you must have heard tales of him.'

She hadn't, but it had been clear William had. There had been awe in William's eyes as Hugh had spun his stories.

'But he wasn't a legend to you—he was your friend.'

'He's dead now.'

He had talked not of one moment with Robert, but of many times over the years. They must have been close. 'I'm sorry.'

Another adjustment of the logs before he threw a new one into the fire and turned to her. The light in the room didn't allow her to see his expression clearly.

'You can't fix him,' he said.

And so they were back to talking of William's trials again, not Hugh's.

Again Alice kept her patience, though it was fraying. 'He doesn't need to be fixed. There isn't anything wrong with him.'

'He lacks the funds and connections for him to be brought to the Church,' Hugh said. 'If he pulls through this then what?'

Her patience was gone. She didn't want to talk of William—she wanted to talk of *them*. But it all had to do with the same thing. She knew it, and she feared he knew it, too. It was as if their talking of William and his childhood was somehow talking of Hugh's. As if talking of William's unknown future was talking of their own doomed future together.

If that was somehow true, then in this she would tell all. She would confess and lay it all before him. Because there was a connection between herself and Hugh—there always had been. Maybe they had been too young to care about it, maybe there had been too many misunderstandings, but now they could understand each other.

'What hope for *you* when you arrived at Edward's Court?' she said. 'I know what you came from, the means you took to help yourself. I appreciate now that when you did need it you gained help from this Robert. If William gains help from others, who knows what will become of him?'

Hugh bowed his head, shook it before he raised his eyes, steady on hers again. 'You think your caring for him will set things straight. Life doesn't work that way.'

It *did* work that way. A traitor amongst them or not. This moment right now was what she had dreamed of all those years ago when she'd demanded that Hugh kiss her. She didn't want only his kiss—she wanted his love.

'What I want for William is love. And he has that—all of it. He doesn't need to be fixed for me to love him. I don't care if the Church won't take care of him. What use is all the Fenton wealth if it can't help him? I'll make sure to help him. That's what love is. It's to be there, to help when you can.'

He cursed and turned away. Pressed his hand against the wall as he faced the fire.

Alice watched his anger and frustration fade to something else. Something darker inside him. They were talking of *them*. This wasn't about William. Except even with that understanding there were still barriers.

'You don't think it's enough?' she whispered.

'What's not enough?' he answered.

'Love.'

He turned his head, his eyes glancing over her before returning to the fire. 'What would I know of it? It's the Fentons and the other grand families who seem to have an ownership over that emotion as well as everything else.'

His childhood again—but there was more. Maybe he was an outsider because he chose to be.

'I never understood why you hated this town so much,' Alice said.

'I never said that I hated it.'

'You never had to. I heard it when you talked to William. I watched it while we grew up. You never tried to make friends here—you always held yourself apart.'

'Unlike *your* family.'

She loved her family, but all families had flaws. Her father and his mistresses were only one of them. 'My family isn't perfect. You know that.'

'Is that what we're to do? Speak of the past? Haven't I done enough of that tonight?'

Hugh didn't want to remember those days. As far as he was concerned he was from Shoebury. That was all he told anyone. Of course, the King, Robert and Eldric knew otherwise. After all, he couldn't have trained as a knight if he'd had no connections. Swaffham and his

father, such as he was, were necessary. But this town—
he didn't want to remember at all. And yet here he was,
actually living here again.

'What else are we to talk about?' she said.

'What do you want me to talk about? The past you
know or the past you don't?'

'Tell me,' she whispered, so softly he shouldn't have
heard.

Maybe he hadn't but had simply wanted to hear those
words. For her to give him permission to tell a tale he'd
never intended to tell.

'What is there to say? That I was born in Shoebury
and my mother was sick, and that for unknown reasons
she sent me to my father when I was only five?'

'I didn't know.'

'Of course you didn't. I didn't let *anybody* know.
As far as any of you were concerned my life consisted
only of this town.'

'Then tell me about it.'

Alice had never thought of Hugh's childhood before
Swaffham. People had talked about it in vague ways,
but never with any kind of salacious whisper or sym-
pathetic murmurings. He had been but a mere child
when he'd arrived.

But now she could visualise it all too clearly. Shoebury was to the south. There would have been warmth,
a mother who loved him. Loved him enough to find the
man who had abandoned him. A father who had taken
no responsibility for him before. Knowing Hugh, who
had his pride, she had no doubt his mother had had her
pride as well.

She thought of her own happy childhood and her
practical mother, her very impractical father, and her

two sisters. Hers had been a busy home, a happy childhood, and one to look back on fondly.

But for Hugh something had been taken from him. Cruelly, forcefully. And he had been brought here to Swaffham. Brought to a knight, a man who hadn't taken responsibility for him in the first place. A man who had served the King, but who had changed over the years. Who had become cold, callous, his drinking increasing as his viciousness grew out of control. If Hugh had been five when he'd arrived, he had been part of the downward spiral that his father had taken.

The whole town had watched it happen. For herself, she'd never forgot that day when Hugh had picked his father up from the middle of the road.

'I wish I'd done something differently that day,' she said. 'When the rains came and your father—'

'Was covered in mud and everything else.' His brow furrowed. 'You were too young to comprehend.'

'Still…' she said. She had watched like everyone else. But she often looked back to that day and wished she had done something. But nobody had. Nobody.

'I'm glad you didn't. That you couldn't comprehend the shame of it all.'

And there was the difference in their pasts, she didn't see any shame at all. She saw only a good deed, and strength. 'Tell me something of Shoebury.'

A muscle in Hugh's jaw twitched. 'I remember nothing except my mother.'

'You never travelled there again?'

'Never. I didn't want to know if…'

'If it had changed?'

'I didn't want to know if she was still there.'

Alice needed to sit. Her legs weak from the storm,

from his story. But she also wanted to hold him, so she stood. How had he endured the jibes of the town, of his father, when all the while he'd worried about his mother?

Before she knew it, she'd crossed the room and grabbed the outside of his arm. He looked down at her hand, his eyes softening from the starkness they'd held. When she went to remove her hand, he clasped it in his own.

Startled, she searched his eyes. There was so much pain there. 'Was that even a possibility?'

He shook his head and released her hand. She reluctantly let it fall to her side.

'She was coughing blood at the end. There was someone else in the room—a local healer, I think, who often tended her. But still...'

But still he wondered if he had been abandoned.

'Weren't there others in the village who could have taken care of you?'

'I never believed so. Why else would she have notified my father and asked him to take me in?'

Why, indeed. And if his father had already abandoned him, why beg him to take in his son?

Then a thought occurred. 'How did she know where your father was?'

'My father was born and died in Swaffham; it probably wasn't difficult to find him.'

'Was your mother...? Did your mother have coin?' She shook her head. 'I'm asking this wrong. Do you know how she got you to Swaffham?'

'I travelled with a messenger from my father.'

From his father. 'So it's possible your father paid for your trip? It's possible he wanted you?'

He raised a brow. 'Trying to soften it for me? My father made his intentions towards me clear when he abandoned his wife, my mother.'

'But he agreed—' Alice started, then stopped and gathered her thoughts. 'He took you in, Hugh. Even if you believe he didn't pay for your expenses to travel. He answered your mother. He took you in.'

Hugh's eyes closed, as if he could not accept what she said. When they opened, they were as clear as she had ever seen them, and completely unreadable. As if he purposely kept what he felt from her.

'Why are we talking about this?' His eyes went to the room where William slept.

'Because after all this time we're here, together.'

Her heart hammered in her chest. Finally they could talk about the dance, his revealing of his past. The accusations in the garden. There would be no misunderstandings any more. No more questions of *what if*?

'For what purpose? I said I would help with the Seal. We'll find it or not, and either way we'll leave Swaffham come spring. Me to my home, and you to inform the King on what has happened.' He looked back at her. 'We'll be going our separate ways...as we have before.'

'No. You kissed me. I know you feel for me.' She took a step and noticed him bracing himself before she stopped. 'I know why you turned me away that day. All those years ago. It was because of your father.'

'He's dead.'

'But he's why you stayed away, isn't he?'

'At the time? Yes. Is that what you want to hear? How could I subject you to a father fallen drunk in the mud? To the shame and humiliation of my lineage?'

Alice's heart soared even as she feared that this

wasn't enough. She couldn't tell what Hugh was feeling, what he was thinking. The storm still battered against the tiny house, but she felt as if it howled and slashed at them. But she wouldn't give up—she'd made a vow.

'But don't you see?' she said. 'There wasn't a reason to stop your kiss that day. I never saw you as you saw yourself. Like you do now. I only saw your strength, courage, perseverance. *That* was the man I wanted. The man I vowed to marry.'

'You saw me wrong. You keep seeing me wrong. To this day I don't look at ale or wine like everyone else—as something to drink every day or, if it's a good vintage, as something to use in celebration. I look at it and wonder if the next sip I take won't wreck me, too.'

She'd seen him at parties, lifting his goblet and staring at the contents. 'And yet you still drink?'

'As a test...a challenge...a game.'

It was no game. He did it to prove he wasn't like his father. If he continued to think that way there would only be bitterness about his past. There was no changing who had sired him, so he needed to see his father in a different way.

'You saw *yourself* wrong. Your father had difficulties, but there was good in him. Your mother may have asked for his help, but he must have paid for the way. He took you in.'

Hugh's legs wouldn't hold him any more and he leaned against the wall again. Alice stood there, looking far more fragile than he'd ever seen her. Her hair was wet from the snow, and she was shivering under the blanket she held.

He could see the blanket covering her. It was his...

and he couldn't quell the feeling of possessiveness that he felt.

She was always beautiful to him, and never more so than now. As she showed her love for that child, quaking and breaking everything inside him until he had no walls.

Then she had brought up his past with his father, and rewritten his childhood. How could she have known? A few words spilled at a dance when he'd been angry and she'd guessed accurately.

She was right. He had never seen what she had, hadn't known such a boy existed. He only remembered the hardship, the shame. His begging of his father to stop drinking. He only remembered the relief when his father's land had been sold and he bought his armour and turned his back on Swaffham.

Turned his back on Alice.

He had thought he wanted her then. It was nothing like now.

He had held her in his arms, felt the softness of her lips. Tasted her until it had driven him to the edge. He had avoided her for days now, just to stop this conversation. He knew she'd have questions about why he'd kissed her.

And all of the answers he could give her would bring him trouble. He had kissed her because he'd needed to distract her from the real traitor. Because he still wanted her. Would always want her.

'It doesn't matter,' he said truthfully. 'The present is too full of lies and deceit.'

She stopped her shivering then. 'What are you saying?'

'Even if we repair the past—even if your words are true, Alice—what is there now?'

'There's *everything* now. There's *us* now.'

'Not for long. I'm selling this house. I don't know why I kept it. I'm a knight, and I find information for the King. It's what is expected of me.'

'But—'

The door rattled, sleet slashed against the roof and Hugh raised his voice to be heard. 'There is nothing else. What did you think? That you could heal me of my past and repair the present? Is this something like William? Do you want to fix me? What did I tell you? Life doesn't work that way. Since I left here, years separate us. More mistakes, more barriers. You and I were never meant to be together. Life has made sure of that. We have no future. *I* see that. Why can't you?'

Tears were falling. Why hide them? She was baring her soul to this man anyway. To one who found the world lacking, one who stormed and raged within himself and never let it go. A few mere tears meant nothing.

'Because you feel something—'

'For you? *Lust.*' His lips curled. 'I used to be as sheltered as you when I lived here. Believing there was a right and a wrong way. But nothing is that black and white. Didn't staying in London teach you anything? Didn't your father show you how flimsy vows are?'

She gasped. Her father. Happy. Adulterous. Yes, she knew how men were, but Hugh had shown devotion and loyalty to his father. She had believed Hugh was different. But if he was, he was denying it.

And he continued to deny *them*. Maybe the years he'd been away had change him irrevocably. Maybe she had imagined their compatibility. Maybe she didn't, but it didn't matter because if he denied the truth of their connection, what was the difference?

Nothing.

And in that, her heart cracked. She didn't want to run away this time, but if he denied there was something between them, then it wasn't her who was turning her back.

She still had a traitor to catch, William to care for and her project with Mitchell. Maybe it was time to say goodbye.

The thread binding them felt more than frayed. As if all she needed to do was yank to break it.

'So that's it,' she said. 'What will you have me do now? Return home by myself? Drag William out of bed?'

'The bed's big enough for both of you. I'll stay out here.'

She clasped her hands before her and arched her brow. 'And what of the Seal and your helping me?'

'What did I say about flimsy vows and the fact that you shouldn't trust anyone?'

She pulled herself up with all the dignity she could and headed to the bedroom. Before she entered the darkness there, she turned. 'I will still seek the Seal and the traitor.'

'I didn't expect otherwise.'

'And neither you, nor any other man, will stop me.'

Chapter Fifteen

Heart thundering, Hugh entered the Fentons' Great Hall and felt again like a gangly youth who wasn't worth the imaginary dirt on their spotless floor, rather than the man he had become.

He almost laughed. The man he'd become was worse than the clumsy poor youth he had been. Shamed for his father's failures and knowing he'd fight against them for the rest of his life. He still had to fight those rumours, those memories, those truths.

And now he had committed even more sins that, though he had confessed to them, he wasn't all that certain God would forgive him this time.

He didn't forgive himself. Especially since he was being so brazen as to grace their home with his presence. He wasn't invited, and after all he had done, he was most likely unwanted.

Yet, this was the Fentons' annual feast, and they kept the doors open for all of Swaffham. Everyone.

Which made it easier and yet more difficult for him to be here. Because in the past this feast and entertainment had been exclusive. Now it was open to everyone, and he knew without asking who was responsible for that.

Alice. Always Alice and her generous heart and spirit. She'd have been the one to insist on inviting the entire town. And it seemed the entire town was here. Dressed in their finery with their jewels glittering.

His years away made it apparent how prosperous Swaffham had become. Everyone appeared in many ways more opulent than those at Edward's Court, for he, at least, had suffered financial woes with his wars.

Not Swaffham, which glowed. Yet, as opulent and joyous as the crowd appeared, it didn't stop him from seeing Alice immediately. He almost walked away. It was better to face the King and the guillotine than Alice and the truth.

It wasn't his past deeds or his traitorous present that made him feel unworthy of being here today. It was how he had treated Alice the night of the storm.

And how *had* he treated her? By spilling his bitter past, his pain, and talking to her with disdain.

Then she had asked whether he'd help her. Her chin raised, her lips trembling from the cold or from her anger—he didn't know.

But he did know how she'd felt after he had told her he wouldn't aid her. Her pride and dignity intact, she'd gone to sleep, safe, warm, with the boy at her side.

He had stayed up all night, hating himself more than he had ever hated this town, and had resolved simply to leave. But the next day had sealed his fate.

The storm had left lasting damage, but the worse was over when Cranley had come to his door, asking if Alice had made it.

Alice and the boy had emerged from the bedroom

then. William weak, hungry, but effusive in his happiness as Alice had fussed over him still. The boy had grumbled, but leaned into her hugs as well. And Hugh had known he was witnessing something he had never had.

Love, unconditional.

It was what he had seen when Alice had hugged the boy over the tub. It was what he had braced himself against and didn't want to see. And the morning after the storm, he had been defenceless.

And love had ripped through him like the unforgiving winds had. For one crystalline moment he had been wiped bare and then, with staggering swiftness, he had felt his body swell with a warmth that had filled every barren crevice of his life, of his soul.

Love. He had felt love. Precious. Delicate. And yet so strong a storm couldn't break it. A storm had forged it.

He loved Alice, could no longer hide the truth from himself and pretend it was mere want or desire. And there was the crux of the matter. Because he loved her, he couldn't leave Swaffham, leave her to think she had failed the King. There was no resolution for him. But he would set things right—or as much as he could without breaking his promise to Robert.

He knew only one way. It was time to tell.

Hugh was here…in her home. Where he hadn't been for far too long, where she had imagined him a thousand times even though she'd denied it a thousand more.

And he was so unbearably striking that that was how she felt. Struck down. By his height, the hardened but fluid way he held himself. At ease and yet ready.

For what? She didn't know him any more. He had rejected her with no misunderstandings between them. It made no sense that he was here, and yet his gaze caught hers just as it always did.

But his eyes were different now. Because she didn't feel merely caught, she felt ensnared. She thought the thread between them broken. Now she felt like wool too tightly wound around the spindle.

He stepped further in the room. Eldric walked right along with him.

Alice forced her eyes away—only to meet Elizabeth's knowing look.

'It's not over, is it?'

Alice tried to relax her shoulders, but Elizabeth raised a brow at her obvious discomfort. She hadn't told her sister of their conversation that storm-filled night. She probably didn't need to.

'It's merely surprising to see him here.'

'He's been here for months and attended all the celebrations since then. How could you possibly be surprised?'

Because every time she saw him, it hit her.

'Weren't *you* surprised when he arrived for St Martin's Day dinner?'

'You could have knocked me over with a quill!'

Her as well. Alice felt the gentle relief inside her. This conversation with her sister would be easier than she imagined. 'But only Father's good graces kept your manners intact?'

'No, it was the paleness of your cheeks. I thought you would faint. For you it was like seeing a ghost, and I thought, "Here we go again…" But then you did spend time with Mitchell and Lyman.' Elizabeth gave a tenuous smile. 'Did you ever mean it? About finding suitors?'

She could never tell her sister why she'd done it, but she couldn't lie. 'There was no way we'd ever suit.'

'What happened when you found William? What happened when you stayed in his home? He didn't...?'

'He didn't touch me—not that anyone would ever believe that.'

'I do, because you're still so sad. I feel that perhaps... did we make you miserable? Was it something I—?'

Alice squeezed her sister's hand. 'No, it was life, circumstances. Something else.'

'Did you and Hugh talk of it?'

She couldn't keep lying—not about this. Her heart hadn't simply broken that night of the storm, it had shattered. She didn't even know where to start to pick up the pieces.

'We did. Some things were repaired between us. Or so I thought.'

'And other matters were...insurmountable?' Elizabeth said kindly, but in her usual dogged way.

There were times Hugh unwillingly acknowledged their connection; more often, he denied it. But he had never said the reason. When he dismissed her so thoroughly, she'd given up on understanding why, and yet—

'He's here tonight,' Elizabeth interrupted.

'It means nothing.'

'But he's heading this way.'

And she was still angry at him. All her life she'd done nothing but lay her heart out for this man. Like a fool. As if she had no pride or didn't know her worth.

She did—she always had. It was he who didn't know

his. But she understood that now—or thought she did, and told him so.

Still, he'd refused her. Yet he walked towards her now, the distance not so great, the room not so wide that his path through the crowds could be anything else.

'It matters not what direction he comes—he'll remember the path to the door.'

Elizabeth released her hand and kissed her cheek. 'Find happiness. That's all I ever wanted for you.'

When Elizabeth turned away Alice kept her gaze on Hugh, weaving through the crowd. Happiness was all she'd ever wanted for him, but he refused it. Now he looked determined. She braced herself.

Then he stood in front of her.

'Would you like this dance?'

Here, now. This was the question he asked? 'You know the answer to that.'

'You did dance with me at one time.'

She looked starkly at him. 'Shouldn't you be dancing with Helen?'

'Helen from the St Martin's Day dinner?' He only just hid his smile. 'So you did feel something that night.'

'I don't think *my* feelings have ever been in question.'

'So mine *are*?'

She tilted her head. 'Didn't we talk of lies and deceits and flimsy vows? You have no purpose here. I meant what I said.'

'I'm not here to stop you from finding the traitor. I'm here to help you find him.'

She'd be a fool to accept his offer of help this time. She'd be a fool to expose herself to the connection that he denied. Even when she'd handed him her heart she might as well have ripped it from her chest and dropped it in the darkest well she could find.

She tilted her head. 'What changed your mind?'

'You did.'

He lied.

'I remember my words and your responses. What has changed?'

'The next day.'

Cranley had accompanied her and William home. 'I left that day.'

'Exactly.'

So her leaving caused him to have a change of heart, when all their lives they'd been separated? 'Is this a game?'

'No, Alice. I'm here because I know who the traitor is.'

Chapter Sixteen

They stood in the alcove by the stairs. Not exactly private, but better. It was quiet enough for him to share his words, to make her understand.

She was angry now, and should be. But he still had her love—he felt it in every part of his body, in his own soul. So precious to him—though he had almost lost it.

He knew the moment he told her the truth he would lose it. He was a traitor and without honour. It didn't matter why he had done it. That was a mere excuse.

He would tell her, and she would do what must be done. She would need to go to the King and tell him who carried the Half-Thistle Seal. She had to protect her family, to protect herself.

He would go to the guillotine. His only hope was that she could protect Robert.

'You have got me here,' she said, gesturing around to the shadows. 'So tell me.'

'I'm a spy.'

'You've already told me that.'

'But not this.'

He took her hand and placed the Half-Thistle Seal in

it. Watched her hand shake before she clenched it and hid it in her skirts.

He took heart in the fact that she hid it. There was still a part of him that had believed she would loudly proclaim his crime and he would be hauled away before he could give an explanation. He deserved it after his cruel words during the storm.

'This can't be,' she whispered, her eyes darting around.

'It is.'

She took a breath. 'Not here, then. Follow me.'

He took comfort in her request, too. As Alice darted around the corner and went up a private staircase. Down a long corridor, her steps ever faster, his own following close. He was trying to quell his heart from gaining any hope. Her wanting privacy only meant that she would listen to him. Nothing more.

They entered a room. He saw a bed, a fire banked low. The room was dark, but he saw the vague outline of soft furnishings without any frills.

'Your bedroom?' he whispered.

'It's the only place I can guarantee privacy.'

'But it's too private. I could kill you here.'

'You could have killed me without showing me the Seal.' She turned it in her hands. 'It's been yours all this time?'

'Weren't you curious when you couldn't find it? I made *sure* you couldn't find it.'

She shook her head. 'This makes no sense.'

'Why? Because of the boy I was when I left here? It's true that he saw only right and wrong, but so much has happened since then. I told you that you didn't know me, that the present was full of lies and deceit. This is what I meant. This is why there are barriers between us.'

'Why would you tell me this?'

'Because I didn't want you to keep looking. To keep risking your reputation or being forced to marry Lyman because he'd caught you in a compromising position. Or worse, going empty handed to the King.'

'You told me to keep me safe?'

'I also told you I'd help you. Foolishly, I thought I could come up with a plan not to reveal the Seal and also to keep you safe, but I couldn't.'

'So you have told me even though you are now... not safe?'

He nodded.

Hugh. A traitor.

She had orders from the King to find this man, to report him. If she did, Hugh would hang.

That was what justice would be. She would be righting a wrong. Except it didn't feel right. Hugh knew she'd have to report to the King and had told her anyway.

He wasn't denying anything now, but telling her everything. About them, about his secrets, and all of it could be the death of him. Still, he did it.

He was keeping her safe. It was what he did with those he cared for. Loved. Hugh loved her. She knew the calibre of man he must be. He was proving it now. And then she had her certainty.

Who else in Hugh's life would he want to keep safe?

'It was all for Robert, wasn't it?'

He stilled; his heart hammered. 'What was for Robert?'

'You have no family to protect. And you respect the King. I can hear it in your voice when you talk about him. This Half-Thistle Seal and the messages it marks has something to do with Robert.'

'Robert's dead. I told you that.'

Her brows furrowed then, and there was a moment of hesitation. He wanted her to keep that doubt.

'Then it's for his family.'

'Robert's mother and father are also dead.'

'Did he have a wife?'

'Alice, stop asking questions.'

'You had to know I would ask.'

'No, I expected you to—'

'Run screaming and report you to the magistrate?' She shook her head. 'I might, because you're still hiding something from me.'

'I'm a traitor—what more do you want to know? Why I did this? A traitor is without honour, Alice. Reasons and excuses have no place. They don't matter.'

'They do. Reasons always matter.'

'Actions do—and mine are full of lies and deceit.'

'If you are a liar and a thief and full of deceit, you would have continued to be. After the storms were over, after this winter, you would have left Swaffham and never returned. And yet you say you have told me because you didn't want me in a compromising position? What kind of declaration is that? You told me because you have feelings for me. You *love* me.'

He did, and his heart burst with it. He wanted to shout with joy at the happiness it brought him. Instead he fought it. But with Alice in front of him demanding answers, demanding *him*, he knew it was a losing battle. Though he could no longer deny it to himself, telling her would gain nothing. There was only one resolution to this, and declaring love for her was not it.

'And if I do, what does it matter? The facts remain the same. I'm still a traitor.'

'As I said, reasons matter. You're telling me this because you're trying to save me. You're trying to save me like you did that day at the well. You beat those boys to get to me. There were three of them. *Three.* They could have killed you. Thrown you down the well and snapped your neck. You did it anyway, because the reason behind it was your feelings for me.'

'They were tormenters and they deserved it.'

'They deserved it long before then. I saw them taunting you about your father and you never lashed out at them. You only did it that day to save me. And now you're trying to save me again.'

'That's—'

'I'm not listening any more about why you told me. The issue is why you began sharing the King's secrets in the first place. You would only go to such extremes to save someone, and I have to know who.'

She couldn't guess. She had to not guess or he'd break his vow. It was the only remnant of honour left in him.

'Don't, Alice.'

'Don't say any more or don't guess?' she said. 'Is it a woman? Are you...have you married and not told me? Is that what all this has been about?'

The very idea—after what he felt for her? 'God. *No.*'

Then he knew he had failed. A moment unhinged and two revealing words had slipped out.

'Then there's only one other you care for,' she whispered.

He looked away from her then; waited for the truth to be told through her.

'Robert's not dead, is he? William talked of how they never found his body; the Scots never sent his head to King Edward like they promised. Robert's alive and you're protecting him.'

A ragged sigh. Defeated. He was always defeated when it came to her. But maybe if he wasn't clumsy he could make her understand and Robert could still be kept hidden.

She'd be lying to the King, and her honour would be blackened like his own. But Robert would live and so would she. Maybe if he told her everything she would fully appreciate why he did it and why he still had to die.

'He's alive. He's alive and married to a Scot.'

Alice gasped.

'So now you see why I had to keep this secret. They met…' Rueful, he shook his head. 'If so light of a word could be applied to them, they met when Robert investigated the massacre at Doonhill. Gaira and four children were still alive and surviving there. Scottish children, whose families had died at the hands of the English. He took them under his care, and along the way…' He shrugged.

'Where were you?'

'I had followed Robert to Clan Colquhoun land, intending to rescue him, only to discover he wanted to stay. To marry. He was happy.'

'And you couldn't take that away from him?'

'Never. But to ensure he kept that happiness he needed to be dead. So I showed Edward Robert's ring he gave him, and detailed the devastation of Doonhill. I let him come to his own conclusions.'

'And the Seal?'

'I gained Edward's trust that day, and I have been

spying for him ever since. Inevitably, I was given secrets that would affect the Clan Colquhoun. I had the Half-Thistle Seal made to send a warning message to Robert.'

'So the Half-Thistle Seal is only between you and Robert?' At his nod, she continued. 'And you doubt your honour?'

'I'm lying to the King and will continue lying to the King.'

'For love.'

'For...friendship. I gave my word to him.'

'You love him. You told William you fought by his side for years.'

'I did. He lost someone very dear to him, and he left everything behind to fight by Edward's side, and I fought with him. But we met long before that.'

'When?'

'After my father died, I had enough coin to buy myself into Edward's Court, but rumours of my father followed me. As a result, I suffered at the hands of men like Allen—except these were well trained men with swords. Robert arrived when I could no longer defend myself. He didn't say a word, or show his sword. He simply stood there and they all stopped. I immediately knew who he was. He'd already earned his spurs and a property. Can you imagine what I felt that day? I was poor, couldn't fight properly, and Robert, who was almost a legend, saw me at my worst.'

'How many beat you?'

'I think four took me down and others followed. It felt like there were others.' Hugh shook his head. 'I was poor. Disadvantaged. I had dreams of making my mark by defeating all of them. But Robert gave them one quelling look and I realised that whatever skill he acquired, I wanted to learn it as well. I was his shadow after that, and he let me be. Along the way he told me he knew of my father, and then he told me of his.'

Hugh turned to see Alice's steady grey gaze. So warm, but determined.

'I know that look,' Hugh said. 'You're intending to fix me. This isn't a project. There's nothing to repair.'

She threw up her hands. 'Of *course* there's something to repair. You have confided a great secret to me. I understand now.'

'What do you understand?'

'You did it for love. You're not a traitor—you're a man who protects. Who gave a vow to his friend and has been honouring it ever since, even at the expense of his own life.'

'You don't understand at all. The facts remain the same. I have been giving information to the Scots. No matter the reasons, my actions make me guilty.'

Every word hit her as truth. It was how the King would see it. He'd told her that himself. That he didn't care for individuals, only for kingdoms. He'd given her a hunting horn to solidify his position.

Her heart hammering, she knew she had to think this through. Had to...*fix* this somehow. There had been wrongs committed here, but there was no justice if Hugh hung for it.

'I'm a dead man, Alice, and have been since I made that promise. I only solidified it when I began releasing information.'

Then she saw a way. She went to the box next to her bed, placed the Seal inside and locked it. 'Only if the King knows about it. He doesn't need to find out. You can go on protecting Robert and his family. You're only giving him information to protect the clan, right? Then it's fine. It'll be fine.'

He shook his head slowly, his eyes wide with her actions, with all the storms in all the land. 'It's not fine. The King will know because *you'll* tell him.'

'Never!'

'You *must*.'

She gasped. 'How could you think I would? Even if I didn't know you, you have told me of Robert's family, and of how he saved those children. You know how important family is to me. I'd never betray them to—'

Two strides and he was gripping her arms. 'Yes, you will! Otherwise Edward will only send more spies here—or, worse, simply lock you in the Tower and torture you until you confess. Your wealth won't protect you because you are not nobility. You wouldn't have the same comforts as a nobleman waiting for the guillotine, and the King would gladly take your family's coin.'

'Then I'll lie—like you do.'

'You're terrible at it. It took me no time at all to realise what you were doing, and I would have realised sooner if I hadn't been blinded by my past when it came to you. You could never pull it off.'

She lifted her chin, her eyes watering.

'It's not your fault you can't do it well. That's only because you're good. You're *good*!'

'And someone…*good*…would kill you and an innocent family?'

'Damn him!' Hugh wanted to roar, but the silence of the room and the situation demanded silence.

So he swallowed his raging emotions, tried to calm his tumultuous heart.

'You say I love Edward, and that I respect him. But you need to know how close I am to hating him now, simply for asking you to spy for him. The moment Edward asked you, he made you and your family a target. He put you in jeopardy.'

But the King didn't care for individuals. He didn't care for her life. The King had asked her to serve, and she'd meant to. She'd truly meant to, but now...

'So I'm in jeopardy like you.'

'More than that—you've marred your kindness and your decency. All are blackened because of lies and deceit. I never wanted that for you.'

'And yet still you're loyal to him?'

He laughed. 'See how twisted it is? I'm trying to be loyal and protect all of you. There's no resolution to it.'

She could see his loyalty. She had seen that when he was a mere child, doing all he could to protect his father.

Again, she wanted to ease his pain. 'Edward didn't mean to put me in jeopardy. It was an accident. I'm the one who happened to win a seal in that game.'

'You think it was an *accident*? With you and me both from Swaffham? What he had to do to manipulate the game, I don't know. But it's too much of a coincidence.'

She gasped. 'You think he suspects you?'

'I can't rule it out. Not when he gave you and I the same task to fulfil.'

A cunning ruler. Intelligent and ruthless; arranging things to ensure she found a seal first. How he must have worried when it had taken her so long. But the King didn't know of her fear of the dark.

He did, however, know how to make her co-operate. 'He threatened my family, Hugh. I would do anything

for them because I love them. I would do anything for
you because—'

'Don't say it.'

'I love you. Always have—'

'A childish vow, and it has no place here now.'

It was something she had heard all her life. 'Did you
see it that way? My vow to marry you? Did you take it
as something childish?'

He stepped away from her then. And another step.
'How could I ever see your vow as something childish?
As merely a whim? If it was, I had the same one. If I
had been worthy of you I would have said it myself.'

Happiness. It could only be happiness flooding her
fast and making her strong. She wanted to run to him.

'Back then you would have said it?'

'Then, and always.'

Her lips curved. 'But I was a child.'

'Even so...even then. I was an outcast, and because
of it I could see how fiercely protective you were with
your family. How you took animals in to shelter them.'

'I don't remember...'

'How could you not, when your arms were full of
the puppies you kept dropping?'

She laughed. Despite everything, she laughed. 'Then
why...why did you reject me that day?'

'Haven't we gone over this enough? I wasn't worthy of you.'

'But I told you—you were. I've explained it.'

'I appreciate that now. I didn't then. But it doesn't
matter.'

Of course it did, it had to. The room was dim, almost black, but she saw it in his eyes. That never ceasing storm.

'I still have to die, Alice.'

She felt terror at the mere words. 'No, you don't. I won't let you.'

'This isn't something you can fix. Your family is in danger. It is better my life than—'

She rushed to him, placed her hands upon his chest. Felt his heart beating as hard as her own. 'No!'

'It's the only way to fix it. Don't you think I've tried to find another way? Since Lyman's party, that's all I've been doing. But there isn't. I have to save your family and save you.'

'I couldn't bear it.'

'Let me,' he said softly, solemnly. 'Let me bear it.'

Tears ran down her face and he brushed them away. Kissed her forehead, her cheeks, kissed along her jawline before pulling away.

She put her hand against his face, held it there. The room's shadows were making it hard to see him fully.

'It's dark in here,' he whispered.

'Yes.' She could barely see him. But she felt his gaze all the same. Felt the heat of his skin and knew it flushed his cheeks.

'I didn't realise… Is it too much?' he asked.

She was overwhelmed with what she felt. 'Yes.'

His hands loosened.

'Where are you going?'

'Finding a candle. The dark…'

And then she understood. Even now he thought of her fear; she hadn't given it a thought. 'I'm not afraid. I can't be—not with you here.'

'Alice.' He bent his head and kissed her cheek, her temple.

She felt the warmth of his breath, the heat of his body.

'You told me to see the light in the dark.' She wrapped her arms around him. Held him tightly. '*This* is the light in our dark.'

She lifted herself to kiss his jaw, his cheek. Felt the scratch of his beard, the heat of his skin. It was Hugh she touched, whom she brushed her kisses against.

'This moment is for us. This is our light.'

Upon a groan he captured her lips with his. His mouth slanting, parting her lips, tasting her. Brutal. Claiming. Her hand twined around his neck, pulling him closer even as he pulled away. She locked her fingers into his tunic.

'Alice...' he said in warning, his breath hot against her skin.

'Please, Hugh.'

'Not like this. Not when I know—'

'This may be all we have.'

A sound choked out of him. 'There's a fire over there—let me make the flames higher.'

She didn't want to let him go. She moved the only thing she could—her lips, her breath. Her heart thumped against his.

'I don't need to see you,' she said.

A sound of disgruntlement or a sound of approval as she continued her kisses, as she caressed and stroked along the cords of his neck, the blades of his shoulders.

'I want to see *you*.' The darkness of the room heightened his voice, heightened the raw emotion there.

She'd let him go and he'd leave. She knew it.

'Not yet,' she whispered.

She skimmed her palms along his face, her fingers clumsily caressing the soft wet heat of his lips. When they had pressed against hers they had felt firm with intent, with purpose. She wanted that purpose and intent again, but he was holding himself away from her even as her thumb caressed the fullness of his bottom lip. More touches along his jaw, below the curve of his ears…

'Don't make us wait, Hugh. Not any more. I won't have it.'

She felt the tension in him increase, felt his control burn hotter. 'But here, Alice? Now? There is so much more for you.'

'Shh…' she said, pressing against him until his body shuddered. 'There's no more than this.'

'Is it enough?' He clenched her tighter, closer, dipped his head. His lips hovering over hers until they shared breath.

She didn't need her eyes to know that this was real. *He* was real. Here…holding her. She'd seen him enough in her dreams, but never to touch. Their touch was the truth for her.

'Is it enough?' he repeated.

'This is all that matters.'

He lifted her, and his lips captured hers. Not in desperation, but in a slanting of lips, of effortlessly pressed desire. And she felt everything between them, waiting for them both.

This kiss was what she had dreamed all kisses with him to be. A slow, achingly slumberous heat, with those threads she imagined tethering him to her, weaving throughout her, making some pattern she didn't recognise, but followed.

Followed the stroke of his hands, the tilt of his head as he kissed along the curve of her jaw, along the downward slope of her neck until he reached the restrictions of her gown.

But he wasn't deterred. He loosened his hold on her, and she slid slowly down. So similar to that day at Court. When in her hurry, in her fear, she had slammed into him. But this time she wasn't buried under acres of courtly dress. He wasn't covered in lethal chainmail.

It was only him, Hugh, who kept his grip against her skirt as she slid, and rucked it to her hips. She felt the cool air, the heat of his hands on her outer thighs.

'Lean against me,' he said, his voice roughened.

It sent shivers through her just as much as his bare hands on her thighs.

Holding her still, he let the heat and something else soak deep within her. Something much warmer that spun fast through her body.

Desire. Need. Want.

She leaned against him, his body and his arms fully supporting her. His hands raised her skirts a little more as she dropped and his fingers spread, his hands encircling the backs of her thighs.

He stroked her until she entwined her hands around his neck and he carried her to the bed.

She lay there while he stood. He wasn't leaving, but he wasn't satisfied either.

'Hugh...?'

'You might not mind the dark any more, but I can barely see you.'

So stubborn. So relentless. But that was what drew her to him. 'Light a candle, then.'

A low chuckle. 'It's dark! And, as much as I have dreamed of being in this room, I don't know it.'

'On the table there.' She pointed.

He turned then, lit the candle. Walked to the fire to increase that as well, until the flames danced light into the room.

Then he stood there, with the fire illuminating him. An errant lock of blond hair across his forehead, his blue eyes dark.

'You're still dressed,' he said.

'You laid me on this bed fully clothed.' She threw her hands over her head, watched his body go rigid.

'I've changed my mind,' he said, and there was a light in his voice to match the flames behind him.

'Does this have to do with the room being well lit?'

'Not lit enough; I need to see more.' He crossed his arms, leaned a shoulder against the wall. 'Take off your clothes.'

An order. There was a lightness to his tone, but his voice was low, raspy, as if the very idea of what he'd said burned through him.

It did burn through her. In all the times she had imagined this, she had never imagined them like this. Because being apart meant they'd changed. Grown stronger.

Sitting up, she leaned her weight on one arm and dangled her feet over the edge of the bed.

Like this, she could see the frayed threads in his composure. His need just underneath. From the way each breath looked purposefully drawn to his unflinching gaze as if he'd forgotten to blink.

'Alice? Your clothes.'

'I will, if you take yours off as well.'

He arched a brow, as if he was amused, but his fingers flexing restlessly along his crossed arms told another story.

'Are you...commanding me?' he said.

The words she'd said to him that day at the market. He had tried to humiliate her, but it hadn't stayed that way.

'I don't know why I said that—'

'To taunt me.'

She almost smiled. 'I suppose that's true.'

'They had another effect. They *haunted* me, and it's all I can do not to show you.'

It hadn't only been him affected by her words. For many nights afterward she dreamed of Hugh like this. 'Won't you?' she said.

His chest rose and fell suddenly, his lids narrowed. 'The fire's lit. I want to see you now. There will be no more waiting, no more stalling, no more longing. And I *do* long, Alice. Even if I have to wait.'

'I don't want to wait.'

He closed his eyes briefly on that. 'You need me to wait. You need me to even if you don't know it.'

His words added to the tension between them, like wool being expertly twisted between the distaff and the spindle. Even the low reverberations of laughter and song downstairs tightened the need to be with him. As if they could be caught.

She felt *ensnared*.

Keeping her gaze on him, she undid each shoe, rolled down each of her hose. Her fingers fumbled as she tossed them aside.

Hugh wasn't looking at her eyes. Instead his gaze skimmed up from her bare feet along her still covered legs and down again. He bent, his movements swift, sure, as he tossed his boots aside.

She slid off the bed. His haste in removing his boots encouragement enough as she untied the laces at her sides, as she shrugged to let her gown fall to the ground and stepped out of the clinging fabric until she stood in only her chemise.

She waited, but Hugh stood still. 'Tell me, Alice.'

She licked her dry lips. 'Tell you what?'

'What do you want from me?'

She felt as if he was preparing her for something—like wool about to be sorted and cleansed. As if she was being readied to be made into something else.

'I told you I don't know why I said that to you that day.'

'I think you do.' He paused. 'I've wanted you all my life, and I feel as if I've been bound to stay away from you. Now you've suddenly given me a way to untie those bonds. But my hands are shaking. I need you to tell me.'

Didn't he know? He wasn't bound *away* from her. He was bound *to* her. That thread she felt—he felt it, too.

His hands might be shaking, but her whole body quaked at his words, at what he implied. He wanted her to...to *command* him. Her heart sped, warmth filled low in her belly. He was right, she wanted it, too.

'Take off your tunic and belt.'

Huffing in a breath as if she jabbed him, he roughly unhooked his leather belt and it fell heavily to the floor. Grabbed the back of his tunic and tugged it over his head. She watched the muscles in his stomach ripple, saw the flexing of his arms as they lifted so light a weight. He threw the fabric as if he wanted never to see it again.

He was bare except for leggings that hid nothing from her. The flames' light illuminated his tanned skin, the light dusting of hair along his chest and down to his breeches. Tall, lean, corded in ways she hadn't imagined. Had felt, but didn't know the full extent of. Magnificent male. A knight. A warrior.

And every glimpse of his skin showed the hours of training, the scars and wounds from past battles.

Some injuries were far more recent. There was a fresh wound surrounded by bruising on his left side. Healing, still red. He'd received that while he'd been in Swaffham. Training or something else?

'Does it hurt?' She pointed to his side.

His brow rose, he looked at his side, and shook his head. 'Worried for me?'

'Maybe.'

'It was Eldric. He's gotten better at wrestling since the last time I saw him.'

She didn't like that he got hurt. But the longer she gazed, the more she noticed his past injuries. The jagged line across his forearm that matched the identical jaggedness of the thin strip across his stomach.

She hated that. Hated that he'd suffered, that she hadn't been there to protect him, to help him as she should have. He loved her—he should have stayed here. Hadn't he realised that when she'd punched him in the nose?

'I am concerned for you.'

A small smile. 'I'll have you know he didn't get another swipe at me, and I won't let him.'

Another pause from him. His gaze was waiting. Watching.

The chemise wouldn't be so easy to remove. It wasn't only the laces at the side, but the fact that she'd have to lift it over her head. Her arms didn't feel as if they'd work properly.

'Hugh…' she said, her voice not indicating any nervousness, but instead a whisper of something else. Desire. Longing. She wanted this. But her hands seemed incapable of completing this strange game they started.

'I'm right here, Alice.'

She could see that. The flames danced behind him. The tips of his hair curled, the light blond shining in the fire's light. His eyes a dark murky blue.

'I don't understand this.'

'I know. I don't either, and it's not how I imagined I'd react.'

'You've imagined this?'

A laugh, a chuckle—low, pained. 'Over thousands of nights and hundreds of days.'

'I don't think I can do this. Shouldn't you be here?' She indicated in front of her. Directly in front of her.

'I should. Yes, I should. But, just as you can't seem to lift that material, I can't seem to move from where I am.'

Something forlorn tugged through her then. Maybe they would always be separate. Maybe they had waited too long.

'Why are we like this?' she asked, fearing the answer, but needing it.

'Because I want you too much. Always have. And it's like a dream that we are even here.'

Warmth spread through her. 'But I'm real. I'm here...
I want you to kiss me. Like at Lyman's.'

'Don't mention Lyman's.' He closed his eyes, shuddered. 'It makes it worse if you mention that room.
What I wanted to do to you. What I'm aching to begin
now.'

Was that how it was for him? Did she affect him so
much? She could see it in the way his gaze went dis-
tant and heated at the memory of what they had done.

And knowing he shuddered simply at the memory
made everything easy again. She simply gripped her
chemise and ripped it over her head.

His chest suddenly stilled before he shoved himself
away from the fireplace and strode towards her.

His eyes didn't roam over her naked frame. Instead
each watchful gaze fell against her skin like his heavy
steps across the floorboards. From her feet to her thighs
to her hips to the indentation of her waist and breasts.
More steps, until his eyes locked on her lips. On her
eyes. Until he stood before her as she had commanded
him to do.

'Too long,' he whispered. 'Too much. You are more
beautiful to me than I could ever dream.'

Warmed by his words, she grew restless and urged,
'Please, Hugh, touch me. End this.'

'Lie down,' he said.

She didn't hesitate—wouldn't, since for every step
she took back he stepped forward. When she sat he took
the final step, but did not sit with her.

She should have felt vulnerable. She'd asked him to
take his clothes off, but he'd kept his leggings and braies
on. She sat while he stood.

Alice could see the fine sheen of his skin, knew this wait was costing him as much as her. She put out her hand as if he might take it, as if she could pull him to her. They were so close and she wanted this.

'Not yet. You don't know what you do to me. How much I want to touch you. Your skin looks so soft...'

'You've touched me,' she reminded him. 'At Lyman's. Here.' She demonstrated with her hand and fingers along her shoulders, and down her arm. 'And here.' Her hand went down her thigh.

He went rigid, watching her hand. She didn't know where this came from—this strength, this need.

'Through your clothes,' he said, his eyes lifting reluctantly from her hand to her eyes again.

There was no relief from Hugh being this close to her. She could feel the heat from his body, smell the scent of leather, of linen, of him. See the curl of his hair against his forehead and that fraying of his control as he'd watched her hand.

She was bound to him, bound by a thread, by her feelings, by their love. But still he kept himself away from her when she needed him nearer. Yet all her life if she saw a problem she found a solution. She'd bring him closer.

'But wouldn't you like to touch me here?' She purposefully trailed her fingers from between her breasts up along her collarbone to the arch of her neck. Watched as his eyes absorbed her every stroke.

'Alice...'

'Your clothes,' she said, stopping her hand.

He shucked his leggings and braies as efficiently and roughly as he had the other pieces of his clothing. Then he stood naked before her.

Never had she seen a male before, and never one like this. Magnificent knight. If she was at the mercy of the master spinner who bound them, she wanted it. Needed it. Demanded he twirl the spindle faster to tighten the thread.

His body shot with tension, his breath ragged, Hugh bent his knee on the bed and dipped his head to kiss her neck ever so softly along the path she'd traced with her fingers.

Supported by the bed, she tilted her head for more of his hot kisses, more of his flickering licks as he tasted her.

He lifted his head, his eyes meeting hers. Waiting for her command.

Watching his eyes, she trailed her finger along the shell of her ear to the curve of her jawline and then traced the other ear.

Hugh lips curved more before he bent again. She shivered as she felt his breath, hot and moist. She shuddered as she felt his tongue and lips along the new path she'd created.

He moved further up the bed and so did she, until she was lying down and he was lying over her on straightened arms. A bead of sweat on the side of his face matched the fine sheen on the rest of him. His blond hair, curled like a halo, made him look like an angel. But the shadows and reliefs, the muscles, cords and planes of his body, were wicked.

She'd never seen a man like this—up close, one she could touch. But she lay still, watching his eyes searching everywhere but always ending with hers. Then her lips again.

He wanted to kiss her; she wanted it as well. It was the logical place for her fingers to go. To trace along her lips until he replaced them with his mouth.

He gave it to her. Brief, not enough. She wanted more.

Keeping her gaze on him, she trailed her fingers from the base of her throat down between her breasts, slowly, slowly, loving and watching the surprise in Hugh's now half-lidded eyes, in the parting of lips that looked swollen and vulnerable, watching as he followed her continuing trail until she stopped at her stomach.

A groan came from him, and she revelled in the heavy weight of him as he lowered his straightened arms, dipped his head to bring his lips to where she'd trailed her fingers, to sample and kiss, to lick at her navel.

She whimpered; he lifted his gaze. Suffused with heat, she shook her head at him.

'Then let me...' He adjusted himself between her legs. His hands and fingers curved to the back of her thighs, opening her for him.

She was no longer showing him where she wanted his kisses, his touch. It was his turn.

His body went tense as hers grew slack. As she curved into the cradle of his arms against the locked tenseness of his body while his fingers glided down from her navel.

'Hugh...' she tried to warn him.

'Let me, Alice. Command me. I want to kiss you here.' His fingers stroked through her curls. 'And then I want to do more.'

It was his words, the loss of control of his breath matching hers, the increase of tension between them— she couldn't stand it, couldn't stand it.

'Alice, please…' The heat of his hand was cupping her. His fingers were rubbing, pressing. 'Let me,' he repeated.

'Yes!' she gasped.

With a wolfish grin, he did as she commanded him to do.

Chapter Seventeen

Their breaths caught; their hearts slowed. The uncertainty of her future with Hugh was more terrifying than the darkness to her now. Still, she eked out as much happiness she could as she leaned her head in the crook of his arm and rested her hand against his chest. She adjusted her hips to tangle their legs even more. It was Hugh with her now, touching her, loving her. More glorious and heartbreaking than she'd ever dreamed this would be.

How could someone be happy and heartbroken at the same time? She lifted her palm, skimmed her fingers through the hairs on his chest, over the flexing muscles underneath. His warrior's training, his strength, were so evident in the cords of his muscles, in the ridges along his abdomen. She would never get enough.

'We have spent so many years apart.'

'And I regret them all,' he said.

Misunderstandings and missed opportunities. And now their monarch was after them, and there was nowhere they could run.

'I cannot regret this,' she said. After he brought

her pleasure, he'd taken her maidenhead…just as she begged him to do.

'Maybe we never had the perfect time, but we did have it—we simply needed to be able to see it. I see it now.' He paused. 'I didn't hurt you?'

'Did it sound like you did?'

Hugh clenched his eyes. 'If you keep reminding me of our pleasures, Alice, we'll never get out of your bed.'

If only they could. Happiness. Grief. Joy. All were somewhere in this moment. 'I like us this way,' she said, curling into him and splaying her hand to feel his heartbeat.

'Me, too.' His shifted, his idle caresses now becoming more purposeful.

Alice basked in the feeling of Hugh's fingers tracing circles behind her knee before trailing up, then down again. Rejoiced in the way he breathed and how his heart thumped under her ear.

'There's something I've been meaning to ask…' he whispered.

'Hmmm?'

He gave a low sound, almost a chuckle. 'Why did Allen lower you into the well?'

She tilted her head to see him watching her with a tenderness she'd never known existed. A happiness she was only beginning to glimpse. 'You never asked me that question before.'

'Well, at first I was preoccupied with saving your life…and then saving my nose. Afterwards—'

'You were trying to escape a six-year-old girl's vow to marry you, and a young woman's demands for a kiss.'

The lightness in his eyes dimmed. 'I regret all those years,' he repeated.

She sighed, rested her head against him. 'Well, the last demand wasn't your fault. It was mine.'

'Yours? I almost killed you that day. I said so much in anger—no wonder you fled.'

It was easier to talk to him this way. So much had already been revealed between them, so much shared, it was simple to share more. 'I didn't flee; I ran away.'

'I told you to, though, didn't I? Told you to run away.'

'I shouldn't have listened. You didn't mean it, and I was a coward.'

His hand stilled. 'I was the coward who demanded that you go. Do you know how long I was haunted by your standing against me like that? I dreamed of how you would have tasted.'

Somehow, even after all they'd shared, her heart still yearned for that moment. She lifted her head and softly kissed his lips before settling down again.

'Well, now you know,' she said lightly.

'I'd like to know more,' he said, his voice indicating that even the slight touch of her lips had affected him. She heard it in his heartbeat, and in hers as well. Their desire was only slightly banked and was beginning to bloom again, and she was more than ready for it.

'Aren't you going to tell me?' he said.

'Tell you what?'

'I'd like to know more about what happened that day.'

Where was her thoughts? Certainly not with Allen.

'It wasn't only Allen who lowered me into the well. It was Peter and Garman as well. It took more than one boy to tie me up and lower me down.'

He chuckled, and she loved how it felt against her.

'And he did all that simply because I told him that

he would never get a wife if he didn't learn to comb his hair.'

His hand squeezed her thigh. 'You were trying to fix him? A boy almost twice your age, with his friends watching, and you were...*scolding* him?'

She giggled, and rested her chin on his chest in order to catch his gaze. 'I suppose I was.'

Laughing, he bent his head and kissed her thoroughly, until their laughter blended and her breath caught with his. And then she couldn't breathe at all as his hands cupped the backs of her knees to hold them wider and make space for him.

'Again?' she breathed.

'Always,' he promised.

A knock on the door. The light from the shuttered window indicating it was still night; the noises down below revealing the festivities continued.

Hugh sprang out of the bed to grab his tunic and the blade from his boot. Another knock—not any louder, but more insistent as it beat again and again on the door.

'Who would it be?' Hugh whispered.

'I don't know, but it can't be good.' Alice whispered back, pulling on her chemise. 'What are you *doing*?'

'I'm protecting you.'

'You can't answer the door!'

He cursed.

'I'll get it. It could be my sister or Esther, enquiring after my well-being. I didn't tell anyone that I was retiring. They may be wondering where I am.'

He scoffed. 'It could be a reveller, trying to get to you.'

'They wouldn't knock, would they?' she retorted as she headed to the door.

'I know you're in there.'

Hugh's stomach dropped and he moved away from the drapery around the bed as Alice opened the door. 'Eldric? What are you doing here?'

'Coming to warn you.' Eldric stepped around Alice. 'Easy with that dagger, Hugh. I come here as a friend.'

'The fact that you'd notice a blade hidden behind my back tells me otherwise—as does your presence here.'

'I think my noble intentions are clear since Alice stands next to me and no harm has come to her.'

Alice gasped then. Softly. But she didn't move. She was brave. And Hugh's faith in her strength blinded him to her vulnerability.

He brought the blade forward and lowered it to throw it under-arm. Just in case.

Eldric chuckled. 'Not very knightly of you to allow a maiden to be your shield.'

'You as well, then,' Alice said with steel in her voice he had never heard before.

Not now; don't let her guess everything now.

'Eldric, leave,' Hugh growled.

'Not a chance. Not now that we can finally get to the point.' Eldric swept further into the room and Hugh watched Alice move behind him, her eyes scanning the room. No doubt for a weapon.

It was the casualness of Eldric's words that punctuated through Hugh's anger, diffused the haze of desire that had burned through him from Alice's love and confession.

Eldric was too casual…too knowing. 'You comprehend now, don't you, why I'm here?'

Hugh knew it was only Alice's presence in the room that kept his knife still. His secret was known. Lives were in danger. Not only his own, but families, entire clans. 'How much does Edward know?'

Eldric crossed his arms across his chest, and leaned his shoulder against the wall. 'Not mincing words in front of her, then? Either you're planning on killing me, or she is with that comb.'

Alice didn't drop said comb, but she came close. She looked mutinous, ready to throw it despite the lack of surprise she'd no doubt been depending on.

'Look at me, Hugh.' Eldric shifted his crossed arms. 'I couldn't attack fast enough for any harm to come about and you know it.'

'How is it you know?' Hugh said, though he had already guessed. Eldric had been too careful with his words and actions since his arrival.

'Because I'm like you.'

'Another spy. Who isn't?' Alice blurted.

Eldric's lips quirked. 'It's not something I acknowledge in front of strangers, but apparently, it's information Hugh freely hands out.'

'Edward sent you here,' Hugh said. It was not a question, but he had to know with certainty how deep this went.

'Long before your arrival. Or his summoning of her.'

Alice did drop the comb then.

Eldric cracked a smile. 'You aren't any good at this you know.' Then he nodded his head. 'And you, rushing headlong to defend her. As if you could protect her when your very presence is the cause of—'

'Enough!' Hugh growled. 'We'll have this *conversation*, since you insist, but we'll do it elsewhere.'

'No, you won't,' Alice said. She'd moved towards the door again; looked as if she intended to bar their departure. 'You won't be leaving this room until I know what is going on.'

Eldric's low whistle did nothing to ease Hugh's riotous feelings. Elation at being with Alice, at her bravery in the face of Eldric. Her understanding that he and Eldric were spies.

Eldric's presence here was either a bluff or meant he knew Hugh had the Seal, though there was a possibility he didn't know about Robert. Eldric definitely knew about his involvement with Alice, and that meant the King could too. She was in danger. If only he could protect her from it.

'How many spies does a king need?'

'How vast is Edward's greed and desire for power?' Eldric replied.

Vast—so vast. Hugh wondered if, given enough time, he'd take over the world.

'Explain it to me,' Alice said.

Hugh's gaze snapped to hers. Her eyes were filled with determination, fear, confusion. She was so open, innocent. And he had allowed Edward close to her. To make her part of his manipulations. When he had had her in his arms at Court—he should have held on and escaped with her. Damned the consequences and the outcomes and simply gotten her out.

But he hadn't known what was expected of her. How could he guess Edward wanted her to spy?

Now Eldric was watching them both for their vulnerabilities. He had waited until this moment to reveal his intent. True, Eldric still stood casually, but his hand wasn't far from his sword.

'How much danger is she in?' he asked, not expecting an answer.

'I want an explanation *now*,' Alice said.

He wanted to answer her, but that could only come from Eldric. He needed to comprehend exactly what Eldric knew. Since Eldric suspected Hugh had the Seal, did he know of Robert?

None of it mattered if Alice wasn't safe.

'I'd say she's in a lot of danger,' Eldric drawled, 'more than you alone can protect her from.'

'Now,' repeated Alice.

When had she grabbed her comb again?

'Edward's need for power is vast, Alice. So vast he wouldn't ask three spies to go to this wreck of a town to find one traitor.'

'A king always has more than one traitor,' Eldric added. 'He couldn't waste the resources of you, Hugh *and* I. Therefore, there was an ulterior motive at play here.'

Alice eyes darted from Hugh to Eldric, and then she shook her head once, twice. As if trying to answer questions.

'Which means he suspects one of us,' Hugh said.

Eldric's eyes narrowed. 'You guessed, and yet you didn't throw your blade at me?' he replied.

It still didn't mean that the King had proof of Robert, and he had to protect Alice. 'Since you've held back your sword, I don't suppose you want to negotiate?'

Eldric drew his lips in, made a dismissing sound. 'You've seen the slashes on my arm. I have my own burdens to bear. Can't be taking on any unnecessary ones.'

'But she's not unnecessary. I'm asking, as a friend, if you know how to protect her.'

Alice gasped at the same time as Eldric laughed.

'You think it's *her* that needs safety?'

No bluff. Eldric did know about the Seal, was about to reveal all.

'The King suspects you, and guessed you had some weakness here in this town, given your less than stellar lineage. I don't think he suspected it was her. But it's ironic, isn't it? That he chose her to be a spy…on you… and she's your greatest weakness. If it was planned, Edward must have some divine given power from God. It has to be luck.'

'Just don't do it in front of her.'

Alice clenched the comb, felt the bite of the teeth into her palm, but none of it was holding in the pain in her heart.

Eldric was a spy, watching, *threatening*, them both. Hugh now wanted to keep her safe.

'What, not in front of me?' she bit out.

Eldric gave a tsking sound. 'Hugh thinks I'll kill him in front of you.'

'Won't you?' Hugh asked. 'You have to kill me or be hanged yourself. I know what is done with traitors.'

She wouldn't allow it. 'You think he's the traitor with the Half-Thistle Seal?'

Eldric shrugged. 'I don't *think* it. I—'

'But you don't know why he's done it. You don't—'

'Alice!' Hugh cried out.

Eldric's knowing smirk was gone. His expression was stunned. 'There's more?'

'Alice, don't.' Hugh shook his head, his expression fierce. 'As a friend. Protect her. If you think it's luck that Edward chose her, then downplay her role in this. Tell the King of her failed attempts. Sever our connection. Keep her safe.'

Eldric pushed himself off the wall. 'It's luck. It has to be. I've been counting on it.'

'What do you mean?'

'I'm not going to kill you, or drag her into this. While you were both pining for each other, some of us were actually planning how to survive once you revealed your feelings.'

'If I were dressed, I would show you planning,' Hugh stated.

'I rather like you helpless. And you won't be able to kill me once you hear my plan.'

'You intend to help us?' Alice said.

'That's *all* I've been doing—but you were both taking so long, and I had to be sure.'

'Of what?' Hugh said.

'Of where your loyalties lie.'

'They lie with the King.'

Eldric raised a brow. 'While you trade secrets with the Scots?'

'You do know a lot.'

'Know this, the King only suspects you have the Seal. I doubted it, and told him so. Throughout your time in Swaffham, your actions of following her made me believe it to be true. This conversation is only confirming it.'

Alice sound was of dismay. 'Tell him why.'

'No.' Hugh swung his gaze to her. 'I'm a dead man either way, Alice. At least this way I'm keeping some of my vows, some of my honour.'

She couldn't stay quiet any more. '*Tell* him. Or I will. You both act like enemies, but you're friends, aren't you?'

Eldric shrugged. 'I've sent no message to the King.'

'I can't trust that,' Hugh said.

'Didn't I ask if we were friends? Didn't I carefully, throughout this dance you have both played, examine the information? I flirted with Alice that first night, which confirmed your attachment. I watched you sneak into rooms with her, followed you when you left the church that day.'

'I'm still helping the King.'

'I know. But if we are friends, I'd like to know why you're doing it.' Eldric replied. 'It makes no sense to me.'

'Tell him, Hugh,' Alice pleaded.

Hugh gave a curt shake of his head. 'It will only make matters worse.'

'Right now I understand that both you and I are dead anyway,' she said. 'How could it be worse?'

'Not only for us, but also for Eldric.'

Alice's eyes widened, and she gave a curt nod.

'I've told nothing to the King,' Eldric said. 'I'm already taking risks.'

Hugh exhaled, and looked to the ceiling. 'I'm sharing secrets to protect the Clan Colquhoun and their families.'

'And why would you have loyalties to a certain Scottish clan?'

Hugh turned his gaze to Eldric, who *was* his friend. He'd been surprised that friendship was there, but it was.

'I don't have loyalties to that clan. In fact, having run into them, I wouldn't mind if a few of them disappeared. But I *do* have loyalties to Robert of Dent, who is alive and married to the Laird's sister.'

Eldric whistled and leaned abruptly back against the wall. 'Well, I wasn't suspecting *that*.'

'Now what?'

Eldric shook his head. 'At least I now know it was a good reason. But what a reason! And one I'll not worry about for now.'

'You won't worry about a legend or the fact that Edward's right-hand most faithful knight has been lying to him? That one of the most deadliest swords is now on our enemies' side?'

Eldric smiled. 'I have my own burdens, remember? The Archer was here.'

Hugh shook his head. 'How do you know?'

'He left an arrow on my bed.'

'Maybe you shouldn't have been distracted by that woman.'

'I only danced with her once.'

Hugh arched his brow. 'And you didn't try to look for her again?'

'I was trying to look after *you*.'

'I thank you for that,' Hugh said, leaving out all humour from his voice. 'You truly are my friend.'

'That's what I've been telling you.'

'So tell me your idea.'

'You won't like it.'

'Will it keep me with him?' Alice asked.

'Yes,' Eldric said, 'and if it goes according to plan no one will be hurt.'

Alice looked to Hugh. Her wide grey eyes were filled with all the warmth they shared, and determination for the trials to come.

'I'll do it,' she answered, her eyes never leaving Hugh's.

* * *

The moment the door was closed Hugh grabbed the rest of his clothes. He threw Alice's gown towards her, but she didn't dress with the same alacrity. He didn't know whether to be amused at her sudden lack of shyness, or frightened because of her serenity.

Alice was never serene.

'We can't let Eldric do it,' he argued. 'The loss is too much for Swaffham and for your family.'

'It can all be built again. My family has more silver and gold than they know what to do with. My father certainly doesn't need another pair of breeches or shoes.'

'Yet to set fire to your new barn! There could be bystanders. The loss of the spinning wheels, wool, tools and supplies will be significant.'

'But it's a plan that's so natural—as if it was meant to be done on Candlemas. All the workers will be gone by then and the town is *always* flooded with candles. It will look like an accident. Believable, too, because I have already had a conversation with Mitchell about the barn being in danger of burning down.'

The plan was eerily perfect. She shouldn't be this full of relief. The building was new, and filled with all of her and Mitchell's plans. And yet, she could see this as a viable way for her and Hugh.

In one way it was like setting fire to her past so she could have a future.

'And Eldric's right,' she continued. 'The trap door underneath and the passageway will make the perfect escape in case someone stops the fire early. No one knows of it except for Mitchell. We could be on our horses at the tunnel's entrance and out of the country before anyone even thinks to look elsewhere.'

He turned away, his shoulders rigid. 'So many years protecting Robert, so many years of openly fighting by the King's side. There's a part of me that feels like a coward even contemplating Eldric's suggestion.'

She could see that. As a child, his shoulders had gone back whenever the crowd had jeered. His head had been held high as he'd half-carried his father home. Then selling the land, taking the coin for armour, training to become a knight... He was a proud man, and planning a fake death, going into hiding, would go against everything inside him.

'Eldric is no coward and *he* suggested it.'

He shook his head. 'I keep thinking there must be some other possibility.'

'If you lived, if you stayed by his side, the King would order your death.'

'But you don't have to go with me.'

'Of course I do. I can't go to the King empty-handed. He was adamant about what he'd do to my family. You're the one who pointed out that I'm not nobility. I won't have the protection of a title and power. If I live, my family dies.'

'He's looking for the Seal, and our sudden deaths will be too suspicious.'

'Maybe he'll think the traitor is someone else—who got rid of us.'

'He'll send people here to investigate. More spies in Swaffham.'

Her home town, with a population of more sheep than people. She could hardly contemplate any intrigue here, even though she was a part of it.

'Which is why only us three know the truth.'

He turned then. 'I won't stand for that. When we are at a safe distance, we'll let your family know.'

Her eyes welled at that. It was the hardest thing, knowing they would suffer. She put a hand to her mouth to hold back the other thought, of the even more painful separation.

Hugh's eyes softened. 'And William, too. We'll make sure he's looked after. He loves you. That isn't going to change.'

'I'm going to miss so many years.'

He strode towards her again, and she went into his arms. 'You don't have to go.'

She'd go where her heart was. 'I won't be separated from you again. It'll hurt, but I have to trust that William will find us eventually.'

He rubbed her arms, exhaled. 'So much could go wrong.'

'And yet you saved the wrens.'

'The wrens?'

'The boys were there to capture them, and somehow you freed them before they could be tied to the poles. That's what we'll be—a couple of wrens.'

'We have no feathers to satisfy those left behind.'

'I have the horn the King gave me. If I leave that, he'll believe I died.'

Hugh looked to the sword at his side and nodded. 'It's winter…our passage will be dangerous.'

'The ice and snow will only make it more difficult for someone to follow us.' She patted his chest. 'You worry much for a knight, a spy and a traitor to the crown.'

He looked at her with heat and love in his blue eyes.

'I have much to worry *about*. You are everything, and yet I now realise how easy it would be to lose you.'

'Do you trust Eldric? Because all this comes down to Eldric and his words, his ideas for you and I.'

He nodded.

'Then stop worrying for me and my family; I worry more for you.'

'There's nothing to worry about with me.'

She gave an exasperated sound and took some steps away to pace the room. 'Leaving for Spain! Leaving England and Scotland and your vow to Robert! You started spying against the King to protect him.'

Ah. It was good that they talked, and they needed to talk more. There were words he wanted to say, and she wasn't going to like them. Alice fought to the death for those she cared about. And…he felt his heart swell… she cared for *him*.

'I won't be breaking my vow to Robert,' he said, and waited for his words to be understood.

She stopped and clenched her hands. 'What do you mean?'

'I can pass information from Spain. I'll work together with Eldric and we'll continue with the Half-Thistle Seal.'

Her hands flew apart. 'No!'

Hugh crossed the room and entwined her hands with his own. 'I *must* continue. There are too many changes in the world, too many chances. I can't sit idly by while others sacrifice themselves—'

She jerked her hands away. 'But you'll be free from all that. We'll leave your sword, the horn, a few pieces of our clothing. It will be as if we died. If we don't stay hidden you might be recognised, and then what? What of our children?'

'Children?' He choked the word out as if his throat closed on him.

'You *have* to know we'll have them. They'll be at risk.'

'I cannot break my vow.'

'But this plan includes marrying me. To do so you need to be alive. You jeopardise our lives by doing this.'

'I have already said I feel like a coward for going into hiding, I can't just abandon my friend, my honour.'

'Did Robert feel like a coward because he faked *his* death?'

Hugh rubbed a hand down his face and across his nape. She was right, and Robert had never cowered from anything or anyone.

'It doesn't sit right with me. Maybe I'm wrong— maybe in this way I am flawed—but I know that if I turn my back on that vow it will be something I cannot recover from.'

Suddenly she stilled, and a look softened her eyes. 'I'm not trying to fix you. You're still unflawed to me.'

'I don't understand—why are you arguing with this then?'

Tears welled in her eyes, and he felt every one of them even before she said the words.

'Because I love you. Because I finally have you, and we have a future. I don't want it to—'

He took the necessary steps and pulled her into his arms. 'It won't end. This is our beginning. This is new for you, but I've been here before. There are risks—'

'Yes, there are risks. I don't know how good a spy

you are if the King suspects you—and now you say you'll continue?'

'I have to. I meant it when I said I regretted those lost years without you. The years you helped people here—I would have liked to help along with you. I liked that day at the barn, and I intend to have more of those days with you.'

He did understand her need to help; he wanted to *share* it with her. 'I do, too. Which is why I want you to stop. Which is why—'

'What?' Hugh said, at her sudden pause.

She sighed against him, but it didn't sound like resignation. It sounded like…acceptance, and something in him eased.

Held in Hugh's arms, it was hard to keep her anger and frustration, and even harder when she knew he was right. The difference of him being a spy before was that he hadn't had her. Together, they would keep each other safe. They would share in this way, too.

'Let him know,' she whispered. 'Send a message to Robert about what we do.'

'Alice?'

She pulled away and was caught in Hugh's gaze. The storm inside his eyes had ceased, and they were more blue than ever.

'Keep your vow. We will be helping together, just as we both wish to. We'll be helping Clan Colquhoun and Robert's family.'

He cradled her face in his callused hand, his thumb tenderly brushing against her cheek. 'I have to confess your words that day of the storm about my father aren't what brought me peace. Aren't what made me forgive the past.'

'Then what?'

'You were here.' He gave her a soft kiss. 'No matter what loss had brought me to Swaffham, no matter what trials I had living here, how could I ever hate this town where I met you?'

She pulled him tightly to her, and rested in the warmth of his embrace.

'I love you,' he whispered. 'The pain, the regrets, the trials ahead we must face—all of it is insignificant to my feelings for you.'

She knew the thread, the years and the love that bound them would spin endlessly now that they were together.

'I knew all along that you'd marry me.'

A huff of held laughter, a shake of his head against the top of hers. 'We'll be careful. If it goes according to Eldric's plan, we simply have to travel for the few weeks afterward before we find a home. If anything is discovered, we'll be countries away from here.'

They would be, and yet... Looking up, she shook her head. 'Then how will Spain work in your vow to Robert?'

'I have sources to follow. If it doesn't work, we'll move to France—but away from the Western border. I can't guarantee to keep you completely safe from this.'

She laid her hand on his cheek. 'I don't want safe. I want you. I never thought I'd have you at all—I'll take what I can get.'

Grasping her hand, he kissed her palm. 'You may take all you can get, but I'm greedy now and I want everything. I want us *this* way.'

She leaned her head against his chest and heard his heartbeat. 'Me, too.'

Chapter Eighteen

Candlemas. A day marking the end of Christmas. For him, it was a day that would mark the beginning of his life with Alice.

The sun was starting to set when Hugh finally spied through the crowds Alice's chestnut-coloured hair against her green cloak.

Entire families were carrying their candles into the church for a blessing and then placing them in the square until every bare spot was covered. The well and cross in the square's centre dripped and flamed as bright as any sun and illuminated the snow-covered square.

And there, as the flickering flames glowed brighter than the dying sunlight, was Alice, taking candles and helping William find places for them.

It was weeks since he'd held her, kissed her. Weeks while he and Eldric had planned what needed to be done and how. What steps he would take to protect himself, Robert and the Clan Colquhoun. What he would do to protect Alice.

Already Swaffham might be plagued by other spies, and they'd agreed they wouldn't be together until every detail of the plan had been discussed. Even he and Eldric had limited their time in the open together. Nothing could be left to chance.

Seeing her here, her grey eyes glowing like the flames, her chestnut hair haloed like some angel, her cheeks red with the cold, he knew nothing had been left to chance. He'd never risk it otherwise. She was too precious to him.

He slowly stepped into the square, simply to prolong watching her take these last moments with William that she wanted so desperately. Theirs would be a difficult parting, but he was a child and wouldn't be able to bear the burden of the truth.

However, he and Alice had made contingencies and William and his family would be well cared for. William would be positioned as a steward-in-training with Mary, and when enough time had passed he would know the truth. Hugh would do everything in his power to ensure Alice would see him again.

She shared a few more words with William, gave him a strong hug that took the child by surprise, before she stepped down from the well's steps to walk towards him.

She was beautiful. Tiny, fierce, determined. Her grey eyes wide, shining. He could barely contain his happiness as Alice stood in front of him. So close he could touch her, hold her. Against the cold of the dying sunlight he felt her warmth.

Children played, animals grazed, adults laughed and chattered. The town centre was as full as he had ever seen it.

They had planned every detail and every possibility. 'It's time,' he said.

She tilted her head. 'You've said that to me before. I kept thinking you had a hidden meaning.'

He tried to think of the past few months and their words exchanged, but couldn't recall.

'I understand it now.' Her lips curved. 'You mean, it's time for us.'

'Always,' he easily answered.

She looked around her, her eyes taking in the beauty, the laughter, and this most familiar and treasured of Christmas traditions.

For himself, he didn't need to look anywhere else but at her.

'Every person and most of the animals are here, and as far away from that barn as we could get them. When we light the fire, Eldric will ensure that all the animals nearby are free to run.'

'I'm not worried. What I am is surprised at how much I'll miss all this.'

She took his hand and placed it on the side of her cheek.

'You're cold,' he said.

'Not for much longer,' she said.

'Don't. Not even in humour. Eldric will ensure nothing happens.'

She nodded. 'We have to let them see us together now.'

'How do you want to gain a crowd? Should we argue? And if so about what?' he said.

She bit her lip. 'What do you think will get their attention?'

His eyes on her lips, he said, 'All I want to do is kiss you, and I don't care if it's in front of everybody.'

Before she could answer he swept his hand along her

nape and tilted her lips to his. What was meant to be brief, warm, tender, quickly turned to so much more— and still not enough. He would never get enough.

When he pulled away it took Hugh a moment to hear the laughter and clapping over the roaring of his own blood. Even knowing that people watched them, he felt his body protest at pulling away from her.

Smiling, laughing, enjoying the ribald jokes that were making Alice blush, his happiness overwhelmed him.

Facing the crowd, he announced, 'I want you all to know that Alice has agreed to become my wife!'

Cheering overpowered the sound of his words, but he knew Alice heard.

'Exactly who proposed to whom?' she said.

He glanced at her. Laughter was in her eyes. He could not love her more. 'Are you ready? They've seen us together.'

'With that kiss, they've more than seen us,' she quipped.

As they hurried away from the town square, Alice's heart expanded. Her love for Hugh was endless, the thread binding them together strong. But there were more steps to take this night, and she grew impatient for their lives to begin.

A few buildings away, Eldric came out of the shadows. While slowly walking past them he whispered, 'It's all set. Good luck.'

All they had to do was light the match. Alice gave him a quick smile and hoped it wouldn't be long before they saw each other again.

A horse ride later, they reached the barn. Slapping the horse away, Hugh looked around. In the distance, they could hear the Candlemas celebrations and the singing.

'It's all clear,' he said.

'Are you worried for others?'

'I only want to make sure it's safe.'

Inside the barn, Alice spied the pile of wool and hay, the large church candle and the lone torch hanging on the wall.

Alice looked at the restored barn so full of possibilities. She had been excited at starting it with Mitchell and his family, and now in one moment it would be gone.

'Sad to see it go?' Hugh asked.

'Happy that it was started. I have no doubt that Mitchell will build it again and continue with our business. Mary and Elizabeth both know of my intentions here—they'll see to it.'

'I wish I could protect you from all this.'

She brushed the front of his tunic as she looked around again. 'And that is why I fell in love with you.'

'Because the best plan I had was to burn down your future dreams of dominating the wool market?'

She shook her head vehemently. 'No, because you're always looking out for others. Your father, William... me.'

He pulled her into his arms, and she squeezed until she could barely breathe. She felt the tender kiss he brushed against her hair. Felt love and warmth and comfort as he bowed his head and laid his cheek to her temple.

'I like us better this way,' he whispered.

Joy soared through her. Together, they had made it.

'As a couple of wrens? Me, too.'

Epilogue

'I'm pleased we can have a few private words together,' King Edward said as the door of his chamber at the Tower of London closed behind them.

'I'm at your service.' Eldric walked further into the room, noting the fact that there were no guards or attendants visible. 'Are there more questions you have, sire?'

With the door closed, no sound from the hallways and joined chambers reached them, though he knew there were many conversations going on.

Eldric had very thoroughly given his account of the fire at Swaffham that had taken a large barn with many supplies and the lives of Hugh of Shoebury and Alice of Swaffham.

It had all run perfectly to plan. Alice and Hugh had started the fire. The burning building, so far from town, hadn't been noticed until it was mostly flames. No person or animal had been hurt.

Chaos in the town had ensued, and it had taken hours before people realised Hugh and Alice were missing. Eldric knew they'd made it. The two saddled horses and another laden with provisions and coin had no longer been tied to the nearby tree.

They were safe, free, and he felt a surprising pang of envy at the life they were embarking on together.

In another two weeks, when he was far away from the King, Hugh would get a message to him. Then they would plan what to do with the Half-Thistle Seal he carried.

Until the King had ordered a private word with him, Eldric had felt confident that Edward believed all accounts of the fire. Alice's sisters and their husbands, grieving, had been convincing when they had spoken of the flames, the confusion, and what and who they lost. Her father, struck blessedly silent by the King's presence, had looked the part of a grief-stricken father. Mitchell had given an accurate account of the restoration project's financial loss.

But it was the handing back of the costly hunting horn that had seemed to appease the King most. He'd clenched it in his hands as if grateful for its return.

Now, Eldric wasn't so sure what the King believed. He was suspicious that the royal chambers were vacant. Edward *always* had attendants.

Edward swept past him to a table laden with food and drink, but he did not pour himself wine nor pick from the delicacies artfully arranged. Instead he sat, and indicated that Eldric was to sit across from him.

Adjusting the chair to accommodate him, Eldric kept his expression neutral. The King offered him the courtesy of sitting, but did not offer any refreshment. Either this was a short briefing over his duties, or the King was letting him know that he wasn't worth the courtesy of a drink. If so, it might mean that Edward did not believe Hugh and Alice had died in the fire.

The King rotated the hunting horn in his hands. 'I understand that Hugh was once your friend.'

'It had been many years since I had seen him.'

'But it was good to share news, even for so brief a time?'

'It was *very* brief time, Your Majesty.' Eldric carefully skirted the full question. It wouldn't do to discuss his shared conversations with Hugh.

The King's brows rose, but he nodded. 'My time with Alice was far too brief. It was a terrible tragedy... the fire, and the loss of income for the merchants and the town.'

It had been wasteful, burning the entire barn, but it had seemed to convince the King that Hugh and Alice had died. No one would burn all that simply to conceal two traitors. Still, Eldric remained uneasy. And it had everything to do with Edward's steady judging gaze.

'I appreciate the workmanship on this horn.' Edward touched the horn's wider bands. 'Did you know there are two tales told here? One is of kings warring and the other of lovers torn apart. Here, by the mouth, we see the lovers joined again, their arms cradling a child between them. It does not show what happens to the kings.'

Eldric was right to be uneasy. The King was toying with him. 'And you think the craftsman should have depicted what happened between the two countries?'

'Of course what happens between countries is important...' The King's mouth quirked, as if in self-deprecation. Eldric knew better. Edward had a healthy knowledge of his true worth.

'But perhaps I am biased,' Edward continued, 'and the craftsman simply believed that what happened between the two lovers was the more important tale.' He paused and raised his gaze. 'Do *you* hold such a belief?'

Eldric had no intention of stepping into that verbal trap. He kept his eyes on the horn. 'Perhaps the craftsman was trying for some...balance. Perhaps he thought the horn would be too heavy for the user with more silver bands, and therefore didn't tell of the kings. Or perhaps the price of silver was too costly.'

Edward rotated the horn again, as if contemplating the truth of Eldric's words. 'Both valid reasons.' Edward gave a curt nod. 'In truth, I *do* find the horn elegantly designed like this. And, since a king's power and rule is for ever, it isn't strictly necessary to tell his story. There is the comforting thought, too, that the love between a man and woman has some worth.'

Like a man facing the executioner's block and axe, Eldric felt every reflex in his body suddenly snap tight. Foolish reflexes. As if there was anywhere he could go to escape, or anyone he could fight against. He had been neatly and swiftly outmanoeuvred.

'Here—I want you to have it.' Edward held out the horn to him.

Eldric was obliged to take it, but he could not quell the slight tremor in his hand. The King did not give anything away without a price, and he more than suspected the price of this particular gift was...his head.

'Why?' he asked, knowing he might be insulting the King, but knowing he was a dead man anyway.

The King shrugged. 'You gave me wise and clever words regarding balance. I want to give it to you as a token of my regard. I believe you are a man who appreciates the power of a king's rule, but also understands the endurance of love.' He waved his hand towards the horn. 'Look for a moment—is it not beautiful?'

Eldric looked down at the intricate silver bands and felt as if he was bowing his head before the axe fell. 'It is very beautiful.'

'And very precious to me, as it was my wife's.'

Edward had been devotedly married to Eleanor for over thirty years. If there was any ruler who understood matters of kingdoms and hearts it was him.

'I will take care of this,' said Eldric, with all the reverence of a vow.

'Oh, I know you will.' Edward's eyes lit with his own private joke. 'In any case, you may have need of a hunting horn.'

Eldric looked around the room again. The brightly plastered walls were mostly hidden by heavy green draperies to keep in warmth. But with their fabric pooling on the floor, they might also hide any feet, if someone was behind them.

'Is there some service, some mission you require of me?'

'Not me. The horn is for your own endeavours.'

He only had one endeavour, and that was to bring an excruciating death to the man who had killed his friends and sliced his arm. How could the King possibly know?

Eldric thought he had avoided every verbal trap the King had laid before him. But somehow he had been caught and snared. He now knew that someone had been watching him and reporting on him for months, if not years.

His mind raced on what had been seen and by whom.

'Isn't there something…or *someone*…you're after?'

Edward continued. 'You could use that horn. And I'll grant you any other assets you might need for your efforts. I don't like you to be distracted.' Edward grabbed the flagon of wine. 'You can go now.'

Distracted. The roaring in Eldric's ears slowed his processing of the King's words.

When he understood that he had been unequivocally dismissed, Eldric forced his body to bow, turned and counted each step across the stone floor. By the time the doors closed behind him and he walked the empty corridor back to the hall he knew two facts.

First, he would never live far from the executioner's axe. If the King didn't know with certainty, he at least suspected that Hugh and Alice were alive. Edward might understand matters of the heart, but he governed by his own rules. His retribution was swift, and often devastating.

The King had made it clear that Hugh and Alice's fate was in his hands. As long as balance was kept, secrets would be as well. Eldric had given Hugh and Alice a vow. He would work and fight to his last breath to keep it.

Second, Edward had just granted him all the time and resources he needed to find his enemy. How the King knew Eldric was tracking him, or why Edward was giving him the means to pursue him, he didn't care.

If there was a price attached to the King's gift he would ensure it was The Archer who paid it.

* * * * *

*If you enjoyed this story, you won't want to
miss these other gripping Medieval stories
from Nicole Locke*

THE KNIGHT'S SCARRED MAIDEN
IN DEBT TO THE ENEMY LORD
THE HIGHLAND LAIRD'S BRIDE

YES! Please send me **The Hometown Hearts Collection** in Larger Print. This collection begins with 3 FREE books and 2 FREE gifts in the first shipment. Along with my 3 free books, I'll also get the next 4 books from the Hometown Hearts Collection, in LARGER PRINT, which I may either return and owe nothing, or keep for the low price of $4.99 U.S./ $5.89 CDN each plus $2.99 for shipping and handling per shipment*. If I decide to continue, about once a month for 8 months I will get 6 or 7 more books, but will only need to pay for 4. That means 2 or 3 books in every shipment will be FREE! If I decide to keep the entire collection, I'll have paid for only 32 books because 19 books are FREE! I understand that accepting the 3 free books and gifts places me under no obligation to buy anything. I can always return a shipment and cancel at any time. My free books and gifts are mine to keep no matter what I decide.

262 HCN 3432 462 HCN 3432

Name	(PLEASE PRINT)	
Address		Apt. #
City	State/Prov.	Zip/Postal Code

Signature (if under 18, a parent or guardian must sign)

Mail to the **Reader Service:**

IN U.S.A.: P.O. Box 1867, Buffalo, NY. 14240-1867
IN CANADA: P.O. Box 609, Fort Erie, Ontario L2A 5X3

HHBPA17

Get 2 Free Books,
Plus 2 Free Gifts—
just for trying the
Reader Service!

Get 2 Free Books,
Plus 2 Free Gifts—
just for trying the Reader Service!

HARLEQUIN *Desire*